PARALLEL*Amour*

by

C.J. Lazar

First print edition: April 2017

Edited by Quoth the Raven Writing Co.

Cover design © Book Covers by Ashbee Designs
www.ashleybaumann.com

Formatting by Paul Salvette

About the Book

Jack: "KISS: Keep It Simple, Stupid. Every coach I ever had from Pop Warner football to the pros taught me that lesson, but my situation with author Helena Bliss is far from simple. I know I should keep my distance, stay professional, and follow my own rules, but she's everywhere I go and I can't escape the feeling that unseen forces are pushing us together."

Helena: "Jack 'Titan' Smith, ex-football superstar turned romance novelist, is an ass of astounding proportions, a manwhore, and everything everyone warns you about. Before I met him my life was stable, secure, and good enough. Since then it's been a roller coaster of pain and excitement. I'd like to say I'll keep my distance, but he's everywhere I go."

We both write romance for a living, but nothing could have prepared us for the parallels in love and life which brought us together.

Dedication

My mother and father: You instilled strength and discipline in me, even if the strength came from earning the discipline. So much of who I am now is because of you and from following your lead.

My wife: "My One", for opening me up to a world of love I was sure could never come my way. With you, I achieve all my dreams and have learned how to love someone more than I love myself.

My daughter: Who helps me grow every day, right along with her. I am the child I couldn't be and, with you, I get to live my most impossible wish, to be a parent.

My brother and sister: My first friends. From you both, I learned how to grow up, to be a protector, to make selfless choices and to shrug off the drama, destruction, and distraction younger siblings can bring. Forever grateful and proud to be your brother.

CHAPTER ONE

Helen

"WELCOME TO THE Austin Grand Hotel, Helena Bliss," said the man behind the check-in counter, his wiry frame carrying a charcoal suit and crimson tie, a ten-dollar smile, and a bulletproof haircut. "We're pleased to have you here for the romance authors convention. We have a fantastic room waiting for you."

It was all I could do to stop myself from bouncing in place. Like a kid on a field trip waiting for the teacher to let us off-leash to play, I was being set free to be Helena Bliss the globe-trekking author rather than simply Helen from Montana. It was like donning my superhero identity and getting the chance to explore a whole new world! "Thank you, I am so excited to be here."

"Is this your first time staying at our hotel?"

I chuckled. "More than that, this is my first time in Texas. Does it show?"

"No ma'am, not at all, and we're glad you chose to spend it with us. My name is Clark, and this fine young gentleman over here," he said, pointing to a bellhop who had appeared behind me, "his name is Bert, and together we can assure that you will have a 'Grand' time while you're staying with us." He flashed a smile I'm sure all members of the staff would describe as 'Grand'.

Where a more sophisticated individual may have given a simple nod of acknowledgment, I wasn't one to care if my old-fashioned country upbringing showed. Raised right, I shook Bert's hand, looked him straight in the eye with a smile on my face, and said, "Nice to meet you."

"Nice to meet you, ma'am. Anything you need, just call for me." He ran his finger across his brass nametag. "Bert."

"Thanks, I don't think I'll need much, but if I do—you'll be the one I call."

He loaded my bags onto his cart as I returned to checking in.

Clark opened a small single-paged booklet, slid in my key card and a couple pieces of paper, and passed it across the desk. "Here's your room key and the food and drink vouchers. I see your reservation is for two. Will your assistant be joining you later?"

The frown I felt sneak across my face was involuntary but accurate. I shook my head no and said, "No such luck, they had to cancel."

His nod was ready, comforting, and without judgment, a skill I know is necessary for working the front desk. "How about I let you keep those vouchers anyway, just in case something changes, or you'd like a few extra treats for yourself?"

"Thank you, that's very kind," I removed the extra vouchers from the packet and slid them back to him, "but I don't believe that will be necessary. I have a pretty straightforward weekend ahead."

"Excellent. Well, you're one of the first to arrive and, in Bert's capable care, I know you'll be fine. Is there anything else I can do for you?"

"No, thanks. You've been great."

"I'm so glad to hear it. Thank you, and have a Grand stay."

Bert had the keen enthusiasm of a young guy who had found his calling, and let it shine through an eager ear-to-ear smile. "Your room number, please?"

I handed him my key, and we were off.

The lobby was truly "Grand". A crystal chandelier, whose sheer size suggested it must have required the hotel to be built around it, cast a kaleidoscope of colors twinkling across the ceiling and the nearby decor.

Following Bert proved an awkward task. While he wasn't pushing the pace by any stretch, I was moving like a strolling sloth. I felt compelled to take in every sight and sound, to make notes, and embrace every nuance of the place. *Not the time, Helen, don't be a nuisance. Get to your room so you can set the nice young man free to do his job.*

The chime of the elevator's arrival brought back my focus. As the doors slid open, I did my best not to gasp at the plush mirrored interior. I entered, and we rose.

Oh my. The things I will write about this weekend.

CHAPTER TWO

Jack

*T*RANSITIONS: *LIFE IS all about how you handle them.* I played tackle football professionally as an inside linebacker most of my adult life until one day a new head coach thought it would be fun to use my speed in a different position. I don't know if he disliked me, but he ran me like he did, or maybe he saw something others may have missed. Either way, I had a transition to make or my career would be over. In hindsight, it was kind of ironic, since moving to that position is what put me on that quarterback blitz and open for the blindside block that rang my bell and gave me a massive recurring headache in exchange for my career. Three years ago when that job ended, I was once again forced into a "do-or-die" transition and, if you know or ever learn anything about me, Jack Smith will never die—so I became a writer. *Surprise!*

It was easier to start writing than you might think. Playing that many years in college and then in the League gave me the chance to see a whole lot of stuff. I just had to find a way to put it on paper and let my agent do the rest. *Well, I can't give my agent all the credit.* At the last minute they bailed on attending this convention, and I was the one sitting here all alone trying to prepare myself for another weekend of hobnobbing and pressing flesh all in the name of my new career.

Outside the limo, new hurdles awaited. If football taught me one thing (and it taught me many), it was how to get psyched up for the moment.

Step one, a little bit of self-talk to get hyped.

Strap in, here we go!

Seek and destroy. I adjusted my tie in the interior reflection of the limo's tinted window.

Time to grab the spotlight. My fingers ran through my hair to give it that perfectly-tousled look that made everyone wonder whose bed I had just conquered.

This is your moment, Superstar, and none shine brighter. I gave a practiced burst of the pearly-white moneymakers before giving a knock on the window. The driver opened the door and I leapt into the fray. *Get yours!*

A brunette in a slinky electric-blue dress and a shiny gold nametag rushed to me with her hand outstretched and begging for my grasp. Cupping it gently, I bowed slightly and gave it a delicate kiss before giving the blushing beauty a spin and an appreciative whistle. "And beauties like you are why I keep coming back to the great state of Texas. Wow!"

She may be a professional rep for the hotel, but she's a woman first and giggled in the awkward way they all did.

Girls like her *are* why I return to Texas, but they're also why I hit almost every other location my books are sold. The devotion of such insatiable and adoring fans has been buttering my bread with enough money to just about rival my days of sacking quarterbacks, destroying wide-receivers crossing the middle, and leaving running backs with shortened careers. On the gridiron stage—or in this life on the page—it was the same cutthroat game, just with a different physicality. I missed football, but the life of an infamous author kept the spotlight bright.

"And we're so glad you do keep coming back to us, Mr. Smith," she said. "Texas loves its stars. The bigger, the better."

"You flatter me."

"Oh no, I wouldn't . . . Sincerely, you—"

I played seven years for this state and won them a title in storybook fashion in front of a global audience—my face could be smack-dab in the middle of the star on that flag. I chuckled and let her off the hook. "It's all good. Thank you. I'm grateful for the opportunity. Should we head to the check-in desk or straight to the conference room? I know I'm cutting it close, probably the last to arrive."

With a cute little squeak, this five-foot-nothing cutie cleared her throat and raised her chin in a way that suggested a former prom queen or pageant contestant.

I do love Texas.

"No sir, Mr. Smith. You are checked in and all set. My name is Tammy and I'll be your concierge. You are correct, most of the other authors have already arrived, but it's your choice where you would like to go next. Bert, here," she gestured to a young bellhop in his early-twenties, silently waiting off to the side as my driver unloaded my stuff onto Bert's cart, "will take your bags."

As I walked over to him, Bert responded with a professional smile that, like Tammy's and mine, was no doubt honed through hours of mirror time to get him to the top of his profession. "Welcome to the Grand Hotel, Mr. Smith, my name is—"

"Thank you, Bert. Miss . . . er . . ." I turned to give Tammy one of my patented "hey, baby" looks. "It is 'Miss', isn't it?" The look was right on target, I could actually see her knees weaken as her cheeks turned a deeper shade of pink.

"Um, yes. I am available. Uh, single. 'Miss' is correct."

Judging by her behavior, it was clear she knew my reputation. Leaving her to hang on the vine, ripe and ready, I returned to Bert. "Miss Tammy here says you'll be taking care of my stuff." I took the fifty that had been waiting in my pocket for this moment and handed it to him. "It's appreciated and I'm going to look you up if I need help with anything else—"

He froze in place, eyes glued on the bill in his hand. "Whoa. No offense, sir, but I think you made a mistake. I—"

Tammy slipped into the conversation on cue. "Mr. Smith, as your concierge it's my job to help you with those needs. Bert is the bellhop."

I chuckled, looking at the two of them, dedicated to their jobs and giving me far more attention than I could ever justify to my father. "Thank you, Tammy, I know that with you I'm in fabulous and capable hands, but there are some needs that only a front-line person like our friend Bert here can meet." I slipped another fifty from my pocket into Bert's hand, closed his fist around it, and, nodding with a smile, continued. "Please take it, there's no mistake. I did two summer seasons and one winter break slinging bags at a hotel back home. I know you've earned it, and if not, I'm sure after a weekend of being harassed by me— you will."

He had been trained well. Before I could finish my words, the money had disappeared into his pocket, "Thank you, sir.

Whatever you need, just let me know. I'll be sure you have the best weekend Texas has to offer." He grabbed the brass rails of the cart. "Shall I get your bags to your room now?"

"Yes, please," I said, and like a shot Bert was off and running.

"Now, Tammy." Her long eyelashes drew my attention to her doe-eyed stare. Stories of my fun and debauchery were reflected there and made me smile. "Let's see what kind of trouble we can find. Please, lead on."

A grin pulled at the corner of her mouth as she asked once again, "To your room—or the convention area?"

Wow. She must be new to be so bold. This girl could be real trouble, or fun, depending on the circumstance. "Right now, let's go meet the people and make friends. The convention hall, please."

She spun away, her heels clicking on the concrete as her hips swayed enticingly.

This will be one helluva ride.

CHAPTER THREE

Helen

"I DON'T GIVE a damn! Don't touch my stuff!"

And just like that, the beautiful pre-conference silence was dashed by the shrill sound of a woman's angry voice. Worse yet, it was coming from the area of my booth.

A male voice oozing cool confidence responded with, "Lady," and an extended pause, "not on your best day. I promise you."

As I rounded the corner, I quickly hit the deck to avoid a small red projectile hurtling my way.

"You pervert, that's not what I meant at—" the woman fired back, her anger now gaining a new layer of indignity.

The man cut in with a deep, rumbling laugh that rolled over her words. "*Pervert*?"

I peeked up from my spot on the carpet to see the back of the man. His blond hair, carelessly tossed like he'd just come in from the beach, or a bed, grazed the collar of a form-fitting jacket that framed his broad shoulders with hard-hitting angles that made me somehow think back to math class—until I arrived at that butt. It danced under his jacket as his arms swung wide around the room to underscore his retort, the words barely drifting over my ears as I stared in awe. They say you shouldn't look directly at the sun but when it is there, so close and magnificent, you have to sneak a peek.

"Really? 'Pervert'," he continued. "Lady, look around this place. We're all perverts, most of us professional perverts, and it's the reason we're here." His next burst of laughter spread across a growing crowd.

With only a collapsible table between them, I saw the slightly gray-haired woman I recognized as historical romance writer, Nancy Coeur, in her business-casual skirt and blouse squaring off as his opponent. Her face was a deepening red that matched the small objects she was scooping up in her hand and flinging his way. Most missed, but a few ricocheted. He stood there unflinching, his laughter growing as they bounced off him like bullets against Superman's chest.

I regained my feet just in time for two more to rocket toward me. Not feeling all that bulletproof, I tried to duck out of the way again just to have one smack me square in the forehead with a surprisingly loud "*thwap!*"

The barrage of bouncy baubles and the surrounding laughter screeched to a halt as everyone stared at me, waiting for a response. I can't begin to guess what a normal person would have done, but I had to be me and grabbed the rubber heart eraser off the floor, lifting it to my face for a closer look. I decided against the obvious "heart-on" pun and deadpanned, "Um . . . anyone else order the conference facial?"

There was a pause as I pocketed the trinket and looked at the crowd, then her, and finally him. We locked eyes. He had lean chiseled features and a dimpled chin that underscored the small smirk forming on his face. That amused look broke my stoic visage and had him roaring with laughter once again. The woman picked up her tray of ammunition and slammed it back down before storming off, roaring for the conference staff.

Like school kids not wanting to be around when the principal arrived, everyone scattered except for the one person guaranteed to be the target of whatever authority she might recruit.

And now I recognized him. Mr. Smug himself in a suit and silk tie: it was Jack Smith. We had never met, but I'd heard enough stories and seen enough photos to recognize him. A former football jock who continued to use his celebrity to bed women left and right while doling out romance novels filled with stories of his conquests. A self-propagating scenario where his reality was spun into fiction to meet his function. I could now guess why the other author must have been yelling at him and regretted missing my chance to join in on the attack.

"Hey," he said, as I locked my chin high in the air and walked by his table. *"Hey", he says. Like he knows me, or like I could be one of his bimbos. "Hey", like I'm one of those girls who would melt under his attention. Yeah, you pegged the wrong woman.* I kept walking.

"Hey, funny girl. I just wanted to say thanks."

Don't fall for it, Helen. Wait . . . I have no reason to be scared of a guy like this! I stopped, then strolled casually up to his table as he threw an overdone, over-rehearsed smile my way. Somewhere in my brain, I had decided to go for full-throttle attitude, and I felt my head tip to the side and my hand land on my hip. "You're welcome," I said, in my best attempt at cold-hearted smooth-as-silk delivery.

He skipped two steps back, hands up and open. "Whoa,

there. My mistake. I thought you were one of those rare laid back and fun ones—"

"Fun ones"? "Ones" of what? Only in his wildest, best-selling fantasies!

"—that maybe I could buddy up with. Guess I read you wrong." His hands slithered back down to his sides. "My apologies. Thanks anyway."

"No problem." I gave him a nonchalant nod as I spun on my heel to strut off into the sunset, having survived my first Wild West-type showdown of the conference.

"I owe you," Jack called after me. "See you at the after-party."

That one almost caused a hitch in my giddy-up, but I kept strolling on with extra-long strides until his angry table neighbor—and a lanky guy wearing an "Event Staff—Todd" lanyard around his neck—blew by me. I got caught up in their wake, or at least in my need to people watch, and edged toward the next table to slip into what I called "observer mode", something I had practiced since childhood, the ability to become invisible to watch the world unfold.

"Him," said Nancy Coeur, her voice screeching at the staffer who appeared to be the law of the land.

Jack Smith rolled up to face his accuser with a small smile and a look of innocent curiosity.

"He was touching my stuff and was rude, trying to humiliate me." Nancy sounded devastated, like tears should be raining down in buckets, yet her face showed no evidence of moisture, just pure unabashed hatred. "I don't know why he's here, anyway. He's not a real writer. He's just some dirty gigolo making a mockery of our hard work."

I wanted to raise my hands up in a great "hallelujah" as she spoke the words many of us were thinking, I'm sure. *Preach, girl. Sing the gospel!*

Unphased as she called him out, Jack gently took the staff member's lanyard in hand to give it a look-over before releasing it back to its surprised bearer.

"You should just get rid of him and give his space to someone else," said Nancy. A crowd had once again formed, and was now nodding and whispering its approval. We were warming up for an Old West-style lynching with Todd playing the role of sheriff. Bolstered by the support, Nancy's voice continued to rise in both conviction and volume. "I've been coming here for years. I've written more books than him. I've—" Her words stopped and dropped to the ground.

Smith had turned his gaze to Nancy with a strength that could be felt. She had poked the bull one too many times, and we all took a step back expecting the worst: a torrential tirade, or whatever guys like him do to people like her.

But when he spoke, his voice had a calm to it that none of us in a similar scenario could have maintained. A calm that said this was not his first rodeo and he'd already decided on the outcome. He licked his lips slowly. A move, I'm sure, which wet more than a few panties in the room. "Lady," he said, and leaned in a little closer to her as if speaking privately. "May I call you 'lady'?"

Her face softened and she gave him a subtle nod.

"You are someone considered prolific in your output. Your delivery. Your mass production. Many of us will never write as many books in our lifetime as you have already written." Jack Smith made an exaggerated bow that perked up Nancy's shoulders. "And I bow to you in that regard. But I can now see why." He cleared his throat and gave a glance around the room to his audience. "You are as loquacious as you are loco. As verbose as you are vain, and as tired as your tirade."

She gasped, and clamped her hand to her forehead with a "Well, I never!" look on her face.

"You have written volumes but have said nothing. Most importantly, I'm sure you know just how many books you have written and you know just how many you have sold, and I ask you, lady: have you sold more books than I have?"

The crowd gasped. Nancy's hand went to her heart, mortally wounded. She stumbled back until she had enough people around her to fall into their arms, doing a passable imitation of having fainted from the shock.

Jack turned away casually. As he did, our eyes met, and he gave me the knowing nod of co-conspirators as if I had somehow been in on the plot—or even on his side—from the start. I may have been swayed, maybe, because he was absolutely right about Nancy, but there was just something about him. Something I couldn't quite put my finger on. Maybe it was my instincts, or something about his casual swagger or his reputation, that demanded my senses stay on high alert. I didn't know and was probably best served if I did not find out.

Jack busied himself opening a box of books and preparing his display, turning his back and dismissing us to go away to wherever we belonged.

Nancy leapt up for a last hurrah, her hands slamming down on Jack's table, preparing for a final attempt to vanquish her nonplussed foe. "Don't you turn your back on me!"

With books in hand, Jack turned to face her and the crowd before firing a look at the poor guy with the lanyard. "Todd, how long is this going to go on? Most of us have work to do for our fans."

"Oh you!" Nancy huffed, and turned her anger on Todd. "I cannot," she said, pulling at the lower hem of her blouse, "nay, sir, I *will* not, share a booth with this scoundrel. What are you going to do about it?"

Now, I didn't know how much, if anything, Todd got paid to do his job. Odds are, he was a volunteer who'd signed up hoping to get a little extra access to the attending authors. I was sure this wasn't what he'd had in mind, and was even more certain he'd reconsider his role next year.

Jack continued to unpack boxes and set up his display. "Rough start for us all. What are you going to do, buddy?"

Todd, floundering in the chaos, took a furtive peek at the crowd, likely looking for any lanyard-laden support nearby, but finding none. If they were there, they were hiding themselves, knowing it was too early to be dealing with this kind of drama and thinking: "Better him than me". Todd stammered, "Well, Nancy, I believe—"

She jumped in on him hard, to make sure he got it right. "That is Ms. Coeur to you." Her emphasis being on the "Ms.", as she underscored the point, "*Mizz* Coeur." She forced out a big smile. "Because I'm all heart."

Ah yes, because Coeur was French for heart. Talk about a misnomer.

A series of thuds resonated as Jack dropped an armful of books, and laughed hard enough that his roars threatened to knock down the nearby stacks.

I, and several others, joined in the laughter, in no small part because of the irony of her statement at such a time.

She tried to continue talking but was drowned out. Even Todd joined in for a chuckle that would surely cost him. "Mizz All Heart" just had to wait it out.

When everyone had calmed down and Jack had regained his breath, he stepped back into the mix with a sigh, ready to take over this situation.

CHAPTER FOUR

Jack

THIS TODD GUY, he meant well, but was in over his head with our sweet little Ms. Coeur, and she knew it. The same way she thought she could bully me was the same way she was working him. She could smell the fear and hesitation on him and was looking to finish him off by getting him to do her dirty work.

Not today. I put my stuff down and stood with just a table between me and our boy, Todd. "Okay, this has been fun, to an extent, but now I feel the need to get to work."

Todd gulped. "Yes, sir. I understand."

"I knew you would. You look like you're a pretty bright guy when not facing both barrels of a shotgun. Am I right?"

He wasn't making direct eye contact but gave a quick look at both of us before his head wobbled a "yes".

"I get it, man. That was more of a rhetorical question, but we've all been there. I know I have." I leaned across the table and placed a hand on his shoulder, trying to let him know I was on his side.

Ms. Coeur rolled her eyes and clamped both hands on her hips. "You guys done makin' love?" She looked around the room for support and came up dry.

"Wait, is this what constitutes making love in your stories? Maybe that's why you aren't selling so well. I can send you a video of my activities this weekend in Texas if you need inspiration, because I promise you . . . " My survey of the crowd showed a much more favorable response. Even the attractive blond witness who had earlier been pegged with a heart seemed to be coming around to my side. " . . . when I make love, you'll know it. Likely, the whole hotel will know it. I might even invite this fine gentleman to be my wingman." I clapped Todd's shoulder for emphasis, which brought a new height to his spine, and a grin. "It would be a whole different scenario than whatever you've imagined, Ms. Coeur, and if you weren't all heart before, yours would beat hard enough afterward to make it count."

Her lips curled as she snarled, "You're a pig."

My smile got just that much bigger, "When the time is right, yes, ma'am, I am."

"Todd!" she cried, grabbing his arm. "What are you going to do about this?"

Before Todd could answer, I felt it was time to let him off the hook, or at least change the direction of this mess. I stepped aside, found an opening, and with two hands on the table, vaulted over. The people nearby stumbled back and continued to give ground as I made my way through the crowd to the beauty doing her best to be invisible. "Excuse me, miss. Could I spend the weekend with you?"

Her jaw dropped but she stood her ground.

No matter how you did the math, at maybe five-foot-six in height the woman was a fraction of my size. I towered over her, but this blond bombshell with the killer smile wouldn't be thrown by me casting the spotlight on her and leading with a double entendre.

Yep, Jack, you picked the right one this time.

"I know it's a mighty big ask," I said, "but you would make me, and most everyone here, far happier if you said 'yes'. You are an author, correct?"

"Ye—yes, I am."

Yep, gold star for me. "Excellent, and probably a fine one at that."

"I will not stand here while he flirts with everyone," Ms. Coeur shouted, demanding the spotlight come back her way. "Todd, get him to apologize, and—"

Time to give her the attention she craved so much. "Excuse me," I said to my newfound, but as yet unidentified, author friend.

She gave a little nod and I made my way over to Nancy Coeur. "Here's the thing. If you want some type of apology, I can give you that, happily and sincerely. I apologize to you for picking up the books that fell onto my table and spilled onto the floor. I apologize for picking them up and stacking them on your table for you. Clearly that kindness, something my parents worked hard to instill in me, was a mistake when dealing with the likes of you. I can promise you it won't change, but I'm sorry that somehow you could be so easily offended by such a thing and use it to try to get yourself some attention and to bully so many people."

"I did no such thing. Slander! Take that back!"

"Sure, consider it taken back. Now, this is what you need to know. This is my table. Booked it last year and the one before that and, as long as they'll have me, I'll be right here in this spot. I've always been happy to share the booth, but now I can't extend that courtesy to you."

Turning my attention back to the crowd I confirmed that, sure enough, my new author friend had started to slip away. In an instant, my eyes were drawn to her once again. "This is where you come in," I said. I took two steps toward her, careful not to corner her with the attention. "My friend, Ms. Coeur, and I need your help. Would you be willing to switch spots with her? I promise, with your permission, of course, to help you move your stuff, take care of any inconvenience, and be on my finest behavior."

Caught up in thought, she blinked nervously. *Likely trying to figure out a polite way to escape the whole scenario.*

And then Todd appeared at my side, his focus now on the blond, which drew Nancy—not yet willing to give up her perceived control—hot on his heels.

"Oh honey," Ms. Coeur crooned, "if you could do that, I would be greatly indebted to you. I wouldn't wish this man on anyone." I could feel Nancy's eyes burning holes in my soul. "But he appears to have a respectful attitude toward you."

Todd, fondling his lanyard, finally chimed in with, "Miss Helena Bliss, you don't have to make this switch. The convention is placing no obligation upon you and also apologizes for any inconvenience or unpleasantness this situation may have had on your experience."

Helena clenched her fists tight. And, as the entire crowd stared—me with a growing grin—she said, "It would be my pleasure." *I knew it!*

Her pleasure? *Interesting choice of words.*

Nancy pounced on her with a grand flourish. "Oh, thank you. Thank you. You have saved my weekend." Like a boa constrictor, Nancy wrapped the poor woman in a hug she couldn't escape without a club or some pepper spray, and gushed, "I do owe you. Anything you need this weekend, just ask and I promise to not be any further imposition."

CHAPTER FIVE

Helen

INSPIRATION STRUCK AS I entered the room for dinner. I whipped out my notepad. It didn't matter what outfit I was wearing, or whether I was carrying the tiniest of purses, I never left home without it. I began to write. *The sign over the door said "The Grand Eatery", and when I passed through the doorway, I could see why. In fact, I think someone may have understated things. There were rows upon rows of tables centered around—*

"Helena?" a female voice with a thick nasal tone called to me, and I tried to ignore it so as not to lose my train of thought.

The rough stone floor accented the cavernous expanse. The creators of this space broadened their use of the word "grand" from that of pure beauty to include massive size, suggesting they originally started serving food here simply because anyone trying to make it to the other side would need a break halfway across to refuel.

"Helena? Will you be joining us?" Apparently my face being buried in a notebook and my furious writing meant nothing to this nuisance as she began to crawl into the corner of my vision.

I nodded with an exaggerated motion, trying to give her a hint, but I clearly failed and she was now firmly in my personal space.

"What are you writing?" she asked, refusing to go away.

I mashed the button on my pen, flipped my book closed, and stuffed both back down into my purse. Snapping my eyes toward the intruder, I said with a matter-of-fact smile, "Ideas on how one could go about killing a roomful of people at dinner before the waitstaff noticed."

It was Sandra Bennet wrapped in what had to be Manhattan's finest skirt-jacket combo that likely bore labels I couldn't pronounce and a price tag I would never pay. I watched as it took three hard blinks before she was able to refocus and respond. "Oh . . . uh . . . that's nice. For a story?"

Wow. These are the people I call friends. Actually, it would have been a stretch to call Sandra a friend. She lived in New York City, and said it gave her the best insight to "the biz" and a never-ending source of material. We'd met in an online writing group and had shared some ideas, done some beta reading for one another, but that was about it. This was our first time meeting in person, and I recognized her from the photo on her website, but I'm pretty sure I was lacking in making a first impression. *Well, I was writing, and if anyone should understand that, I would think it would be another writer.*

"Yes, for a story," I said, "a future story, maybe. I like to jot down things that strike me as interesting, and this room is pretty incredible." I raised my arms up, gesturing around the room. "I mean it is absolutely cavernous." *"Cavernous". Add that one to the notepad when I get a chance; it has a lovely, echoey sound.*

A condescending smile pierced Sandra's tiny oval face, her cheekbones set impossibly high beneath smoky brown hair that curled its way over her shoulders. "This isn't even the big room."

"It's what?"

She shook her head to underscore the point. "Nope. This is the biggest one they rent out for private parties, but it's not the biggest restaurant in the place. The upside is it's likely one of the few places in this hotel that you won't catch any signs of the Grand's link to football hidden in the midst of its beauty, especially promo pieces with Jack Smith's face all over them."

"That's good, right?"

"Oh yeah, it is. Come on, join us. You're right on time. We were all just talking about Jack, what he did to poor Nancy earlier, and how you got roped into taking her spot and sharing a booth with him."

Her cold, bony hand took mine and sent an awkward shudder up my arm.

This woman has no concept of personal space.

She dragged me past rows of empty tables to the center of the room. "Look everyone, speak of the devil. Here's my friend, Helena, right on cue."

"Everyone" was seated around a gigantic table of the most impractical design. It appeared as if three tables had been pushed together to form some type of "T" which had people wedged in at the corners.

The only thing more awkward than the seating arrangement was my wave. *What does one say in such a scenario?* I went with a tried and true "hello", and received a smattering of responses that were indiscernible in the mix, but on the whole seemed warm and friendly enough.

Once again, a yank on my hand had me moving again with Sandra the Guide. "You're sitting beside me. Everyone was set up with the rows they're in on the floor so you would be with familiar faces." She stopped in front of two empty chairs patting on one in front of a place setting with my name. "This is you. Pretty brilliant, don't you think?"

Unless you hated your booth mate, then it was one of Dante's circles! "Uh, yeah. Clever . . . " It really wouldn't be worth trying to explain, especially knowing she'd likely be offended and I'd spend the rest of the night trying to make it better. I sat down in my assigned chair as she leapt into place.

"Tell us," a loud and boisterous voice called out across the table. I followed the sound to a slender man with thinning hair whose fragile spectacles perched precariously over his nose. *There's no way he wore that outfit on the floor—unless he writes slapstick romance.* Apparently he had used his time between leaving the conference hall and coming here to switch into something "more comfortable", a lime green shirt with eyesore orange letters that read: "Same shirt, different day" and had a giant yellow laughing emoji as the background. "What's he like?" He rammed part of a sloppy Hoagie-style sandwich into his mouth without breaking eye-contact.

"Me? What's who like?" *Where's the server? Maybe this is the night for some drinks.*

"Jack Smith, the Texas superhero-of-his-own-mind."

He admits that he doesn't even know Jack and yet already calls him out like that. Wow. While I couldn't disagree that Jack had rubbed me in entirely the wrong way, mostly, I couldn't let anyone talk like that behind someone's back unchallenged. "He's all right," I replied.

The man took a drink from an oversized mug while still

working hard to maintain eye contact. Then I noticed that it wasn't just his beady eyes staring me down, but the whole tableful of people. The man licked his lips clear of the greasy sandwich remnants, causing my stomach to have second thoughts about dinner, before replying, "You're too nice, you. You're a newb, so you're still a sweet girl. My name's Bob Pauly, and that's okay, we already know about him. Don't we, Nancy?" he said, gesturing across the table to where I saw the grey-haired sharpshooter from this morning proudly sporting a white neckerchief dotted with crimson hearts.

Clearly one to always enjoy the spotlight, Nancy Coeur stood up to tell me, "He's a chauvinist pig and a hack. I know he would've hit me if security wasn't there today. I'm so glad I got away from him and feel so sorry for you, sweetie."

Sandra nudged me with her elbow as I sat dumbfounded. She whispered, "Is he really that bad? Maybe you can get moved before the morning. Blame it on being sick, or wanting to be with me."

Without thinking, I leaned away from Sandra before answering, "No, he isn't—or wasn't—all that bad. Our booths were pretty busy so we didn't talk much, but he was actually kind of nice. Once in a while I caught him carrying on with fans and he seemed like a bit of a manwhore, but I don't think I'm his type so I didn't have to worry."

"Well, I'm just glad he didn't hit Nancy, or hit on you. He—"

Thankfully, the server arrived and I was able to semi-politely tune out Sandra, Nancy, and Bob, and order my dinner. By the time our orders were taken, Sandra had forgotten about me and was talking it up with a few of the others in the group. They continued to bash Jack Smith for a while more before moving on to talk about upcoming writing events. Many of the faces were familiar from previous years and previous conferences. Inevitably, at this time of year, authors are in full swing and you could spend months on the road touring if you had the resources and either an empty home, or one you wanted to escape.

That definitely wasn't me.

I was already homesick.

CHAPTER SIX

Helen

I WAS ENJOYING the most fantastic chicken and shiitake risotto with winter squash and pine nut dressing when beside Bob, some bald guy in a worn-out football jersey, of all things, jumped to his feet and yelled, "Titan!", like a crazed fanboy.

The path of his gaze led straight to the man, the myth, the manwhore himself: Jack Smith, dressed all in black with silver accents and the most ridiculous oversized black cowboy hat.

"Evenin' everyone," he said with a smile and a wave, then stowed his hat under his arm.

Why couldn't I have made an entrance as smooth as that? I wanted to stand up and say "hi", but as I was second-guessing myself, Bob's neighbor ran up to be sure he wasn't missed.

"Mr. World Champion, himself. My name is Eddie Turner and I am honored to be here in this room with you."

The eye-rolling flooded the place like a tsunami and the number of us on the Bad List for being loose associates of Jack reached a record high of two.

"I need to shake your hand. Please?" begged Jack's fan.

He got his wish, but yanked his hand back before it could touch Jack's. "Holy fucking mother-of-pearl, is that The Ring?

The World Champion ring?"

Jack nodded, loving the spotlight, a big grin on his face. "You know it is. Want to hold it?" and before the guy could respond, Jack was wriggling it free. Before it could even clear his finger about half a dozen others had tentatively made their way to envelop the main star of the spectacle.

"You know, it's too bad he's a jerk," said Sandra, "because he's actually kind of attractive. If you're into the big burly hunk of man-meat thing."

I shrugged, and went back to the well with, "He's all right."

She gave me a playful swat. "You know he poses for his own covers?"

I giggled. *Add that to the notepad: check out a few of his books.* "No, come on. Guess he really does have a huge ego. Who *does* that?"

She leaned in through the walls of my personal space again, and said in an alcohol-laced whisper, "His ego isn't the only thing that's huge . . . if you know what I'm saying." She crashed into me, shoulder first, laughing her dirty head off.

I shoved her. "You're terrible. Aren't you married?"

She teetered back into her seat. Her index finger came up over her lips. "Shh. We're in Texas, miles from home. Besides, it's okay to at least look."

I laughed, threw my napkin at her, and began a dessert of crème brûlée. Two bites later, a small ruckus started and Nancy's voice—in a tone that was beginning to make me think I was going to be hearing it in my dreams—came rumbling my way.

"No way. He's not sitting with me."

Every instinct screamed "don't do it", but I gave in to my

curiosity and stole a quick peek. Sure enough, it was a mistake, because Jack and Nancy had started Round Two and this time it was Nancy who caught me looking.

"You. Missy. You like him so much, you should be sitting with him. Trade me spots again," she demanded.

I wish there had been a way I could have pretended she wasn't talking to me, but everyone in the room was already staring. Time to make it clear that it wasn't happening. It wasn't my fight, after all. "I'm already settled in and I'm in the middle of eating. I'm sorry, you'll have to figure it out some other way."

Sandra jumped up so fast her chair fell against mine. "I'll do it," she squealed, waving her hand in the air like a gameshow contestant. I went back to my food in an attempt to return to normal programming.

Nancy seized the opportunity. "Yes. Her. If that other little thing won't help, let that other one do it." She teetered slightly as she poked a pointy finger into Jack's chest four times to underscore each word, "You're. Not. Sitting. Here." Every thrust forced a gasp from the audience.

Would he really hit her?

Sandra was racing her way around the table as Jack smiled, looked down at his chest, then at Nancy. "You are one strange old woman—I'm beginning to like you."

"Wha—?" He had knocked the pseudo-eloquent Nancy speechless.

"No problem, we won't sit together," he said.

Sandra's hands splayed across his back. "I'm here!"

Despite the tight quarters between fan and foe, Jack managed to turn around. Sandra's fingers seized the opportunity to roam his chest in an obnoxiously brazen stupor. Jack took it in stride, or maybe as a boost to his pride, as he watched with a smile and let her play. Her fingers ran across his chest, wandered freely up to his shoulders, then gently grabbed his neck as she and Jack made eye-contact, before raking her nails down his silky jacket to his stomach. The overused phrase "rock-hard, chiseled abs" popped into my mind, recalling every bad romance novel I'd read. Likely from the seed Sandra had planted. Clearly I was feeling a little more than just homesick.

We all sat there taking in the surreal scenario in a mix of shock and suspense. This stuff happened in our books but not so often in real life, yet here they were, she so drunk and he so . . . living up to his reputation.

He raised his arms with a dirty little laugh as she continued to explore his torso. When her hands arrived at his waistband, she stopped a moment and looked at me, her mouth hanging open with a look that made me expect to see a string of drool falling from one corner. Sandra nodded my way, seeking my approval like we were at some bachelorette party.

But there was no way I was having any part of this developing debacle. I sat completely stock still, refusing to even blink for fear it would somehow be mistaken for encouragement. *Maybe that was where I went wrong.* Maybe my absence of disapproval is what triggered her. Maybe my silence was the sign she had been looking for, because she let out a loud "Woop!" and ferociously began tearing at Jack Smith's clothes, flipping his shirt up and going for the massive silver belt buckle that protected a realm she should not have been entering.

Jack let out a sound that was somewhere between a laugh and

a gasp. His eyes protruded slightly, and I got the feeling that maybe this had gone farther than he'd expected, especially in front of our group. Gently, but with firm intent, he grabbed both of her hands, raised them up to his chest and did a slow turn. Now facing his back again, Sandra went right for two handfuls of Jack's butt. He lurched forward, almost bumping into Nancy who had held firm in steadfast observation the entire time, whether in disgust or enjoying the show, I wasn't sure. She would no doubt debate either position, if asked.

Jack turned again, popped his hat more firmly onto his head, took Sandra in his arms and proceeded to dance her around to the sort of up-tempo Latin beat that was playing overhead. Another loud "Woop!" from Sandra and her head flipped back to give me that look again, this time accompanied by a thumbs-up.

I really need to reevaluate my social gatekeeping online.

They danced a few steps, Jack leading the way, until the music stopped. With one hand, he tipped his ridiculous hat, and said, "Thank you, darlin'," with that tinge of a quintessential Texas accent that I'd heard cropping up throughout the day. With the other hand, he escorted Sandra to her new seat.

"My pleasure, Jack Fantastic. Hey, that should be your pseudonym," she slurred.

He chuckled, "I love it. That's brilliant, but I think people already believe my ego is big enough."

"No shit," mumbled a man to my right.

I gave him a look to see if he was familiar.

He rolled his eyes and looked away.

One less stranger for me to deal with.

Acting the part of the proper gentleman, Jack pulled out

Sandra's chair. She dropped into it with a giggle and continued to stare up at him with lust in her eyes.

"On behalf of myself and our dear Nancy, here," Jack said, popping a thumb toward his nemesis, "we thank you, Sandra, for helping salvage the night." And then to Nancy: "Don't chase this one away too fast. You're running out of people to make switches with." He scampered away like a boy who had just kicked a beehive and left the two of them dumbfounded, with mouths agape, looking at each other for answers.

"Wait! I thought you were goin' to sit with me and get rid of this one?" hollered Sandra.

"I'm not going anywhere, sweetie. This is my spot," growled Nancy.

And I laughed. In spite of myself, as inappropriate as the timing may have been, I laughed. I tried to keep my indiscretion quiet, but apparently it had carried well enough that I got a mix of curious, frustrated, and angry stares. Except from Jack, who was now headed my way.

"Is this seat taken?" he asked, pulling out Sandra's now vacant chair.

"Yes."

His eyebrows raised incredulously.

"I mean it was, but, get out of here, you know what—" and before I could finish, he had already removed his hat and taken the seat.

"Those two are gonna love each other in ways I couldn't even write about," he said with a smile. "Sorry to have traded off your friend like that. You—"

"Whoa." I had to stop that train of thought right there.

"She's . . . well . . . actually, she is my friend, but this is the first time we've actually met."

"Well, good. Now this gives us our first time to actually meet."

I braced myself. It was clear he intended to stay. Clearer still that I was not going to be able to get through the rest of my dessert without him trying to make some sort of small talk. This was the part of the conferences I always found the toughest.

Time to pull up your big girl panties, Helen. Let's see what this sex-driven narcissist has to say before we can escape.

CHAPTER SEVEN

Jack

TIME TO SEE what this Helen's all about. She's clearly expecting me to press the play with small talk. To leap right in like some desperate adolescent horn-dog. If she only knew . . .

Resisting the urge to start a conversation, I looked around the room aimlessly. The gargantuan fireplace with the roaring fire at the far end of the dining room was impressive but, like everything else in the place, I had seen it a dozen times before. But she didn't know that, so I allowed myself some extra time to take it in before casting a glance back to where she was hiding in her food.

Perfect. I began, "I'm sitting here and all I can think is, 'what kind of friend does a person have to be for Helena Bliss to travel all the way to Texas to'—wait, I'm assuming you don't *live* here in Austin, correct?"

"Uh, yes, that's correct, but—" she said.

"Beautiful. Well, then, back to my thought, ' . . . for Helena Bliss to travel all the way to Texas, to meet them for the first time in a hotel that is wall-to-wall with intense, sexually-creative energy?' I need to know or that question will keep me up all night."

"I didn't . . . I didn't come to meet you," she stammered.

"No? Okay, maybe not this time, but—"

With a big gasp, she slapped my arm. "Oh! You mean *Sandra*. It's not like that—"

"She's not your type?"

"I'm already—"

"She seems attractive enough," I said, continuing to feed Helena the bait by taking another look at Sandra. While I hoped it looked like I was checking her out with dirty thoughts, the reality was that I just had to see how the new pairing between Sandra and Nancy Coeur was working out. Much to my delight, their body language of crossed arms and distant leaning said all I needed to hear.

Helena's voice was firm, on the verge of forceful. "Cut that out."

I gave her a small portion of my attention, unwilling to take my eyes off the Sandra/Nancy lovefest. "Cut what—"

"And that, too," she said. Her hand snapped toward my face, index finger calling me out. "If you're talking to me, look at me. Either you want to talk to me or you don't. Which also means giving me a chance to talk without cutting me off. It makes no difference to me. Everyone else in this place is more than happy to lend me an ear. I know you can't say the same." She quickly snatched up the knife by her plate, and, for a brief moment, I had a flash of my name in the obituaries with a cheesy photo of a rosewood-handled steak knife sticking out of my skull. Thankfully, her blade landed in a piece of chicken, which she cut with two shaky hands that belied her confidence but not her fire.

Maybe I did find the one for tonight. "Okay, then. I think we understand each other," I said.

She didn't bother to look my way, but she nodded her head and finished her bite of food.

"So let me apologize and start again, the way my momma would have preferred." I grabbed my hat, stood up, and stepped back from the table, drawing irrelevant eyes my way. "Good evening, ma'am. My name is Jack Smith. Is this seat taken?"

She took her napkin and dabbed her mouth in a clearly casual pace.

I grinned, knowing full-well I deserved it.

When she was finally done, she said, "Nice to meet you, Jack Smith. My name is Helena Bliss, and you are more than welcome to join me."

A woman to my left groaned loudly in disgust as I sat down. Now it was time to try a unique approach—my best behavior—and see if it could land me Helena for the weekend.

Helena continued to eat as if my presence meant nothing to her, and maybe it didn't, but that wouldn't be the end of it yet.

"I'll cross 'do you come here often' off my list of questions for a few reasons, including the fact that I know this is your first time at this particular convention," I said. "I would ask what you write, but I know 'A Long, Hard Road' is your most recent offering."

Her body tensed slightly.

Set the hook.

I could see the expression on Helena's face flicker, like changing the channel between radio stations, a small difference, but it told me she was wrestling with some sort of decision. She slipped me a little look from the corner of her eye.

"So, instead," I continued, "I'll start with the cliché. Why write romance?"

Carefully, Helena laid her knife and fork down on each side of her plate before giving me a cautious look. "You write romance."

"Yep, I do. Many disagree with it, have other words to describe my stories—and me, for that matter—but I'll leave that to them."

"Right. So are you asking because I'm just an average-looking farm girl and not some buxom blond bombshell from the big city?"

"'Average'? The world wishes that you were merely average or, if so, that they, too, could move up to being 'average'. I see that fight in you, that spirit, and that gleam in your eye that says you are anything but average." I had her on the ropes; the look of surprise in her eyes said that she was reeling. "And if that fire has found its way into any of your writing, I'm looking forward to a hot and unforgettable time—"

She recovered, set her jaw firmly, and snapped her head in my direction, fast and close like a cobra striking its prey. Her teeth bared, and she hissed, "I am not sleeping with you."

I sat back, took a deep breath, and smiled. And, whether she wanted to or not, a small smile began to appear on her face, as well. We had connected and an understanding was being formed. *Sometimes conflict is the fastest way to real friendship.* "All I asked was, why do you write romance?"

The guy to Helen's right who thought he was too clever to be noticed eavesdropping took what he thought was his opportunity. "Buddy, why don't you back off?"

"Buddy"? Come on. My shoulders rolled as I fought unsuccess-

fully to stifle my laughter. Back in the days before I'd signed my first contract in the League, I would've just taken his ass out right here and now and let my agent cover the bills, but, lucky for him, times had changed. Once I'd signed, the media said I was "showing growth and maturity" but they had no clue about the ass-kicking my agent was giving me and the way the guys on the team busted my balls. That training carried through well into my post-football life. I learned it was a far better strategy to let comments from guys like this roll off my shoulders until they either walked away or went far enough down the road of trouble with me that nobody would bat an eye at me for putting an end to his night.

"Funny, am I? What're you laughing about?" He stood up from his chair and stared me down, all five-foot-ten, buck-eighty, and receding hairline. "You know you don't belong here." He put his hand on Helena's shoulder and I found my teeth beginning to grind. Her eyes were locked with mine and I could feel her probing to figure me out. "You don't gotta put up with 'im," he said to her.

The way she smirked at me, I knew we were good, and I felt some of the tension release from my spine.

I stood up, and, like one of those Slinky toys, he fell back into his chair.

She turned his way. "Thank you, I'm fine."

I stood firm. The place had gone silent again, and all I could see was him, his hand, and her. "She said she's fine. You can remove your hand—"

"Buddy, you—"

My heart was beating again, my blood beginning to pump

faster. "Remove the hand before I beat you with it."

The corner of his eye twitched. He glanced at her, then me, while trying to maintain a strong and steady look, but it was a lie.

The signal from my brain to my body had barely left the station, but he saw what was racing toward him and immediately his hand came up and away, denying me an excuse to move to the next stage.

In fact, my newest critic raised both arms to the watching crowd. "He asks her why she writes romance. Isn't that a joke?" Some of those in the dark corners of the room, out of my sight, gave him the encouragement he desperately sought. They snickered along.

I looked at Helena. She looked around at the room, then back to me, and mouthed the words, "You got this?"

Goosebumps ate my body, covering me in an instant, and I responded with a quiet, "Yep, all day." *Showtime!*

"It's a joke that a guy like him is even allowed in our midst," the critic continued, as Helena and I quickly swapped seats. "And the freaking nerve, to ask an established and talented writer like Helena here—" When he turned to look for Helena but found me, his face hit the floor. His expression changed quickly from cocky and hoping to score points with a woman to "Please, God, don't let him put me in a hospital." It amused me and made his supporters gasp the same prayer for him.

"You were saying?"

I'll give him credit. Others may have tucked their tails, apologized, and cut their losses, but not him. Maybe it was too much wine or some long-standing attraction to her that made him decide this was his one shot, or possibly he just lacked the sense his instincts were trying to deliver. Either way, he stood on wobbly legs, inching back slightly, and continued. "You—Mr. Smith and his monster cock—" an entirely different wave of gasps went through the group, tinged with dirty giggles, "—who can have any woman in this place. How about *you* answer the question: 'Why do you write romance?'"

I let the challenge simmer in the room. I savored its aroma. I—okay, I milked the moment, but it felt so good to have someone like that set the platform for me and the rest of my weekend.

He slunk back down in his chair, his nerves getting the better of him. He had made his best volley and took whatever pride he felt he salvaged and sat down to let me suffer under the full weight of his question.

I cranked up the big smile, the special occasion cheek-buster, and put my hand on his shoulder as he had done to Helena and watched him squirm. *Not so great when it's done to you, is it?* "Thanks, buddy. Thanks for asking." I gave him a squeeze I knew had to hurt a little before releasing it for a "friendly" little slap on the shoulder. Moving toward Helena who was sporting a smile that had to match, or even surpass, mine, I looked to her and offered, "Before I explain, Helena, I must apologize to you if I offended you in the least."

She giggled. "Thank you. No offense taken."

"Excellent!" I put my hat back on, adjusted it with a two-finger nudge, and began a casual stroll around the outside of the tables, wandering behind the other guests who were sitting and staring in that all-too-familiar way. "You know, *buddy*," I said looking briefly back his way, "You're not the first to ask. In fact, not even the first this weekend. I get it all the time." I stopped, and turned back to cast my gaze across the crowd and pull in any who were missing. "Believe me, I get it all the time." I let the innuendo hang a moment before continuing my trek. "Who am I to do this? Who am I to do that? How can I call myself a real writer when most of the stories I write are true?" I was now standing beside Eddie Turner, my original- and only fan, who now had a beer in hand, his face lit up in the way that only alcohol and super-fandom can ignite. "My first book, 'Drafted'? Truth. My first year in the League I messed up a lot but kept getting heaps of tail." Eddie nodded along eagerly in support. "'Sophomore Celebration: Twice the Fun'. Oh hell, yeah! You better believe it was true."

"I do. I do," Eddie squealed.

I took off my hat and put it on his head. "Damn straight, my man," and gave him a high-five as I got back on the trail of working the crowd. "I write romance for all the right reasons. It's not money. And contrary to popular belief, it's not just for the women, either. What many write can be labeled fiction. Me," I stopped mere feet from Nancy and Sandra, their eyes fixed on me, "I write fantasies. Find me a guy who reads my stuff and doesn't want to be in my place, with those women, doing those things. Find me such a guy, and you will have found yourself a liar. On top of that," my eyes met Sandra's as I slowly moved her way, letting the heat build between us, and I was certain it was more than her chin getting wet with drool, "I also give women the fantasies they seek."

Her fingers cautiously landed on my knees.

I smiled, and gave her the green light with a wink.

Off to the races. Her hands began sliding up my thighs toward my hips. She tugged a moment at my belt buckle before it fell open, along with many of the mouths in the room.

"I give it to them on their terms, in the way they most want it—"

Sandra grabbed my shirt, quickly tearing it from my waistband.

"I give it to them how they want it and where they want it—"

Her hands slid under my shirt to touch my stomach. I flexed, my abs rippling under her touch, unseen by others and left to their imagination, as Sandra let out a deep groan of pleasure.

"I give them what they need, in the form of a book. In the form of a fantasy." I turned to walk away, leaving Sandra's hands hanging in the air, sweat on her brow, and a grin that said she was two breaths away from needing a cigarette. *Yep, every town. Every one.* I grinned a large, private, self-satisfied smile away from their stares. *This room is mine.*

I rounded the final corner, heading back to my seat. "And, in the end, isn't that what we're all here for? To deliver those fantasies? So, when you ask me, *buddy*," once again I slapped the man on the shoulder, "why do I write romance? I say to you— because I have to. It's my life. It's my goal, and all of our goals. It's about the fantasy—and I deliver." That did it. Cheers and applause roared throughout the dining room, and even Nancy, it appeared, was—at least for the moment—a fan. "Buddy" raised his glass toward me, nodding and accepting his defeat.

I looked at Helena, who, much to my surprise was casually finishing up her entrée with a clear lack of interest in my performance. *Can I pick 'em or what?* Kneeling beside her, I asked, "Excuse me, Miss. If I haven't bored you too much already, would you mind slipping away to one of these other tables with me? I think I've worn my welcome at this one."

Finishing off her drink before giving me her attention, she said, "Sure. But you better do up that belt and tuck in that shirt before sitting down with me. I think everyone's had enough fantasy for one night."

Chuckling, I muttered: "Yes ma'am, can do." I stood and turned away demurely to fix myself up before leading the way to one of the smaller tables against the wall to get back to learning more about Helena Bliss.

CHAPTER EIGHT

Helen

I CAN ADMIT, the way Jack Smith worked a room was impressive. He was worthy of being a character in a novel—but in his own work? I don't know . . . there's a big ego under there. Would I ever let him know that I'd watched, took him in, and was impressed? *Nope. No fangirl or groupie, here.* Whatever his game was, it could only spell trouble for me. However, the people-watcher in me and my "writer's brain" definitely had their curiosities piqued.

After he was done his monologue and came back to our spot at the table, I threw myself into focusing on anything but him. Unfortunately, with his type apparently that challenge only attracts them. When Jack asked if I would join him at a private table, I should've said no . . . but how could I? I needed to learn more. My notebook demanded it. I would simply keep the conversation light, stay sober, and get to bed by eleven o'clock. *There was no way I could get into too much trouble before eleven.*

It was a nice surprise when he pulled out a tall wingback chair for me. This courtesy was not something I expected, but there was something undeniably nice about having someone treat you like someone special. *Like a lady, I guess?* Maybe that was it.

"Thank you," I said, easing myself into the soft seat as he sat down across from me with a smile at the small table near the fireplace.

"My pleasure," he said.

Sitting here together after our long day was both comfortable and awkward. We had spent all day less than ten feet apart, but had said very little to one another. Then, just minutes ago, Jack had drawn all that attention to himself, yet now he was hoping to be able to move twenty feet away and disappear with me? I know the other authors had to be watching; some of them—if not all—looking for stories to tell, write about, or at least remember to gossip about later. Yet "here" felt like the right place to be.

He stretched back in his chair, the soft black leather molding to his frame. It was then that I noticed something a little different than what I had observed in him before. Yes, he was attractive, strong, and his physicality could be intimidating to some, but there was a softness in his eyes that I had either missed or that hadn't been there earlier.

The calm and quiet we found was strangely comfortable, and I put aside my natural inclination and my upbringing to simply start a conversation to be polite. Instead, I felt compelled to let the feeling grow, to let the moment breathe, so that the silence could stretch out for as long as we could keep it within our grasp—which is when the server appeared.

Like a switch being turned on, I saw a change take place. Jack's body became much more rigid, his eyes alert and focused, and an entirely different smile appeared out of nowhere. *All in the blink of an eye.* So seamless and quick that it could have easily been missed if not for us sitting right across from each other.

She slid a plate of steak and veggies in front of him, and a tall glass of amber liquid. "Your food and beverage, Mr. Smith."

"Thanks, beautiful," he said, giving the meal an appreciative sniff. "Smells and looks just as good as I remember," he said, looking up at her, "and just one of the reasons this is my favorite stop on the tour."

The server's mouth, widening to impossible proportions, revealed perfect teeth that glistened in the dimness of the room as the glow from the fire danced upon cheeks now sporting their own natural pink tint. "It's always our pleasure to have you at The Grand," she said.

His gaze returned to me as she stood by waiting. "Something for you, Helena? Another drink, more to eat?"

"Yes, if there is anything either of you would like . . . " she said, her focus snapping my way as if she hadn't noticed I was there until now.

Apparently my invisibility cloak was still working. "Yes, please. Another glass of Chardon—" I looked over at Jack, who drank thirstily and in one move had already emptied nearly half his glass. "Actually, just an orange juice, please."

"Pardon?" they both asked.

"Yes, a glass of orange juice, please." *Sober was the plan, and sober I'll stay.*

"Are you not staying at the hotel?" he asked, "Because if not, I'm sure we can get you a driver, if that's your concern."

"No, no. I mean, yes, I am staying at the hotel, I'm just done drinking for the night." I nodded reassuringly to the server. "Just some orange juice. Thank you."

"Excellent," she said with a nod and a regular, non-Jackinduced smile. "And I'll grab another drink for you, Mr. Smith," she said, and dashed off.

Her silhouette had barely disappeared when Jack leaned in and chuckled at me, "Playing it safe, eh? Don't want to risk getting tipsy and falling in love with me?" He gave an exaggerated wink. "Smart girl. I understand."

Unable to restrain myself, I burst out laughing. On one hand, he was spot-on with his assessment about me playing it safe, but falling in love, afraid of risk? *You've picked the wrong girl.* "Do you wear that cowboy hat to help keep your head from swelling so you and your ego can both fit in the room?" I said.

A small smirk appeared as he did a double take.

"I told you already," I continued, "I'm not going to sleep with you, there's no worry there. I'm not one of your groupies. We're simply writing colleagues out for a night between shifts."

"It's all that cut and dry to you, is it? This place and my company . . . " he waved his hand toward his face as if revealing some supposed work of art, " . . . is so awful?"

"I'm not saying that at all. I'm just letting you know."

He leaned across the table now, much closer, and the feet that remained between us seemed consumed by the energy that continued to build. "You want me to know you won't sleep with me, but did you ever think that wasn't even a thought in my choosing to spend the weekend with you?"

Ouch. My ego took its first hit of the night.

"That maybe it was exactly the opposite reason," he said, "knowing full-well you wouldn't? Maybe I was the one playing it safe?"

Double-ouch! Clearly his ego was maintaining its healthy

fighting weight. "Oh yeah? Then why did you 'pick me', as you say?"

"Because you are gorgeous, intelligent, and clearly have your act together." Bomb delivered, he lounged back comfortably in his chair with a grin.

He says he picked me to spend the evening with, but doesn't want to sleep with me, yet finds me gorgeous, but safe. Oh, Helen . . .

Once again, silence. A new equilibrium.

This time, it wasn't going to be our server who started things rolling. It would be me, with my foot removed from my mouth. "I'm sorry."

"Huh?" He twisted up his face, cupped his ear. "What was that?"

I cleared my throat and spoke again, a little louder. "I said, I'm sorry."

"Oh, sorry. You're sorry?" His focus on me as he tried to piece together my meaning somehow made me feel even more embarrassed.

"I'm sorry for saying that and—"

"Saying what?"

"Saying that I wasn't going to sleep with you, that I'm not—"

An immature sly smile crossed his face. "Oh, so you *will* sleep with me?"

"What? No! I . . . " I searched for something, anything, and for whatever reason it was a Brussels sprout from his very own plate that I snatched up and hurled his way.

With the greatest of ease, he plucked it from the air, held it out my way, and gave a smile and wink before popping it into his mouth.

No way in the world is he going to twist this on me. "You know, comments and behavior like that are probably why people talk about you the way they do and make most of us at ill at ease around you," I said.

"Maybe."

"No, not maybe. Definitely. Between your oddly contrary nature and trying to sleep with everything that moves—"

"Am I?"

"Okay, knowing what we—Hey! Your own little speech just a few minutes ago let us all know about you and your," I curled my fingers up for air quotes, "'fantasies'. So, of course, any woman alone with you assumes you're looking to sleep with them for more fodder for your novels, and so we squirm and run away. Or jump right in your lap."

Sitting forward, elbows on his knees, chin on palms, he said, "Believe me—they all squirm, especially when they jump in my lap."

"Okay. I'm done here." There was no getting through to him. I had tried to help. Maybe he wasn't aware of what he was doing. *Real people don't act like he does!* I got up to leave as the server returned with my orange juice.

Quickly, Jack was on his feet. "Helena, please."

I couldn't look at him. I was leaving.

"Please stay. Let me apologize for my behavior," He took my glass off the tray and extended it my way, "over a glass of thirst-quenching, mouthwatering, soul-satisfying orange juice."

Jack and the server chuckled at his display, and I felt my resolve weaken. Slowly, I turned back toward him and said, with the driest humor possible, "Okay, one drink, and only because I know there's nothing like an orange juice on a Saturday night." I took the glass from him, had a small taste, and we sat back down.

Taking his seat, he raised his glass for a toast, "To guys who can't be taken out in public, and the people who call them on it. Here's hoping for the best finish to a weekend, ever."

Our glasses, his alcohol and my juice, clinked together with a mutual, "Cheers."

This was the cue our server was looking for to excuse herself. "If there's anything else you two need, please let me know. Otherwise, I'll be back in a while to check in."

We thanked her, but before she left, she surprised me by whispering in my ear: "You've got him." She stood up, and we shared a look where she nodded and gave me a wink before scurrying off, leaving me to wonder, *What the . . . ?*

"What was that?" asked Jack. "Am I trouble again already?"

I took the upper hand. "Maybe. You can just call it 'sisterhood'."

"Oh no, I'm doomed!" he said with a laugh. With that, he began to dig into his meal and I became immersed in what was actually a surprisingly good orange juice.

Jack ate with startling and impressive speed and efficiency which prompted me to ask, "Do you always eat so fast?"

He stopped, mid-chew, the fork with his next delivery hanging in midair. It may have been the lights playing tricks on my eyes, but I swear I saw him blush, if just for a split second. Wiping his mouth with a napkin, he swallowed his bite. "Honestly, I rarely ever eat at one of these things, or with the other authors, at all. Usually, there's too much going on. Everyone wants to talk. Everyone's so eager to gauge and gouge that you have to be careful you don't miss anything. When I'm alone, it's usually only for a very brief period of time, so I will admit . . . " he looked down sheepishly, " . . . I *do* tend to inhale my food." He shook his head a few times, then his eyes returned my way. "I'm sorry, especially when you're not even eating. I must be a sight."

It was sincere, and appreciated. We've all been there, maybe not to this degree, but . . . "Not at all," I said. "I completely understand. It's no big deal, and, frankly, I was enjoying the silence."

"Ow!" He sat back hard in his chair. "Got me again. Blindsided."

I laughed, "No, crazy man, I sincerely meant I was enjoying the silence. When you're not being that other guy, you're pretty nice."

He perked up and stared quizzically my way. "Wait. Was that a compliment *pour moi?*"

"Maybe, but don't let it go to your head. You'll never find a hat to fit it again."

He pursed his lips in thought then nodded my way. "Y'know, you might be right," and we shared another laugh.

"All right, you made a toast about 'best finish to a weekend ever'. To be able to properly assess that, we need a standard to measure it against," I said.

"I'm listening."

"Tell me about your worst weekend, or worst conference, ever."

Without hesitation, like he had been waiting for the question, he started out with, "Well, there were these triplets—"

Ewww! Make him stop. "Save it for one of your books. An actual event-related story, not sexual."

He pouted, big and deep, his lower lip puffed out far enough to be able to catch buckets of water. "Well, that makes it a whole lot more difficult. Let me think on it. What about you?"

"Hmm." It was no contest, immediately I knew the one to share. "Okay, one time, at a place I will leave nameless—"

"Was this one recent, or have you been waiting a long time to spill it?"

I giggled before continuing. "It was quite a while ago when I was just getting started. I was new to the romance writers' conference scene. I was nervous and not nearly as outgoing as I am today—and that's saying something.

"The day had gone pretty well. I didn't know what to expect, and I was just grateful that the organizers had given me the chance to be there. Still am grateful, and so I mean no disrespect to them, but many of what I've come to realize are the usual amenities were missing. Not only did we have to pay for all of our refreshments, but we were paying the markup prices the vendors were charging. The conference staff was essentially invisible before—and even during—the whole event, unless they were coming to us with some type of new fee we owed or needed a favor. Which is what got me sucked into drawing a poster for them while I was working my booth and people were wandering by." I took a sip of my juice. He sat forward in his chair and pushed his empty plate aside.

"I hope you did stick figures. I would have."

"Stick figures would have been an improvement over what I did. I was too nervous and frustrated about not being able to focus my attention on my job, especially getting to meet fans. Thankfully, their standards were low and the poster was pretty much just kids' stuff where a great amount of talent wasn't required. Anyway, after all that, cut to the send-off. It was the capper. When I tell you the venue where we ate was nothing like this place, you have to understand—it was *nothing* like this place."

Once again, he chuckled. "I'm under contract to say that there isn't anywhere else like this place. This is *Grand*."

I rolled my eyes and shook my head. "Prince of Texas, you have no idea. This other conference site was just a meeting hall basement. The musty aroma was just there to hide the smell of the mold, and the sweaty men who grew old in there swapping stories and smoking cigars."

He cringed and shuddered.

"I swear it," I said. "And the food was like from some sort of low-ball stag-and-doe where close relatives did it potluck style, but were in the middle of a family feud. I'm talking cocktail-weenies-on-sticks—"

"No!" He nearly spat out his drink, laughing.

"Yes! See? You get it. Apparently the only ones who didn't get the irony of serving cocktail weenies to a group of dirty-minded romance writers were the organizers."

"Please tell me they had melons, served in some sort of form-fitting cup, or—" His laughter cut through the ambient noise of the crowd, loud and boisterous, so full of life it drew attention from the rest of the room in a way that had even a few of the other authors chuckling without having a clue about the cause.

I took another breath for the homestretch. "That may have

been part of the finale, but I didn't stay to find out. Technically, I helped organize a rout, of sorts. When everything settled down, a few of us snuck out secret agent style to a nearby restaurant. It wasn't anything fancy, standard mid-range comfort food stuff, but it was the best time and I made some lifelong friends that night. Even though my tunneling out ended up getting me removed from any further invitations to that event, I chalk that one up as a win."

Jack continued to chuckle, his palms and fingers still facing up like little cups for the imagined melons. Our laughter trickled into a natural finish.

"So, that's my story, mister. What have you got?"

"Melons," he laughed again, and he pantomimed juggling fruit until we watched it hit the floor. "Like those," he watched the invisible melons roll away, "I have nothing to compare. I bow to your misadventure, but at least you made some friends out of it. Maybe that was the point of running the event like that. Something small, familiar and conducive to bonding—"

"That basement was more conducive to bondage than bonding," I said, and we were off laughing once again.

When we stopped, he gained a more serious look. "That basement you described. I can see it, smell it, almost *taste* it. Is that what your writing style is like? Did I just get a sneak peek?"

It was my turn to pause, sit back in my chair, and think. "Yeah, I guess. Well, maybe," I shrugged my shoulders, "maybe you should read it for yourself and see what you think." Without a thought, I switched into my role as promotions manager, "My newest is—"

"'A Long, Hard Road'. Is that where I should start?"

"Yep, it's a standalone about a woman—"

"Is it sweet or steamy?"

I gave him a look I had practiced in the mirror many times to be my most authorial and intriguing. "Like me, it starts off sweet until it's time for the heat, then goes long and hard until steam is all you see."

"Ohhh, really?"

I nodded. "Wait until you see the two main characters at the barn. You might need a cold drink or something stiff handy—" *Oh God!*

That did it. The serious and focused look he had was gone in an instant. The respectful and mature guy I had just been sitting with disappeared in another roar of laughter, yet, even though I knew what was going through his mind, he kept it inside. No crude comments, though they were deserved, just his ongoing laughter. Part of me wished he would just make the lewd joke and move on, until the voice of reason chimed in. *Lighten up, Helen. This is how it's supposed to be. With anyone else, you would have peed yourself laughing by now.*

And it was then that the dam officially burst, and I joined in with the laughter. I tried to explain how I was more accustomed to speaking with female readers. My spiel was never meant for men. But I was too caught up in the hilarity. In fact, after a time, I think we were both giggling just for the fun of it, and that, in itself, was entirely freeing and satisfying. Soon, we were both laying back in our chairs, comfortably spent, with huge smiles on our face.

"Thank you, Jack, this has been . . . " I didn't want to offend him, but let's be honest, " . . . it's been surprisingly 'nice'."

He sized me up with a sideways stare and then a smile. "I know that must've been painful for you to say, so I'll take it as a compliment."

"Well, that's how I meant it. So, good. But I'm really going to have to call it a night," I said.

But before I could get out of my seat, his hand was on mine and he was leaning closer in to talk.

"Could you," he said, then paused to look around the room. When he was sure there wasn't anyone in earshot, he continued, "Could you tell everyone you're calling it an early night because you're not feeling well?"

It was my turn for the sideways glance, but with an added double take. "What?"

"Please?"

"First of all, I'm feeling perfectly well, thank you. Second," I checked my watch to confirm that it was in fact almost eleven o'clock, "it's not early." This time, as I stood, he had nothing. He just gave me a look. It was surprising to see him speechless and there was something in those eyes . . . *Sadness? Disappointment?* I didn't know, but either way, I was heading to bed—in a minute. I sat back down. "Why?"

He laid on a grin that looked far too much like the guy I met earlier in the day being pelted by heart-shaped erasers. The cocky and arrogant Jack I thought I had escaped by coming over to this private table. Apparently, I was wrong and as I stood again he let go of my hand. I went to the table where everyone still sat comfortably nursing drinks and sharing stories. *Maybe I am going to bed too early.*

"I'm going to call it a night. See you all tomorrow," I said, with a smile and a wave. I had been polite, even courteous, and yet received numerous gasps and exaggerated looks where people looked at their watches and then at me as if aliens had arrived. I had a good mind to—

"Yeah, she's not feeling well," said Jack, now by my side, his hand resting on the small of my back in a comfortable, far-too-familiar way.

Subtly, I sidestepped just enough to let his hand fall away and gave him what I hoped was a look that was more about keeping him in check than showing how much I appreciated the support. "Yeah, it must've been something I ate," I offered weakly.

He turned and gave me a childish grin. "Probably the melon balls."

I don't know how he said it with a straight face! It was all I could do to contain my laughter. The cheek on him. The giggles hit me, but thankfully everyone at the table was still looking at Jack, and then at Bob, as he asked, "Melon balls? I didn't see any melon balls. How come we didn't get any melon balls?"

CHAPTER NINE

Helen

A S THE OTHER authors segued loudly into a tangent about the mysterious melon balls, I took the opportunity to exit stage left—Jack Smith on my heels. We roared with laughter the moment we escaped into the hallway. It was probably a good thing it was only eleven o'clock, because I'm sure we would have woken up the first two floors.

Jack's face was beet red and I'm sure mine matched the shade of his as I asked, "What is wrong with you? 'Melon balls'?"

"What, am I wrong? Or was it the cocktail weenies that turned your stomach?" He doubled over, slapping his knee, and sent me into fits not only at his jokes but at him laughing so hard at them.

As we stood there in the empty hall, I was becoming increasingly aware that we may have both had a few too many drinks, even if I had ended with OJ. *I shouldn't have thought "drinks". My poor bladder.*

I picked myself up off the wall. "I really do have to get to bed. You coming?" That slip of the tongue was like a sobering shot of ice water in my face. *Oh no, I hope he doesn't think—*

He snapped upright and extended me his elbow. "I would be

honored to escort you to your room, m'lady."

My giggles returned as I took his elbow and we made our way down the hall.

Abruptly, he stopped, the motion so sharp it almost sent me ass over tea kettle, and he looked at me with a deadly serious face. "Wait, do you think this is a mistake? Are we being selfish? Shouldn't we be helping Bob find his balls . . . er, his *melon* balls?" His face turned bright red again and I nearly spit out my teeth as we returned to full-on hilarity.

We continued like that to the elevator, up to the tenth floor, and right up to my door. It was then I realized that I'd continued to occupy his elbow the whole way. It was also then I got that awkward feeling of arriving at my door at the end of the night with a man. And not just any man, but one who looked like this and had such a reputation. I felt a faint tremble in my stomach as I tried to figure out what to do.

Gingerly, he removed my hand from his arm. As we looked at each other, the giggles faded away and a new look came over him. "Thank you, Helena Bliss. This has been a blast. I don't think I have ever had such a night at one of these conventions, and I am exceedingly grateful."

He leaned in, arms wide. I stood there, locked in place, my mind spinning in a way I wished I could blame on alcohol but I knew I was only fooling myself. Then Jack engulfed me, his arms tight around my waist, his chest pressing firmly against my breasts. The musky scent of his cologne wafted into my nostrils, making my toes tingle. It felt good in a way I knew it shouldn't and couldn't, especially with him. Yet, before I could protest, he let me go and was rolling down the hallway in his one-and-only

"Jack Fantastic" swagger.

I had to stop him. "Jack?"

He stopped mid-stride, and with a silly little hop turned back my way. "Yes?"

"Why did you want to leave the party? Why did you need me as a cover?"

He grinned, and his head bobbed thoughtfully. "I'm afraid you wouldn't understand."

Like an icepick, a horrible thought ripped through my brain. "I think we've had a good time tonight," I said. "You told me you'd never had a night this good and I get that might just be part of your, um, complimentary nature, but please do one last thing for me, if it's at all true. Answer a question for me—as honestly as you can."

"Uh-oh. I have a feeling jokes or a smile won't get me out of this one." His steps away looked almost subconscious. "Okay, fire when ready. If I can answer, it'll be honest."

That icepick had begun to fade, but my ego turned on me with the little voice that cautioned, *Do you really want to know?* Yes. I did. "Did you leave with me so that the other authors would think I was about to become another notch on your bedpost? And did you think it would actually happen?"

He gave an exaggerated sigh of relief and wiped his brow. "You cheater, that's two questions. I'll answer the first and leave you to figure out the second. Simply put, no, my reason for leaving with you was not to give other people that impression." He slowly walked back my way. "I am aware that some people may think that, and I apologize to you for whatever part of my history may fall on you. If there was a way I could've prevented that, I promise you, I would." We now stood within arm's reach of each other, and the look I had seen when he first asked for help had returned to his face. "I knew when I first saw you at the conference today that you were someone I could trust. I—"

If it weren't for me becoming collateral damage, he wouldn't have noticed me. *How could he say that?* "Why?"

"Instinct. Sounds hokey, sure," he said, shrugging his shoulders, "but it's all I can offer. I know to trust my instincts. My ability to read people on the fly got me where I am in life. When I said earlier that I thought you were different than they were, someone I could buddy up with, I meant it. And I meant it with the greatest respect." His face flashed the impish look I had come to know too well, and had me giggling again before he continued talking. "If it helps, I've spent a good part of the night picturing you with a mustache," he said, and he blew up with laughter once again.

I swatted him hard in the arm. "You are a fool, Jack!"

"I am! I truly am."

I gave him another swat. "Good. I've been picturing you with the head of an ass!" It was lame, but it was all I had.

That sent him stumbling down the hall with renewed energy and humor, saying, "You, my friend, are too funny."

"Oh, go away," I said. I stood there, hanging in the wind, trying to find a quality parting shot.

"I'm going," he said with an awkward wave as the elevator doors rolled open.

"Don't be too hungover in the morning. I'll be waiting with the coffee at the booth."

He had become nothing more than a floating head hanging

out of the elevator. "You better. Good night, see you tomorrow."

"Not if I see you first." *Oh, Helen, really?* I waved my arm, shooing him away, and he disappeared. I ducked into my room, closed the door behind me, and flopped back against it. "Did you really just say, 'not if I see you first'? This is why you're not allowed to stay up past eleven o'clock."

CHAPTER TEN

Jack

*L*AST DAY OF *the convention to make an impression, Jack. Time to have fun.*

Playing it cool would be the best way to handle Helena this morning, I'd decided.

And here she came around the corner, bearing a great big smile and two coffees, so I threw myself into sorting today's promo photos of me in uniform and on set for *Drafted* as if I hadn't seen her.

The look of surprise on her face as she realized I had beat her to our booths was worth all the extra hustle this morning. Out of the corner of my eye, I watched her pace slow until she came to an eventual stop near my table.

"Good morning, Jack."

I gave a quick, off-hand wave, a "Mornin', Helena", and kept unpacking my books and swag. "Your coffee is in your booth, waiting for you. I hope it's still hot."

It was difficult but I stood expressionless, watching her startled face as she noticed the piping hot drink sitting on her table with her name on it.

Yep, continue to underestimate me. You're gonna learn today.

Like most people, she likely wouldn't understand that the reason I had such high energy was that I still kept a steady training regimen which was now, in many ways, superior to my playing days. Now I trained for health instead of performance. It's the reason I could be bright-eyed today even though I got less sleep last night, due to a sudden surge of writing that had me burning up my laptop screen. There would be time to catch up on sleep tonight, but in the meantime, I had a lot planned for today, and this was just the preview.

Helena walked back to my table. "Thanks, Jack. I, uh, also brought you one. Like I said I would last night."

"That's really nice of you, thanks. Please just put it beside my other coffee. I'll save yours for later."

She stopped just before the cup landed, I don't know why, and hustled back to her table with my coffee still in hand.

Odd. Dropping a stack of "Game on the Line" bookmarks back in the box, I walked over to the boundary between our booths. She turned her back to me, and her body took on a strange motion.

Is she shaking? I tried to peek around her but had no chance from this vantage point. "Everything okay?"

"Yep. All good," she said, and kept up with the erratic movement.

"You sure?" I wandered back over and grabbed my half-full coffee cup, accepting the minor burn as I chugged it down. "Because the coffee you brought me isn't here, and I just finished mine."

She adjusted her position so that her back still faced me. "Oh yeah? Hang on, I'll get it to you in just a second."

Something didn't sound right. "Um . . . great. I'll just wait over here, then." I returned warily to my booth.

She kept shaking for just a few seconds more before her shoulders slumped and she stopped. With what looked like a sigh, she sprung around with a big smile on her face and bounced over to me with the cup held high. "Your steaming nectar of the gods, sir," she said, and made a big display of delivering the holy relic before scooting off as fast as her little loafers could take her.

Cup in hand, I eyed it suspiciously. *What in the world? How badly did I offend her last night?*

I gave the drink a smell, and, as expected, it was spectacular. "Hmm." *No obvious signs of poison.*

Helena dove into her boxes in the way I had just moments before, and it added to my discomfort. "Okay, I have to ask," I said. "You didn't spit in this or something, did you?"

My question hit her hard and fast. She maintained her act of being busy for maybe ten more seconds before stifling a laugh and standing up red-faced, shaking her head at me and pointing.

Being part of a team usually involves a wide variety of practical jokes so I knew her look well. *Prank alert!* I snapped the cup out and away from me as fast as possible. I switched it between hands to see if there was any sticky or otherwise disgusting material now transferred onto my hands. *Thankfully, no.*

That put her over the top and she fell onto her chair.

My hands were clean, so I had to assume it—whatever that may be—was inside the cup. I lifted the lid and gave it a swirl to check for hidden nasty stuff that I could hear or feel moving around, but it felt okay. I turned the cup around to tear away the opening flap and that's when I saw it.

Funny girl! I worked to replace my look of surprise with anger, and shot her what I hoped was a terrifying look.

Silence. Her hand came up over her mouth and she turned away.

I looked again at the cup to read the now blurry, grease-pencilled scrawl, the thing she had been working so hard to erase: "Jackass", above some barista's crude drawing of the animal. I kept my eyes on the cup, knowing if I looked her way I wouldn't be able to keep my serious, offended visage intact. Instead, I put the cup on the table and lightly stomped my way back to my booth and continued organizing everything.

After a couple of silent minutes, she said, "You're not mad, right? It was just a joke. Y'know, breaking the ice and having fun?"

There was still no way I could look at her without laughing or giving her a high-five, so I continued in my stone-cold manner, keeping an eye on her with my peripheral vision.

She caved. "Uh . . . sorry?"

"I thought we broke the ice just fine last night, and that you wouldn't think of me like that anymore. Guess I was wrong," I said, with a weak shrug.

"We did, but—yeah, sometimes maybe I read people wrong and, well, I've been given grief before about my sense of humor. So, again, sorry."

She sounded sincere, and I felt a little guilty for playing it out like this, but I knew it would only be a matter of time before she—*There it was!*

Helena stood in front of a banner bearing her image that she had left up overnight. A gorgeous piece of work, it caught her essence perfectly. Highlights in her beautiful blonde hair glowed, her icy blue eyes staring off in a way that made you want to join whatever fantasy she was creating in her mind. As promotional material goes, it was great, without crossing the line into cheesy. The only thing that some might consider a blemish was the small Three Musketeers mustache that her image appeared to have grown overnight, or, more accurately, in the last hour at the hands of my dry-erase marker.

Gone was that apologetic, contrite woman. In her place was a fearsome figure clenching and unclenching her fists, ready to go ballistic. Just when I thought she would go off, I ducked back into my box of books and watched her carefully.

Much to my surprise, she took a very deep breath and let it out slowly, like she was doing yoga. Her fingers moved in sequence, like she was counting to ten. Either way, she hadn't fired a volley at me. Yet. *Maybe she didn't realize I was the artist?*

A piercing look came my way. A glancing blow, enough to correct me. She did, in fact, know that I was the graffiti villain, I think, but then her gaze drifted away as if I was just an incidental part of the scenery.

I watched curiously as she walked over and pulled up the matching banner on the other side of her booth to find it was as close to a carbon copy of the other one as I could produce. Then she grinned and nodded appreciatively, like an art critic in a gallery.

"Something wrong?" I said, nonchalantly. I had to keep stoking the fire. We were even now, at least in my books. The question was, did she feel the same? I didn't want to risk a repeat of the Nancy Coeur incident.

With an Oscar award-worthy smile, she said, "Nope, everything's good. Great. Really." She adjusted the position of the banner slightly before returning to her unpacking.

Silence and *a smile. I've known enough women to know that's a bad sign.*

There was a quick screech of feedback overhead, then a woman's voice blared over the public address system. "Five minutes until doors open. Have a fantastic adventure today!"

"Good luck," Helena called, as she sat down in her chair for some final prep, organizing her pens and checking her hair and make-up in a small pocket mirror.

"Thanks, but I don't think I need luck, I've got jackass powers," I said, giving her a flash of the "gun show", doing a quick double-bicep flex in her direction.

She shook her head with a chuckle.

CHAPTER ELEVEN

Helen

CLUTCHING A PAPERBACK to her chest, a woman in her late-twenties stood at my table blinking at me with a big smile and the cutest little dimples.

"Well, good morning to you," I said. "Thanks so much for coming out."

Her subtle nod touched my heart. I will never understand what I did to have such loving fans, but they meant the world to me. Rising from my seat, I glimpsed 'A' and 'Road' on the worn spine of her book.

I tried again. "I see you've read my book. That's—"

That was the necessary trigger. Her face lit up and she gushed, "Oh yes! I've read all of them. I've read this one three times already. I read your blog, your Twitter, and whatever else you share. Your stories are everything good."

"Why, thank you. Can I sign it fo—" A couple of people jostling for position on their way to Jack's booth bumped her aside. They apologized, and she looked none the worse for wear, but it was getting out of hand. "I'm sorry, my neighbor has picked today to make a spectacle of himself."

A goofy grin spread across her face, and she nodded rapidly.

"Oh, I know. I'm going there next to get him to sign my boobs."
She stared at Jack like a dream struck teenager. "I can't believe
you two are together . . . he's so hot. Don't you think?"

*"Hot"? "Together"? Judging by the modeling pictures I found of
him online last night . . . yeah, maybe, but he's also a narcissistic
piece of work.* "He's very successful, I'll give him that."

"Oh God, yeah. I'd let him *success* me," she said, sharing a
giddy laugh with two other women nearby. One of whom added,
"I drove two hours to get here in hopes of him *successing* me. He
does that, y'know?" The third, swooning even harder than the
rest, crowed, "That's how I got into one of his stories. Do it right
and he'll write about you." That started them squealing again.

I interrupted the droolfest. "Still want me to sign that book
before you go over there?"

My fan quickly found her composure. "Yes, please. Sorry. I
just got caught up in—"

I took the book delicately in hand. It was far worse for wear
than it had initially appeared and required careful handling when
opening the cover. "That's okay. I understand. Now, who should
I make this out to?"

"Shannon. I want you to know—"

I prepare four or five different messages for these events.
Nothing is worse than seeing an author, someone you have given
so much time and commitment to, rubber-stamping your book
with the same trite thing you saw the people before you getting.
This time I went with, *Dear Shannon, Life can be "A Long, Hard
Road". Enjoy the journey—Helena Bliss.*

Shannon continued chattering as I passed the book back,
"—your stories help get me through my job, my relation-

ships . . . " She picked up the book to read the inscription, but appeared suddenly distracted. There was a soft tearing sound. Her mouth fell open as her book hit the table, the cover dangling from her hand. In a whisper-shriek, she said, "My. God. He's. Coming. Over. Here." Her voice went up in both volume and pitch. "He's coming over here!"

I followed her gaze and, sure enough, it was Jack, again, returning for more mischief. As he got closer, so did the women, or, as I had to call them—the giddy girls—as they lost control again. When he got to the barrier between our tables, he gave the ladies that big, devilish smile while somehow making his eyes sparkle on command. I watched him look over the crowd, and could almost read his mind. "*Not her. Not her. Did her and her friend already. Not her, maybe that one* . . . and it turned my stomach. Finally he gave them a wave, and a "Morning, ladies", which sent them shrieking again.

I couldn't compete with him. We were only two hours into the day and it was already looking like a loss. I'd just have to find a way to deal.

"Hey, Helena. Can I bug you for a minute?"

A minute? Could I be so lucky to have it only last a minute? I stood up, adjusted my skirt, found a smile, and tried to talk over the ruckus. "Sure can. What's up, booth buddy?"

He leaned in close. "Sorry, didn't want to keep shouting—" Strangely, he stopped speaking and seemed to pause to smell me, my perfume or something.

I snapped my head back a few inches. "Yes?"

"Yeah, um, can you watch my stuff a couple minutes? I'm planning to do a reading and need to get a couple things."

My head shook, involuntarily, in shock and disbelief.

A self-satisfied grin grossly crossed his face.

"A reading? I didn't see you scheduled to do a reading today. I thought you'd be at your table the whole time."

In the most matter-of-fact tone, he said, "I am. I'm going to do it right here."

That wasn't allowed. Maybe it wasn't explicitly stated in the rules because they had never had someone with such selfish arrogance to do such a thing, but it was implied. It was convention etiquette, at the very least. I could run and tell, but I bet that's what he wanted. *That's it! He's testing me.* I won't give him the satisfaction. Let him hang himself. "Are you allowed to do that?" I said calmly.

"Guess we'll find out. I assumed it was for this kind of freedom that they keep on giving me a corner booth with so much space near the entrance. To let people see me and all I have to offer. It's not like you're going to tell on me or get me into trouble, right? Worse yet, throw rubber hearts at me?"

I giggled, legitimately, the image was funny, but it was all still ridiculous. *Oh, and selfish!* "You know I have a booth here, too? That's going to create such a problem."

"We'll see," he said, with a smile that had probably been used a thousand times to placate interrogations. "I need to go find Bert. Will you watch my stuff?"

Whatever. I flipped my hands up in surrender. "Sure, whatever. Just be quick, please. I have stuff of my own to do and I can't be responsible for your—" Before I could finish, he leapt over his table and was running off like a kid freed from detention.

That's it, you know? He's a kid. Like most men, but the prototyp-

ical example that furthers all stereotypes.

With a deep breath, I tried to escape the annoying distractions and get back to the fun of it all, another pair of early-twenties readers waiting for me. "Good morning to you both."

"Mornin'," the man said, followed by an enthusiastic "Good morning, Helena!" from the woman.

The way they held hands, fingers interlaced with early relationship passion, was beautiful. The stuff we all strive to capture in our stories. I smiled at him. "I don't get many men at my tables, not nearly enough, but it's great to see you supporting your girlfriend today. That's real romance."

They both laughed, she a little more boisterously than he, and in unison replied, "We're married," and they held up their hands to show off their rings. He continued with, "And we're both fans. We read in bed together every night."

She finished his thought. "Sometimes as foreplay, other times as part of the cooldown," and they both shared a dirty, yet cute, laugh.

"Well, I'm flattered. Glad I can be part of the fun," I said with a wink. "Be sure to get some swag." I pointed them toward the baskets of goodies at the end of my table, lingering on the little vials of massage oil with a not-so-subtle point of my finger.

"Oh, yeah?" they chimed, and both grabbed a vial. "Thanks."

I don't know what delivered the spark of motivation right at that moment. I no longer question my muse, but rather make the most of what I'm given. Right then, it was so perfect. *Jack thought his little mustache prank was so funny? Time to dish up a serving of sweet revenge.*

"Excuse me, be right back," I said to the next woman in line.

Surveying my stack of markers, I went with the green and made my way quickly behind Jack's table to one of the gaudy cardboard cutouts of him dressed in a football uniform. I spun it around away from prying eyes and went to work, letting my limited artistic ability do its thing as fast as it could.

Once done, I raced back to my seat just as the line that had built up in front of his table, and was now spilling behind my fans, started hooting and hollering, with several people calling out, "Titan!"

Sure enough, when I took a look, there in the middle of the melee was Jack, shaking hands and waving to the crowd, his other arm carrying some signboard and a three-legged stand.

He looked my way and our eyes locked.

I tried telepathically to let him know how much I still disapproved.

His bass voice rolled over the crowd, "Almost ready. I've got a special treat for everyone today." He gave me a wink that made my eyes roll.

Once again, my attempt at psychic powers had failed me, my message of disapproval wasn't received.

He propped up the stand and wrote on the sign. When he finished, he held it up to show "Special Event Reading. Here. 11 a.m." with his signature in chicken-scratch below it, just in case someone might think there was some other egomaniac in desperate need of attention. He leapt back over the table into his booth, and the crowd went nuts.

My jaw locked tight. My teeth began to grind. "Do you mind?" I hissed.

"Nope, can't say that I do!" he said, with a grin so big it fit his

75

claim to Texas.

He jumped into his seat and we returned to greeting fans and signing books, both anticipating the 11 a.m. storm he had summoned.

CHAPTER TWELVE

Jack

A S THE TIME for my reading drew closer, I noticed a few staff members—including Todd—were now part of the massive crowd which had formed. It extended out in both directions from the front of my table and around the corner, while also creeping into Helena's space. Funny enough, it felt like the staff might be there to give me trouble, but, maybe because of the way I stood up for Todd yesterday or some other stroke of luck, they were standing down so far.

Maybe they're waiting for me to hang myself and totally cross the line? I smiled and waved at them and then to the rest of the crowd. I swallowed hard, forcing the butterflies in my stomach into silence. *Time to shine, Superstar. Go big or go home!*

I grabbed the book and jumped up onto the table. "Thank you, everyone, for stopping by for this impromptu reading."

Right on cue, they cheered, and I ate it up. *Mine! This is what you were made to do.*

I walked across my impromptu stage, avoiding whatever paraphernalia I could but whatever couldn't be missed was sacrificed to the show, either stepped on or kicked aside. "I love each of you for your devotion. Your commitment is what drives me to succeed."

"We love you too, Jack!" someone called from the crowd, quickly echoed by a few others before a chant of "Titan!" started the place rocking.

They love me? Yes, they do! I let them have their moment before calming them down so we could move forward. "Thank you. This is why Texas will always be my home away from home." As I opened the book and began to flip pages, I took a slow stroll toward where my table met Helena's. Arriving at the right page and the border between our domains, I announced, "Today, you're in for a very special treat. You've all heard much of my story, but I need to share something with you that I discovered last night."

Looking at Helena, she met my gaze with a mix of anger and confusion. Actually, at this very instant, she had probably already progressed past anger and was heading to a place I didn't want to see—but that made it perfect.

I gave her the smile that had been working so well for me, and when it missed, I continued to talk to the choir. "I've discovered something so hot it may very well be the fuel for all of my future conquests. It's a steamy love story called 'A Loooong'—" I gave a dramatic pause before continuing, with an emphasis on the obvious innuendo, "'Hard' . . . ahem, 'Road', by my friend, Helena Bliss."

Helena's eyes blinked rapidly as she asked, "What? What are you doing?" I don't know that I really heard her words over the cheering or could just read her highly agitated lips, but it didn't matter. We were rolling now.

I gestured to her in a grandiose fashion to be sure the crowd knew she was the author of the book.

She gave a long, hard blush and my heart beat even harder.

"Okay. I have it on good authority just where to start. Brace yourselves." I could feel all eyes, my crowd, her crowd, the event staff, and Helena, hanging on every word.

Oh God, yes!

And I read, in a deep, resonant voice:

As Brock approached, I could feel the heat of his gorgeous brown eyes devouring every inch of me, as I wished he would. My heart pounded in my chest, racing against the wind that whipped through his auburn hair.

I wanted to say "hi", but my willpower had left me and I struggled to find words. I wanted this, I wanted him and only him. I had fantasized about this moment since the days when I first learned about my body and its needs. In those days, he was just an abstract fantasy that all girls had, but, in this moment, I knew the face of that passion and it was Brock Hargrove. In this moment I belonged to him.

When he stopped, barely two feet away, staring down into my eyes, I was sure I would die. I could see drops of sweat glistening as they drifted from his throat into the crease of his muscular chest. I imagined what it might be like to follow that drop on a journey down into unexplored territory.

In the barn behind me, the horses whinnied at the approaching storm. The clouds were gray, but the electricity was building right here.

"Jessie . . . " His brow furrowed, deep in thought. "Jessie, I don't know how to say this, but—"

Something came over me. To this day I can't put it into words, but I became so painfully aware of the seconds ticking by. Seconds that had been accumulating all my life. I couldn't take anymore and blurted out, "Then don't!" I grabbed a handful of his hair and pulled his head down to meet my lips. I kissed him as if I had never kissed anyone before. I kissed him deeply, as if my life depended on it, because, in that instant, I believed it did.

His rough hands took hold of my face. His firm, yet soft, lips devoured mine.

My nails bit into the fabric of his worn blue denim shirt, and I pressed on, my body quivering in anticipation.

Despite my hold on him, he stepped back and ended the kiss. His hands came down upon my plaid work shirt and ripped it free, exposing me to the rapidly cooling air. His eyes drank me in as he mouthed the words, "Wow . . . ", and I felt empowered.

I didn't care about the surrounding world. That others in the main house barely two hundred yards away might see my breasts heaving heavily against a black bra that was far less practical than I would have worn in my equestrian days. I didn't care, and I tore open his shirt. His bare skin was covered with a thin sheen of sweat, and rose and fell rapidly in time with the deep animalistic breathing he now produced. I needed my skin against his. I stripped off my shirt, unhooked the front clasp of my bra, and let it fall away.

We watched it float away on the steadily-building wind before landing with a soft sigh in the nearby dirt.

Then he leapt. Firmly seizing my hips, he lifted me up, and with a thud, I landed hard against the old wooden barn door. Once again, his lips returned to mine as my legs laced around his waist. Our breath became one, our hearts beating a unified tribal beat. We poured our energy into each other, creating a whirlwind of excite-

ment as the rain, in large massive drops, fell upon us, each spot of contact virtually evaporating upon contact—

"Thank you so much, Helena Bliss," I said. "Every morning should start off like that!"

The look on Helena's face was priceless: flabbergasted and at a total loss for words, with an expression that said she would give anything for two minutes of invisibility. The wish would've been wasted, as the red in her cheeks became a beacon no-one could miss.

She gave in to the attention with an awkward wave of her hand, which she quickly interrupted by stopping to blow me a kiss. "You're too kind, Jack—and modest, since I'm sure most of your mornings start off as the inspiration for such scenes."

Nice. A lob my way. I slowly turned to the crowd with a knowing look and a grin, baiting the hook with anticipation. "It did *this* weekend . . . "

Her reflex was a giggle. We were playing along well, until she gave me a double take and then clammed up to abruptly end the game.

Not about to lose the crowd, I fanned my chest to let them see I was still catching my breath. They waited anxiously for me to continue. The snippet had effected them as much as it did me last night, and again just now. We were one big heaving, horny mass—and that felt like the right place to leave them. "I think, for the sake of each and every one of us, I'd better stop right there before we set off the sprinklers." I took an exaggerated drink from my water bottle that I knew they gulped along with me. "If you liked that, and want to find out just how hard that road can get, you better hurry over to see Helena Bliss before she's sold out again." I pointed over at Helena, who stood at her table staring at me with wide eyes. I smiled and mouthed the words, "You're up."

She stepped, almost staggered, back before regaining composure. "Thank you, Jack. I don't think I've ever heard it read quite like that. I may have just found the voice for Brock."

Touché!

Right then, I saw a whole new side of the Helena persona as she worked the crowd. "What do you think, ladies?" The crowd squealed, and it was my turn to feel overwhelmed. It was one thing for it to happen under my control, it was another thing to be ambushed and have someone else orchestrating it. Some may call it humbling, but I'm not that guy.

"If you think your Brock could be a Titan," I called to Helena, then tore open the top two buttons of my shirt, let it flap open and then kissed each bicep before delivering my trademark double-bicep shot, "then maybe we should talk. It sounds like he's got the stuff."

The look on Helena's face changed as we made eye contact again. There was something different. "He's got it all—and more," she said. The words hung in the air beautifully, and the crowd applauded and cheered.

Game. Set. Match. Together, she and I had played the round perfectly, or so I thought.

Just as I was about to move on with the day and let us return to work, Helena reached down, and, looking me dead in the eye, brought up a marker and her hand mirror, and drew a small Three Musketeers mustache on her upper lip. "Thank you, Jack," she said with a smirk, before moving to stand beside one of her banners. "I want to be sure everyone can recognize me."

It was my turn to be speechless. People were laughing, even though they may not have been in on the joke, but I was having a hard time reading things. Was it a smirk of contempt, were we still on the outs, or—?

Then she broke into a good and proper laugh, before announcing, "Welcome, everyone, let's have some fun. Line up here if you'd like to get a book signed by a lady with a mustache," and I knew the game was still on.

CHAPTER THIRTEEN

Helen

W HAT HAD STARTED out as potentially the worst conference day ever was rapidly rolling toward me in record
numbers. The buzz of the crowd all swinging my way due to
Jack's efforts was overwhelming and incredibly unexpected. I will
have to be sure to give him a thank-you.

An unruly row of women pressing against my table brought
me out of my thoughts with the question: "So, did you sleep with
him?"

"What? No! Oh, hell no!"

The next one asked, "Are you going to? Clearly he's hot for
you and you've gotta be hot for him."

*If that's his angle, he was already warned right up front. Forget
it. Move on, Helen. Smile. Be professional.* "Yes, Jack Smith is a
very attractive man, but, no, I most assuredly am not and will not
be—actually, if you have any other questions you'd like to ask,
I'd love to answer them for you."

Again, the first one spoke, "One copy of 'A Long, Hard
Road', please."

The second one purred, "You mean—'A Loooong'," and she
gyrated her hips, "'Hard'," and gave a pelvic thrust, "'Road'!"

The rowdy row burst into naughty laughter when the third shared her brilliant breakthrough, "Ooh, maybe we can get *him* to sign it, too!"

And they celebrated as I grabbed copies and wrote my personal message to each of them. By the time I'd cleared the first wave of fans, things seemed to be falling into place (even with the overwhelming numbers), when a sudden burst of laughter came from Jack's side of the world. Just as quickly as it began, it was muffled. I took a quick peek and saw him standing in front of his cardboard cutout, which he hadn't yet turned back around. A wave of guilt washed over me. I had forgotten about my payback from when he was being such an ass. I should've warned him, but there had been no time with all the commotion.

I watched, waiting for a reaction, hoping his laughter had been a good sign and he wasn't too offended. There was a chance he was laughing just to save some dignity. *How does a guy like that handle his manhood being challenged?*

He shook his head, a small scowl now on his face, and hurried over to his boxes.

I snapped back to attending to my lineup, hoping Jack would do the same, and that we could just move on.

No such luck.

I had barely said, "Hi, thanks for coming out," to the next person in line before Jack was *ahem*-ing and fake coughing in a clear attempt to get my attention—and it worked. I looked back, and sure enough, he was waiting for me to look at him. Once I did, he turned back to the cutout, and then clearly looked down at his own groin. Back to the cutout, and then his focus went to his groin once again. It was odd and becoming awkward to watch, but I felt compelled to see how this was going to play out. He turned the cardboard version of himself to face my way so the entire crowd and I could all see the tiny, bright green cocktail weenie I had drawn over his cardboard bulge.

From behind me, I could hear several gasps.

I giggled.

His eyes snapped my way and he wagged his finger as if scolding me. His hand went down to the image as if measuring. Then, his other hand, bearing a marker, drew. Soon, my small rendering took on longer, thicker, snake-like proportions. Like something you'd see at a filthy sideshow. Again, he did another hand measurement before extending the image slightly further. He stood up with a slow, deliberate, and approving nod. When he turned my way, he had a dirty little grin on his face and a full-body look of pride. He stared at me. I couldn't help feeling he was waiting for me to flinch, but it was then I realized my jaw was now hanging way too low for such a sudden movement— until he gave me that nod and a wink.

Sandra's words from last night rang loud and clear in my ears: *"His ego isn't the only thing huge . . . "*, and I felt my cheeks blushing in a way hers should have when she'd said it.

Oh no, Helen. What have you done?

I snapped back to my fans with a new commitment to ignore him the rest of the afternoon. There was no chance anything good could come from further games. Things had taken an unexpected turn . . .

CHAPTER FOURTEEN

Jack

THE REST OF the day went off without a hitch: the usual fun of signing breasts, giving hugs, doing photos, and selling books. *If only I had been able to enjoy it.*

When Helen's jaw had dropped after the "weenie drawing incident", I'd thought it was all in good fun and we were making real progress in our friendship, or whatever we would call it. Since then, she'd been silent, barely initiating or responding to any chances for contact beyond the necessary. Now, here we are about 6 p.m., stepping on the toes of the evening with the conference long since over and it seems that my usual skill for reading people has failed me.

"That everything, Jack?" asked Bert, as I dropped the last box on the trolley.

Putting on my hat and taking a last look around, I was still amazed at how fast cleanup went. Each time, it seems to go a little faster yet I wind up leaving later. "Yep, it is. You have everything taken care of?"

He rubbed his hands together with a conspiratorial grin. "Hey, it's me, Bert. You know I've got it under control. You're gonna love it."

Clapping him on the shoulder, I nodded. "I have no doubt. You, my friend, have been a godsend this weekend. Thanks for everything."

His smile grew even bigger. "Thank you! There aren't many perks doing this job, you just hope to be treated with a little respect rather than like a servant. Man, you've done all that and much more. I've been looking forward to coming in. Today, at breakfast, even my wife said I looked happier than normal for a work day." Before I could respond, he had me in a big bear hug. "Thanks, Jack."

I wrapped my arms around him, giving the ol' double-hand-pat-on-the-back.

"Have no doubt that when I come back next time," I said, "I'll be looking you up again. Maybe get to meet that wife and those kids of yours?"

As he stepped back, we shook hands. "Deal," Bert said. "Now I'll go get you loaded up." He disappeared as fast as his rumbling trolley would allow.

I felt a tug at my elbow. "Looks like you're winning over more than just the Texas women," said Helena with a chuckle. "You have a bromance going there?"

I shrugged. "Just being me. Speaking of which, I do believe I owe you an apology."

Her eyebrows raised. "You probably do. Anything I should know about?"

Such a smart ass. "You're funny. I mean for earlier, the, uh, 'weenie'. I—"

She gave me a swat on the arm and laughed, "You mean the weenie I drew?"

"Well, yeah. But then I kind of augmented it and—"

"Hey, I'm glad you did, how else would we have learned you could also be a cartoonist? Now I know who to call the next time someone asks me to draw stick figures or weenies."

Get in your digs now, girlie. I gave a little laugh. "So, you're not mad?"

"Only if you don't help me wipe off this mustache before we go to the send-off event," she said, wiggling her upper lip.

"Oh, yeah! I had forgotten about that," I said, and that sent me into a full laugh, "but it was kind of growing on me. Maybe it could be your hook?"

Another swat in the arm, this time a little harder. "Funny guy. We don't have much time, help me out."

With my water bottle, I wet one of the custom workout towels I had stashed away as swag for the convention send-off and handed it to her.

"Really? You better be planning to help more than that," she said, "because my mirror's packed away and I can't see it."

Snickering, I shook my head and began to wipe. Thankfully, much of the mustache had faded during the course of the day and the rest came off easily. I gave her the towel; it was habit to be handing them out, and without a word she stuck it in her bag.

"Okay, so what's your plan now?" I asked.

"Are you going to the send-off?"

I shook my head in surprise. "You kidding?"

She shrugged. "I dunno. I heard it can be crazy."

"Hell, yeah, it's crazy! This is Texas. You know how they say 'everything's bigger in Texas'? Well, this is no exception, I promise you."

"Someone told me there'll be fireworks and everything."

Oh, the infamous fireworks farewell. I laughed. "Yeah, sometimes, and not always intentionally."

She giggled, "That's both ominous and intriguing."

"Why, thank you," I said with a grin, and once again got a swat in the arm. "I'm going to need to ice that by the time we're done."

"Don't start."

A few other authors wandered by carrying Rubbermaid totes and bags full of unsold books, stopping to give Helena a pat on the back or wave. They called: "Have a great trip, Helena," and "Hope to see you back next year, Helena," as they trailed out the exit toward the lobby. Naturally, they gave me a wide berth, but I returned big waves, smiles and a "See you next year!" that left them shaking their heads.

I couldn't tell if Helena was laughing at me or with me, when she asked, "You just like to push buttons, don't you?"

"Yes ma'am, I do." I tipped my hat her way. "And it's always earned me a nice paycheck."

She shook her head and walked away.

Whoa. What the . . . ? "Hey, wait!" I got two steps into sprinting after her but that darn hat flew off and threatened to be washed away in the wake of those heading in the other direction. "Come on!" Scooping it up like the fumble that had made me famous, I spun back to find that she had disappeared.

Racing through the crowd, my old football skills were put to use finding the openings and using oncoming traffic as blockers to get me to the next level in hopes of finding her again. As I broke through a pack, I glimpsed Helena Bliss standing at the doors to the Grand Gala Room. She gave me a cheeky little wave and rushed through the doors.

This girl . . .

CHAPTER FIFTEEN

Jack

T HE GALA ROOM was packed for the send-off, as always, by
those who cut out of the conference early to get to the
drinking and partying. *And yet they talk about my behavior. Ha!*
The retractable roof was open and everyone was in a well-
deserved mood for celebration. I had just one thing in mind:
finding Helen. I stayed on the outskirts of the crowd, circling
around to hopefully catch a glimpse of her. Sure enough, after a
few minutes I saw her standing by an oversized floral display,
hands on hips, as if she had known this was the path I'd take.

I laughed, shook my finger at her, and was making my way
through the crowd to join her when two things happened. First,
the deep boom of an explosion ricocheted off the walls, followed
by bursts of color falling over the room. Second, Helena started
speed walking away while still looking at me over her shoulder.

I shook my head and mouthed the words, "Not this time."
There was no way I would make it through the thick crowd of
reveling authors by throwing my shoulder into them, so I kept to
the perimeter, shadowing her the way I had done years before,
paralleling a speeding opponent on the football field.

A second explosion, followed quickly by a third, sent everyone cheering.

Helena scooped up a drink from a tray held by one of the serving staff, and stopped to raise it up and offer me a "cheers" from across the room.

So, what's her game?

She chugged it back in startling fashion.

I gasped, surprised and impressed. I made my move to join her, but she carefully placed the glass back on the tray and we were on the run again, with fireworks now casting strobe lights backed by rapid-fire bass beats as the firework display reached its crescendo. The partygoers stood between me and Helena, all looking up, entranced, with their mouths gaping.

As the flickering lights and bangs faded away, an advantage finally broke for me when a couple stepped in Helena's way to engage her in conversation, no doubt to congratulate her for selling all of her books today. Seizing the opportunity, I worked my way through the crowd, small elbows busting out when necessary to make headway.

The fireworks now over, spotlights came on and everyone's ranks closed in front of me as they pushed toward the stage and the start of the main event: awards and recognition. *Oh, come on!*

Helena cast a quick look back to where she had seen me last, and her inability to find me felt like an advantage. But it was lost quickly when our eyes met. From this distance, there was no mistaking the sparkle in hers as she gave me a big smile and an approving nod. Just when I thought the chase was over, she gave the couple quick hugs then bolted again.

The public address speakers came to life as whom I assumed to be one of the convention hosts boomed, "Welcome, everyone, to the Austin Grand Hotel Rom-Con send-off party," to a rowdy smattering of applause and cheers.

No time for any of that. I was in hot pursuit. While I had closed some of the distance, it was now slow-going again through the closely-packed crowd of people pylons.

"We thank each of you for helping make this an incredibly special and memorable weekend," continued the host.

For a second or two, I lost her again. I scanned the crowd, and saw nothing. I had to do something, but there wasn't much room left the way she was heading. The rational voice in my head started in. *Don't do it! Don't embarrass yourself. You're a—*

Forget it, Rational Voice, we will win this. At six-foot-three, I'm already taller than most in the crowd, and if I had been rational, or if one of my other voices had chimed in, maybe I would have realized that, but right now, I had tunnel vision.

I jumped up like a jackrabbit to look over the heads of the crowd and pretty much everyone near me stumbled back in surprise.

I jumped again and caught some movement breaking against the grain of the crowd. My name in mixed tones of disdain rippled through the surrounding people who felt affected by my actions. But I'd caught sight of her again.

"We know you're all eager to get to the party part of the fun, so I'll make this short and sweet. We have three people we'll be bringing to the stage to speak and accept acknowledgments."

The looks of disgust from those who had been so offended by my jumping made me stop the chase a moment to offer them a word. "Thank you, I love you too, but you'll have to wait for autographs until another time." Satisfied, I ran off, calling back over my shoulder, "And don't forget to tip your server." I was closing in on her now.

"First up, best-selling sweetheart, Roxanne Tierney," called our host. Applause broke out.

When Helena ducked behind a large floral display, she broke sight again, but I pushed on.

"Second up, a romance icon of film, *and* a model gracing several book covers on display here this weekend: *Marissa.*"

And then I found Helena again, at the edge of the crowd just twenty feet away, casually lounging on a couch like she had been there the whole time, just waiting for me. She had a martini glass in each hand, one extended my way.

"And, third, our one-and-only, the pride of Texas, a killer on the field and apparently in his scorching tell-all tales: Jack 'Titan' Smith."

If I were to be honest, I heard my name called, mostly, but when the jobs you do regularly involve your name being yelled out on the intercom quite often, it's easy to begin to tune it out, even on a subconscious level. The louder it's called, the less likely you are to hear it and I was focusing on only one thing: her.

As I finally broke through the crowd to reach her, Helena stood up, offered me my drink, and, with an acting job to rival the previously-announced Marissa, asked, "What took you so long? I was thinking you wouldn't show up."

Gratefully taking the cold glass, I shook my head and laughed. "Sorry, traffic is rough at this time of day," and our glasses clinked together before we shared a drink.

The announcer didn't care about my on-field victory, and continued to bray, "Calling Jack Smith to the stage, please.

Where are you, Jack? It's not like you to miss a party."

Helena gestured with her glass to the stage. "I think they're calling you. Know anything about that?"

I chugged back the last of my drink. "Yeah. Work calls. Will you be here?"

"Sorry, my plane leaves at 8 p.m. I only had a few minutes to spare—"

"Jack Smith? Anyone see him?" the impatient host cut in, as people around us looked our way.

I took a quick peek at my watch. *There's still time.* "Care to escape with me?" I offered her my elbow.

"Again? Absolutely." She grabbed hold and we bolted—well, speed-walked—our way toward the nearest exit as people made comments I couldn't bother to hear.

"I guess we've lost Jack Smith to another adventure. Wherever he is, I'm sure we'll hear about it in his next book," called the host, trying to maintain his professionalism and save the day. "Let's get on with the show. Roxanne, come on up to the mic—"

The exit door slammed behind us, and we were in an empty lobby of the Austin Grand Hotel.

CHAPTER SIXTEEN

Helen

M Y HEAD WAS spinning—and I loved it. This was not the end of the convention I had planned, nor one I'd ever experienced before, yet here I was, skipping out on the biggest send-off on the tour with a guy I barely knew. *And drinking!* It's not that I don't drink, I love a good wine, cocktail, or even martini just as much as the next girl, but not during an event and especially not while racing through a crowd of my peers. And then there was Jack.

He focused a steely gaze on me that probably would've made me nervous if I didn't already know there's a jovial clown under that rugged exterior and asked, "What was that about?"

Then it hit me. "Aren't you going to get in trouble?"

He shrugged his shoulders and shook his head dismissively, "I dunno, it's my first time."

"And probably the last time they'll invite you to speak at one of these things."

Jack's laughter was sudden and natural. "I doubt it. They kind of own my rights. I bet there isn't even a single person on their staff who has actually read a thing I wrote, but I know they'll get every bit of work out of me that they can. We have a deal of sorts."

The wine, or champagne—whatever it was I chugged back there—was now making my tongue a little numb and my extremities tingly. "Not good."

"Nah, it's all right. I—"

I waved my hand to cut him off. "No, I mean 'not good' that I'm feeling a little tipsy."

"You weren't running like you were tipsy," he said with a laugh. "If only a couple guys I played with could run as well as you when they were tipsy, we'd have won more titles!"

My brain was a little fuzzy and I knew it was time to get moving, maybe get some fresh air. "Let's walk," I said. I put my hand out for his arm and, before I realized what I had done, he was right there with his big smile, ready to lead the way.

"I thought you'd never ask."

The plush carpet of an adjacent hallway swished below our feet as we slowly made our way past a variety of images on the walls, one of which I was sure featured Jack with some over-sized scissors cutting a ribbon. A part of me wanted to stop and look, or at least ask, but I was too wrapped up in the comfortable flow we had going and didn't want to potentially put him on the spot.

Finally, we stood in the main lobby at a crossroads of sorts. Straight ahead, the check-in desk for those wishing to stay the night; to the left, the elevators back up to our private rooms; and, lastly, the doors home waiting to our right.

While it had only been a few minutes, the walk had served well to sober me up. I was still feeling buzzed, but it was clear I wasn't heading into my own little drunk tank.

We stood there in the empty lobby as two receptionists

worked on balancing the impression of looking busy while still appearing available. They were likely wondering what we weirdos were doing just standing there in the middle of the lobby looking lost—though I'm sure they've likely seen far stranger things.

Jack was the first to break the silence and interrupt my internal ramblings, saying, "So, what's your plan now? Time for a bite to eat?"

I shook my head, and surprised myself with a little pout. "Not really, my flight leaves pretty soon, at eight o'clock."

Oh no. Suddenly, it's goodbye. How did it sneak up on me so suddenly? Worse yet, why does it feel so awkward?

He shifted slightly on his feet. If I didn't know better, I would say he was fidgeting before he said, "Oh, hmm. Well, I don't know what time mine leaves but I know it's later than that. Let me go with you to the airport and we'll get something to eat on the way."

"Yes! Great idea."

Without hesitation, we were moving again. Following his lead, I said, "I was hoping you would say that," and we were heading to the right.

As we approached the doors, Bert appeared and swung one open, and greeted me with a "Good evening, ma'am," and a small bow.

"Thanks, Bert. Yes, it is," I said with a smile.

He took a quick glance at his watch before saying to Jack, "Right on schedule. Everything good?"

"Yep, her flight leaves at eight. All good with you?"

Bert let the door glide closed behind us and hustled ahead to where a black limo was parked. He gave two raps on the roof to wake the engine and swung open the rear door.

I slowed abruptly and whispered to Jack, while maintaining a smile for Bert, "What's going on?" Once again, things seemed to be taking an unexpected turn.

"My buddy, Bert, here, took care of everything," he said, tipping his cowboy hat to Bert, who gave a big smile in return.

A weird, warm feeling twisted in my stomach. I couldn't place it. Quite possibly it was the alcohol still working its effects, or possibly the oddity that a man who was still such an unknown was being so forward. *Keep your guard up, Helen, but have fun. Wasn't that the plan?* "Oh, wait! My luggage!" I had packed this morning and left my baggage in the holding room until it was time to leave. A quick look up and down the walkway to where my bags were supposed to be waiting with an attendant came up empty. "Not good. I—"

Jack squeezed my hand, still on his arm. "We took care of everything."

"Your luggage is stowed in the trunk already," offered Bert.

I looked at the two of them and gave a sigh. "Okay, I'll roll with it. Thank you both."

I ducked into the back of the limousine while the two guys clapped each other on the shoulders and said their goodbyes. My courtesies were lost as I was hit by the most wonderful aromas demanding my full attention. Firmly entrenched in the middle of the seating area was a small table bearing a variety of silver serving dishes.

You've got to wait, Helen. It would be rude . . . I was really hungry. I hadn't had time to have anything but coffee all day. *But maybe I can just take a peek.*

My fingers had barely wrapped around the handle of the first cover when my stomach let out a loud, lingering rumble that immediately made me self-conscious. I looked outside and Jack was inching his way to the door, wrapping things up. With a sigh of relief that he was still occupied, I took the plunge. Opening the lid unleashed a wave of steam and a mix of spicy fragrances that temporarily blinded me, coming from heaps of grilled meat and vegetables laid out beside a stack of soft tortillas.

"Oh, yeah, a woman after my own heart," said Jack, dropping into the seat beside me.

Busted!

"I guess 'stomach' would be more accurate," he said, "but whatever. Glad to see you diving right in."

"No. I was just—"

"Don't worry about it," he said, leaning in to lift more lids to reveal an assortment of food. "I didn't know what you would like, so I got a variety. I even got vegan options," he pointed to a lower shelf and looked at me with eyebrows raised, "just in case."

"You have really outdone yourself, Jack Smith."

"Sweetheart . . . oh, sorry, bad habit. *Helena*. Let's just say we earned it."

"I don't know what you mean, but thank you."

"If not for you . . . well, you really helped make this weekend right. Who else was I going to hang out with? Bob, or maybe your friend, Sandra? Bless her heart, but no."

I could feel my cheeks flushing slightly and needed to change the topic. "Okay, load me up. What have we got?"

"Yes! Now we're talking," Jack said, rubbing his hands together with excitement. Before launching into the full reveal of the food, he pushed the button on the intercom for the driver. "Ready to roll, Ed," and we were off. "Courtesy of Executive Chef Etienne of the Austin Grand Hotel, we have filet mignon with . . . " and it all became a blur from there. Once the food introductions were done, we ate in silence like we had been starved all weekend. Between the food and the drinks, it was far too easy to forget that we were in a vehicle, and even easier still to ignore that it was the ending to a trip, rather than the start—until the car stopped and Ed's gravelly voice came over the intercom, "We're here, Mr. Smith."

Jack looked at me with an expression that said what I was thinking. *Already?* "Thanks, Ed. We'll be a few minutes. I'll let you know."

"Sounds good," came back over the intercom, and Jack and I sat in silence. The food had been finished a short while ago, but the drinks and smiles had continued right up until this abrupt stop.

I wasn't ready for it to end yet. I didn't know where to look, or what to say, and soon found myself drifting toward the window, looking at a plane taking off. I had never been less interested in the miracle of flight than I was right then.

In the reflection of my window, I watched Jack mimic me by looking out his window at a view of concrete and glass. *Could he, Jack "Titan" Smith, the chauvinistic bachelor, be feeling the same way? Impossible.* Yet, there he sat, every ten- or twenty seconds turning my way as if to check on me or to start saying something, but then turning back to his window.

Finally, he made the first move. "I hate to be the one to spoil it, but we're already at seven fifteen . . ."

Jolted, I jumped in my seat. "I'm late! You're supposed to check in at least two hours before. I need to run."

An amused look came over his face as he shook his head. "Like I said, we took care of everything. We're at the express entrance. You're good. Unless you've got some big secret stashed in your luggage that we need to know about," he said, with a laugh.

Don't we all? "Wow. What a relief. Thank you . . . but I'd better head out now."

"For sure." He activated the intercom again. "Ed, we're ready."

We sat there smiling at each other for a moment until my door swung open to reveal a massive man whose frame completely obscured the world outside the car. I gasped in surprise.

Jack chuckled, "Yep, that's my boy, Ed. Best defensive tackle I've ever seen and protector of my behind for more than a decade." I felt Jack's body press against mine as he leaned over me toward my door. He had a woodsy smell mixed with some kind of citrus, an intriguing mix that lingered as he said, "Say hello, Ed."

"'Hello, Ed'," said the mammoth monolith with a laugh that was strangely jovial, yet a little scary at the same time.

"You kill me," said Jack, joining in on the cheap joke before sitting back on his side of the car, leaving a cool spot on my shoulder where he had been leaning.

As I slid out the door, Ed offered his massive hand. I took it, and exited the vehicle to see a chiseled face that was in stark contrast to my expectations. He quite simply radiated joy. *Way to jump to conclusions, Helen.* "Pleased to meet you, Ed."

"My pleasure, ma'am. I hope you have the most amazing trip."

"Got 'em," called Jack, and we both turned to see him closing up the trunk with my luggage at his feet.

I gave Ed a hug. I don't know why, I'm not usually a hugger. But it felt like the right thing to do and his friendly squeeze gave me confirmation. Scurrying over to Jack, it was time to hustle and catch my plane. Before I could grab a bag, he had them both in hand.

"Be right back, buddy. Escort duty."

The word "escort" sent an ugly shiver down my back. Casting thoughts in my brain of: *A guy like that could definitely be an escort. He gets around enough. Could that be what people thought? That it was the only reason he was hanging around a woman like me?* I felt all the build-up of my great weekend being washed away in a building wave of self-doubt and negativity.

The smile he sent my way now looked too rehearsed, until he said, "Come on, beautiful, time to put those sneakers back into high gear," and laughed as he raced to the door.

I shook my head to ditch the negative thoughts and get back to the moment.

"Better hustle, ma'am," said Ed, with the sigh of a friend who'd played this game one too many times. "If he beats you, you'll never heard the end of it, trust me." Smiling, I took off after Jack.

He beat me through the doors. The express entrance's lounge was pretty empty, and those who were there were already comfortably absorbed in books, laptops, TV's, and/or drinks, and wouldn't be a hazard in our two-person race. Jack beat me to the turnstile, barely, but by the time we'd made it to the gate, both of us breathing more heavily than we wanted to show, we were neck-and-neck in a photo finish.

"Ha! In your face, 'Ti-*tan*'," I sneered playfully. "What happened to all that talk about how much you train? Caught by a girl in comfy shoes."

He ran his hand over his face ruefully. "Maybe I need to join one of your Pilates classes?"

Laughing, I landed a swat on his arm as the overhead speaker announced that my flight would leave in forty-five minutes.

"Well, this is as far as I can go. I'll let you check-in, wish you a safe trip, and thank you again for . . . for making this an incredibly memorable weekend."

I wrapped my arms around him in a big hug. *Maybe I'm more of a hugger than I thought?* "Thank you. It was a blast."

His arms wrapped around me, and I felt the heat of his hands, each finger a clear and precise point of pressure on my lower back. The feeling of his breath against my neck, innocent yet somehow provocative, quickly created an uneasiness that was far too comfortable and awkward at the same time.

As quickly as I started the hug, I ended it even more abruptly.

He looked at me quizzically. His arms still outstretched as if I had disappeared.

If ever you looked the freak, Helen, this was it.

Thankfully, he let it slide. Maybe it didn't feel as weird to him as it did to me. *I wished.*

The sweetest smile lit his face as he said, "We'll have to do this again sometime."

"Yes, absolutely!" *So much for playing it cool.*

He nodded slowly. We stared again in silence.

Once again, the uneasy goodbye. Just pull the bandage, Helen. Lacing my fingers around the luggage that somehow felt heavier than I remembered packing, I made my way through the gate. I looked back to where Jack still stood, smiling, watching me leave.

He waved. I nodded and then was hustling off as fast as I could make myself move. Almost running, picking up speed as I went, the bags weighing heavier against my straining fingers with each unbalanced stride.

Check-in was quick and seamless. In a flash, I was on my plane, notebook out, and heading back to stability, security, sanctuary, and the life that had always been good enough.

CHAPTER SEVENTEEN

Jack

T HERE WAS A fantastic ambrosia hanging on the air in her wake. Watching her go, struggling to make headway with her bags, was somehow amusing and yet sad at the same time.

Next move, Jack-O. I sighed, a smile still on my face. She glanced back and gave me a quick look back that I couldn't quite place. *Did I do something wrong? Is she that eager to leave, or does she want to stay? Check your ego. She wasn't into you. Keep it that way.*

I waved, and she gave me a polite nod before rushing off.

It was clear everything was fine as she passed through her check-in. My job complete, I pulled out my phone, picked Angelina's name from the list, and sent the text: *Missed my flight, next one in 2 hrs. Be home soon.*

It was time to find a new flight, get my stuff from Ed, and start heading back to stability, security, sanctuary, and the life that had always been good enough.

CHAPTER EIGHTEEN

Jack

"WELCOME TO CLEVELAND, Ohio, everybody. The local time is 9:37 p.m. We hope you enjoyed your flight and will choose TransAmerica Airlines again for your travel needs."

Around me, spring-loaded people jumped from their seats, only to have to wait to move.

I dug my phone out of my jacket pocket, and turned it back on.

James, the guy from across the aisle, popped his hand out my way. "Hey, Titan. Thanks for the heads up on the restaurant. Was great talking to you."

We shook hands.

"My pleasure, man. Have a great trip," I said.

"I will, and you better know, me and my girl are looking forward to the next book."

I smiled. "Thanks, James, I appreciate the support. Believe me, it'll be a hot one and'll heat up those sheets."

"As long as she's not calling out your name," he said with a laugh.

"I can't promise—" My phone interrupted with an alert; a

new message had arrived.

"I'll let you get that." Once more for good measure, he shook my hand. "Thanks again," he said, and he was off.

Four new messages: Angelina, Troy. Naturally, I hit Angelina's first while I waited for the rest of James' row to exit.

> **Angelina:** *Welcome home! Called to Philly for work. Be back in a day or two.*
>
> **Angelina:** *Or . . . I'll see if I can find a work excuse to get you here.*
>
> **Angelina:** *Troy will be there to meet you.*
>
> **Troy:** *picking u up fuckface. be rdy 2 drink*

I chuckled, muttering to myself, "That guy's going to be the death of my liver." Not one to needlessly wait in line, I sat until the aisle cleared then made my way out.

Clearing customs was a breeze. We saw each other often enough that I knew many of the officers by name and had the routine down as well as any play I had ever run.

Unfortunately, most major airlines didn't fly directly to my hometown of Erie, Pennsylvania, and rather than take a connector, I always enjoyed the drive from Cleveland and the chance to regroup in peace.

"Jack, you ugly prick!" a deep voice boomed over the crowd. Women cringed, parents covered children's ears. I buried my face in a magazine, hoping to avoid eye contact.

The baritone laughter was downright ridiculous. "Don't make me come over there. You know you can't hide from me. Bad enough your Mommy couldn't come get you and I'm here."

As Troy lumbered toward me, the same thought I've had

since high school ran through my head: *I can't believe I'm still friends with this guy.* The magazine had failed me and went back into my bag. "Do you need to terrorize the entire village everywhere you go?" I called back. "It's bad enough everyone has to see your ugly mug lurching through the place."

Closer now, Troy lowered his voice to the dull rumble he considered conversational, "Ugly? Who got more tail back in school, you or me?" He grinned, that unmistakable, uniquely-Troy grin full of mischief. "Better yet, who got to get down with Cathy freshman year?"

The ridiculousness of the question scrambled my brain, and I had to shake my head to clear it. "Um . . . *everyone?*"

And we both laughed, but naturally his roar was the only one that could be heard all over the airport.

"Maybe, but I got her before you did." His massive chest puffed with pride.

"Said it before, and it's still true. I wouldn't have done that deed even with your dirty schlong," I hissed.

"Hey, show some respect," he said, then grabbed his crotch and thrust his hips my way. "Woman love this coc—"

I gave him a quick punch to the gut that took his wind. "Too easy!" I said, with a laugh. *Two minutes with the guy and we're back to the immature kids we always were.* Mom always said he brought out the best and worst in me.

Troy aimed his razor-sharp brush-cut and mud-puddle brown eyes at the crowd that was not-so-subtly trying to scramble away from him, then reached over to grab me up in a bear hug and spin me around like a child. He had been an all-pro offensive lineman pretty much since birth, so throwing around guys my size—and especially linebackers—had always been his specialty.

"You losing weight, Jack? You not eating right on the road? Good thing you're home, we'll take care of all that," he said. I could see it in his eyes, the spinning already taking its toll. But even through the dizzy haze which finally forced Troy to drop me, his eyes were still twinkling. "First, we hit the bar!" he shouted. If he didn't already know the location of a bar, I knew he'd find one fast with his uncanny and innate alcohol-finding ability. "Grab your gear, pipsqueak. Let's roll."

Shoving him out of my way, I went to the baggage carousel, and, after a surprisingly short wait, grabbed my stuff, and we were off.

CHAPTER NINETEEN

Jack

S URE ENOUGH, TROY and I flew across the concourse at Mach 2 to find an airport bar called "The Last Stop". Judging by the small and somber crowd, the name fit.

The waiter dropped off my 151 rum and Coke, and a water with a lime twist for Troy.

"Man, you and your drinks," I said with a chuckle.

"Hey, I'm driving. No booze for me, and no chance I'm letting you drive my car."

"No booze is a good thing, even if you were the one to call for us to hit the bar . . . "

Troy took a small taste of his drink. "How long's it been, anyway? I wanted to catch up. Sue me. Plus, I know you're happy to finally be drinking real booze instead of that non-alcoholic crap you drink at those convention things. So, uh, pot, kettle, whatever."

I shrugged while savoring the taste of the 151, a long overdue and welcome treat. "Okay, most regular people would consider our drive home a chance to do just that, but that wasn't my point. I'm talking about your choice of beverage."

"What? Hydration is important. Watch *The Waterboy.*"

"I don't know what's worse," I said, "that you'd reference an Adam Sandler movie as a supporting argument, or that a guy your size—who looks like you and has done what you've done—feels he has to add a lime twist to disguise his drink because he worries about looking soft, not drinking alcohol at a bar."

"I played eighteen years in the League, man, in the toughest position of them all. Coulda done more if not for the knee. You know how it is . . . *no weakness*. So, stuff it, dude, and tell me about your recent girlie weekend."

"'Girlie' weekend? Men write romance—" I started to answer.

Troy's sudden sputter and laugh transformed him into a short-burst fountain as the water flew everywhere, most of it landing in my face. "'*Romance*'? You mean *smut*. You write cheap, git-yer-rocks-off porn."

Here we go again. I smiled, patience wearing thin in a scenario I knew I couldn't win. "It's not smut."

"Hell, I've rubbed a couple out to it when stuck somewhere there weren't any chicks or if I couldn't get some video action," he said, wiping up some of his mess off the table with his sleeve.

I slapped my hand over my face in mock disgust. "You know I didn't need to know that, right?"

He swatted my hand away. "How many years were we roomies? I broke you into the League. You know how I get down."

"Yeah, well, I didn't need to know that I've been getting you off—"

That did it. Troy's full-on laughter boomed across the bar. Every eye, drunk and sober, snapped our way. "Aw, sweetie, be proud. I've gotta say, I think you're the first dude to do that for me."

I shook my head. "You '*think*?" I chuckled, "And why would I—"

Troy suddenly stood up, and took a big swig of his drink. "Y'all know who I'm sitting with here?" he said to the crowd, many of whom were now regretting their choice of layover hangout. "Nobody'll remember *me*. And that's okay, I was just one o' the invisible guys blocking for the glory boys. But this one, this one right here . . . " He snagged my hand and waved it to the crowd.

I knew from experience it would be best just to let this happen and hope it was over quickly. "Hey, everyone," I said.

" . . . this here's my boy. It's Jack Smith. Some of you may know him as 'Titan'. He was a straight-up killer on the field." He stopped to take another big glug of what he hoped made everyone think he was drinking vodka. "That don't matter, though. What we're talking about is his smut writing."

Old habits came back fast as I scanned the bar and then the rest of the room to see if there were any security types considering a move that might get them hospitalized. *Thankfully, nothing.* Like me, the few who might be otherwise obligated to step in were a mix of amused and patient.

"I told him his porn stories get me off. Anyone else?"

The room was silent, as expected, though that little voice in the back of my brain had been hoping someone might say something that would quiet Troy and make me feel not so unknown in my own neck of the woods. Though I likely would've questioned any person who would speak up in this situation.

"Just me?" He gave me a punch in the arm. "Maybe you're

not so famous after all, eh?" He walked toward the center of the bar.

I jumped out of my seat and put my hand on his arm. "Don't do it."

"But I know they're lyin'," he said innocently enough. I saw an all-too-familiar look of good intentions in his eyes, along with a tortured reminder that whatever we'd done back then in the League, on that stage, under those bright lights, simply disappeared for the most part the second the bosses flipped the switch on our careers. It was one thing to be anonymous amongst a group of stars. It was another to be unknown because you'd been tossed aside.

My voice sank low with emotion, hoping I could put him at ease. "Yeah, I know."

Troy took a last look around. "Honestly? None of you have read any of my brother Jack Smith's stuff? Nobody?"

A young woman, likely just out of college, surrounded by several floral-print bags, tentatively raised her hand.

"Her!" Troy screamed, jumping up and down, "I knew there'd be someone else! That girl's got taste. *Yeehaw!*"

An older woman also raised her hand with a giggle, as did her silver-haired male companion. Before we knew it, there were a good half dozen or more people with their hands up, smiling away at my buddy, the biggest, hairiest cheerleader they had probably ever seen.

"Yes," Troy said, pumping his fist in the air. He looked at me again with a look I hadn't seen in years, not since we won the title on The Play, with that same look of pride and selflessness as he celebrated my success. "They know you, man. See? People are reading your stuff. You still got the juice."

There's something to be said for finding a following in such an unlikely and random place. It did feel good, there was no denying that, and I was at a loss for words.

Troy didn't appear to be suffering from a similar affliction as he called out, "Bartender, next round's on me and my panty-dropping friend, Jack Motherfuckin' 'Titan' Smith!"

The half dozen fans suddenly multiplied into a roomful in one big cheer.

CHAPTER TWENTY

Jack

T O SAY I had a chance of making it out of The Last Stop with any semblance of sobriety would be like saying the Titanic had a bit of a leak; neither the ship nor I had a chance in hell.

Normally, when I was with Troy and we were drinking, I could hold my own. Often because he'd be chugging two or three to every one of mine, but on a night like this where he was our designated driver and we became best friends with the bartender and at least half of the customers, it became *Apocalypse Now* for my liver and brain in a way they hadn't experienced since I first got drafted.

"Du-ude," I slurred, "We gots ta go."

Troy's head shook vigorously. "No, no, no. I got one more song and then maybe we can go." He returned to rocking out to the Armani Twins, Harold and Joe, singing their rendition of AC/DC's "Back in Black". They were stock brokers, accountants, I don't remember what. We'd met as they were whining about their delayed flight to somewhere that sounded like it had to be on the other side of the world. Troy brought them into the party with open arms—as he always did.

In the same gregarious way, he wound up mysteriously getting an electrician or somebody to rig up a microphone to the bar's sound system and turned the place into a karaoke joint for the night. *Just another day in the life of Troy Unleashed.*

"You know this ain't even a karaoke place, right?" I asked blearily.

It barely registered. In Troy's current state, there was no room for negativity or stoplights. "If it's not, then why are we all singing and having a great time?" His point made with bullet-proof logic, he flipped me the bird and continued watching the show. "Enjoy it," he said. "Mom's away, time to play."

"Stop that." I gave him an unbalanced shot in the shoulder that buckled my wrist and threw fire up my forearm.

Troy shrugged.

I drank.

We enjoyed listening to the classic track being soundly mur-dered until the world itself went back in black.

I opened my eyes some time later to see stars shooting by, my head full of cotton, and my stomach juggling the day's food. Trying to sit up was impossible. I was immobilized, and a jolt of panic ran through my body that sent me wriggling for freedom. It quickly became clear that I had been strapped down in three areas: at my shoulders, waist, and feet.

"Help!" I screamed, though in such a deep state of drunken-ness, it's hard to imagine I made more than a garbled sound.

"Wakey-wakey, Sunshine," Troy called, and he laughed.

I squirmed to roll in the direction of his voice, and realized I was in the backseat of his car. Looking down, I found seatbelts strapping me into place. Images of Gulliver and the Lilliputians came to mind, sending me into hysterics as I re-enacted the scene of their meeting by struggling against my restraints. "Aarrggh, I'm a giant," I roared.

"You're a fucking drunk is what you are," snickered Troy. "Go back to sleep."

"But. I. Am. A. Giant!" I hit a new level of laughter, and that's when the next wave of nausea hit and my bladder screamed in bloated misery. "Oh no, pullover . . . I gotta go!" I shouted to Troy. Then I was back in black again.

When I woke up with a towel as my pillow, everything had once again become predictable. I knew there'd be a porcelain throne nearby, a drain and faucet at my feet for the shower, a bucket, a face cloth, an aerosol can full of some sort of hideous air freshener to augment the night of drinking and potential puke. The only difference between now and previous years was the quality of the facilities. Back in the day, it had been a hard water-encrusted showerhead. Now, it was a multitude of jet streams and rain showers able to cover you from every direction. And instead of being wedged in a filthy dormitory bathtub knowing my back would need a couple of hours on a table with a chiropractor and masseuse, I was now rolling around in a tub big enough for four. Despite all that had changed, one thing had stayed the same: the feeling of a nail being hammered through my head. *The hangover.* I groaned as my eyes adjusted to the dim light of the sun peeking through a large frosted window into the otherwise unlit room.

Should I even bother getting up now, or pray that I could sleep my way through this one? Rolling over evoked another groan, which turned into a dry cough from a parched throat.

Boom! The door was kicked open. I heard an "I gotcha, buddy," and before I knew it, Troy had me in his hands flipping me over like a burger.

"Whoa!" I hollered. "Leave me alone, ya doofus."

"Aww, Sleeping Beauty is waking up grumpy. He—"

I cut in, "I'm not sure if I'm waking up yet. I feel like—"

"Yeah, you're getting up," Troy said. I tried to focus my eyes on his movements blurring over and around me. He virtually sang the next words, ones that had been a common refrain when waking up one another during our days as roomies: "Wake up, champ. Time to attack the day!" *Oh, and the insidious cackling hadn't changed.*

There was a screech. It may have been me, but I'll blame it on the showerhead that suddenly rocketed icy pellets of death all over me, my boxer-briefs useless against the wintery onslaught. I jumped up hard, and tried to dive for the apparent warmth of a big furry rug on the floor, but the Troy barricade would have none of it.

"Now, you're—" Overwhelmed by hysterics, he gasped for air. "You're awake *now*, aren't ya?"

"Move, you fucking moron!" I screamed, still flailing in the bathtub.

That sent him into even bigger fits of laughter. "Move me, little bitch. You know the routine. You want out, you gotta blow that stink off you first. Or move me."

To this day, I could never complete the second option. A record he remembered all too well as he pointed to a bottle of body wash on the ledge. "Use that."

"At least turn the warm water on. Jesus!" I muttered. My body was now in full-on convulsions from the frigid water, my hangover a distant second place in the order of suffering. "We're not kids anymore, y'know—"

"You washing up, or trying to move me with your rotten breath?" he crowed.

"Such a loser . . ." I said. I gave in and I grabbed the bottle. *I'm sure he was right. I probably stank, especially if I had puked, but . . .* "You planning to stand there while I wash my balls, too?"

He cackled. "From the way you're shivering in the shower, you might need some help finding them." He shrugged, and headed out the door. "Good luck. Food and drink are waitin'."

I stripped off my drawers and finished the scrub down, now wide-awake and full of ice-induced energy.

CHAPTER TWENTY-ONE

Jack

ALL CLEANED UP and wearing a fresh set of clothes from my suitcase, I joined Troy at the table where a huge plate of steak, home fries, biscuits and gravy waited for me.

"That was one of the only things I liked about living with you," I said. "You cook like we're all about to die."

"Damn right. If not for me and my cooking, you would've never made weight," he said, and raised his glass of orange juice. "You're welcome."

I looked down at a glass of Troy's patented hangover cure with dread. The question was never whether it worked—it did— it was the potential ingredients which worried me. "Thanks," I said with a sigh, as I took a sip under his amused stare. Once again, that all-too-familiar tangy, sour, and somehow sweet taste fought its way down my throat, leaving a trail of disgust in its wake. "Gah. How did this not cure us of drinking?"

"Hey, I didn't get drunk last night," he said with pride.

"Yeah, you were driving—"

"But you really put one on. What's up with that?"

I took a second to reflect on the night's events. "You were buying. Something like that happens, I know to jump on it."

He shook his head. "Nope. I know you have no problem saying no, even to free booze, and I haven't seen you drink like that in a long time."

I shovelled home fries into my mouth as I thought on it. "It was nothing, man. Chalk it up to just one of those nights."

He chuckled, and said, "The tally on those nights is pretty big, but covered in cobwebs."

Like old times, we fell into the routine of a quiet disturbed only by the sounds of cutting, chewing, scraping of plates, and drinking, which, in my case, also added moans of disgust.

He'd cooked, so I cleared the plates and put them in the dishwasher before going to find my phone. "Troy, my phone's dead. Where can I plug it in?" I called out to him from the bedroom.

"Oh, yeah! Your agent called."

Phone in tow, I popped back out to find my friend with selective amnesia. "Angelina called? When?"

"Coupla times, while you were sleeping it off." He took my phone and put it on the wireless charger.

"And you didn't tell me?"

"What part of 'sleeping it off' don't you get?"

He had a point.

"She was just checking that I picked you up for her and that all was good," Troy said. "And that she might have some work for you to do out of town, so get your phone ASAP."

"Out of town? Looks like another year of logging some big mileage." Too impatient to wait for Troy's charger, I took the phone, plugged it in, and turned it on. Sure enough, a couple of text alerts waited for me that had started coming in at 8:15 a.m.

Angelina: *Hope you guys are upright today. Rumors of work, want it?*

A few minutes later.

Angelina: *Guess it was a good night. Call me.*

Forty-five minutes later.

Angelina: *OK, I'll call Troy's*

I looked at the clock showing 11:10 a.m.

Troy peeked his head over my shoulder as if stealing a look at my phone, "Uh-oh, you about to get canned? You know I got room."

"Yeah, you do, but somehow I wound up sleeping in the darn tub."

He laughed and gave me a shove that almost knocked me over. "You know the protocol, brother. It doesn't change."

I chuckled, "Don't get your hopes up about another sleepover anytime soon. I'm just going to give her a call and see what's up."

As if on cue, and to our surprise, the phone rang and displayed a '406' area code. I showed it to Troy. He shrugged and shook his head. "Your phone. No clue."

"Hello, Jack Smith here. What's up?" I pushed the button to turn on the phone's speaker.

"Good morning, Mr. Smith. My name is Sam Proctor and I'm the producer at KTAL radio in Montana."

"Hey," I said, with a smile. "Good morning to you. What can I do for you, Sam?"

"Well, I have a very odd and big ask to throw your way."

Troy and I snickered quietly at our own childish humor. "Great, that's right up my alley," I replied.

"Okay. First, I want to thank you for taking this call and I apologize if I'm interrupting anything . . . " Proctor's lack of confidence was telling as he let the silence hang a moment to give me a chance to cut him off. When he didn't get an out, he continued. "We're hosting a roundtable discussion with several romance authors, and wondered if you'd be interested in being part of the panel?"

A list of questions ran through my head and I started with the one that was always supposed to be first, "Did you speak with my agent? Everything goes through her."

"Yes, sir. Yes, we did. She told me to tell you she gave the green light and that it was up to you. It's how I got your number."

Makes sense.

"But I also know you're just getting back from Texas and—"

Angelina knew my schedule better than I did. If she had given this guy the green light and my number, it was probably a good deal, plus I didn't have any other bookings at this time. I looked at Troy, who was nodding his head vigorously and mouthing the words, "Do it!"

Nothing more needed to be said, we had decided. "I'm in."

"Uh, you are?"

"For sure. Just get my agent the date, time, details, and all that, and I'll be there ready to roll."

"Sir?"

"Yep?"

"It's this evening. Six p.m."

"You're screwed," said Troy, grabbing a pillow off the nearby couch and flinging it my way. Of all the skills he may have had, throwing wasn't one of them. There was a reason he'd protected quarterbacks rather than becoming one. The cushion went flying by and skidded across the table to take out both of our glasses. They shattered on the floor, spilling their contents.

I stopped right there, checking Troy's reaction from the corner of my eye. He stood there in disbelief, staring at me. We both burst out laughing.

"You're an idiot," I said, busting a gut as Troy hustled to get something to clean up the mess before the liquid made its way across the room.

"Sir? Are you still there? Is everything all right?" asked Sam.

"Yes. Yes, I am. Sorry, my man. Did you say six tonight?"

"Uh, yeah. I did."

My phone chirped an alert. "Please hold on a moment, Sam."

"Sure thing."

I checked my phone and saw that I had just received an e-ticket for a flight leaving in two hours from Cleveland Hopkins International Airport. "That girl's amazing," I whispered under my breath. Switching back to Sam, I said, "Okay Sam. I'm in, and should be there in four or five hours. Maybe less, with the time zones."

"Wow. Okay, I'll have someone pick you up at the airport." I could hear him saying in hushed tones to someone, "*We actually got him!*"

I snickered to myself. "That's great. Thanks, man. See you then."

We hung up just as a wet vac roared to life to suck up the

mess. I laughed again at Troy, and he flipped me the bird.

"Okay, I guess that saves me from unpacking or heading home."

"Damn right, you lucky fuck. Git movin'. Oh, and you might have to ride in the front this time. We still gotta catch up, and having you strapped into the back, as fun as it was, didn't work too well for talkin'," Troy said, with a stupid grin.

"You're a fool," I said, as I hustled for my bags.

The trip back to the airport was far better than the one to Troy's house. Being vertical and not tied down made all the difference.

CHAPTER TWENTY-TWO

Helen

*P*RICELESS.

Mr. Always Witty, the reader of the room, the "I-got-this-under-control" guy—Jack Smith—was actually surprised.

"Good afternoon, Jack," I said, with a smile.

He chuckled. "Wow. Don't *you* look proud of yourself?"

Jack was on my home turf now, so I could be the one to play it cool. "Naturally. Always am."

"Oh, really?" I could see his brain hard at work as he looked at me with a smile. "I like it. But, tell me, what's the deal? Why are you here?"

"You mean, why am I here at the airport surprising you with a limo? Feels kind of weird when someone else calls the shots, makes assumptions, and takes the initiative like that, doesn't it?" she said.

"Ouch. It wasn't as bad as that, was it?"

It was my turn to chuckle. "No, not at all."

"Okay, well, consider me happy to see you," he said. He stepped toward me with his arms open, and I accepted the invitation to be wrapped up against that muscular chest once again. "But why are you here, waiting on me with a limousine?"

"Get in and I'll explain."

He grabbed his bags, and I cut him off. "No need, Jack. Ben here will stow the bags for you." It was all going as planned, every beat. I had discussed this with Ben earlier, and, when I gave him a nod and he sprung into action, Jack stood there dumbfounded. Without giving Jack a second look, I was spinning around to get back into the limo when Jack sprinted a few steps to get by me and opened my door.

"I guess this is your show, so allow me," he said.

I slid across the fine leather seat and he ducked in right behind me, eyes alight with energy.

"So, spill it," he said, "what's going on?"

"What? No food or drink for you?" I waved my hand at the small table of food and drinks I'd had prepared.

"No chance. I need—sorry, thank you for that, but I'm way too curious to eat right now and . . . " A strange look came over his face as it seemed to tighten.

Could this be embarrassment?

" . . . I, well, I had more than enough to drink last night. Was catching up with an old friend."

"Oh, a lucky lady, I'm sure." I could only hope the words didn't sound as bitter as they tasted.

Jack looked off across the plains to the distant mountains and shuddered, an exaggerated full-body shake. "Oh, man, that's an image." He laughed lightly, "Nah, it was my buddy, Troy. Played ball with him for years and we were roomies. I was at his place when I got the call to—hey, you haven't answered me. Is that intentional?"

I giggled. "Maybe. It's fun to see you as the one in the hot seat." I took a drink to squeeze out every possible delay, and realized that I was not only delaying the truth because I wanted to have some fun, but was also now second-guessing my choice. *There was no mistake, Helen. Did you see the smile on Sam's face after that call?* "I'm here because I'm part of the roundtable today."

"Oh, yeah? That's awesome."

With those words, the weight slid off my shoulders. "Yes. Oh, and I also live here."

"Doubly-awesome. Sorry, I had no idea."

"You thought some little radio station in Billings, Montana just decided out of the blue that they needed to send out the Titan signal to get you to save their broadcast?"

His face tightened again—*definitely embarrassment*—and he paused before answering, "Got me there. Good point."

I gave him a swat on the knee. "Yep, the show had a guest cancel and asked the rest of us if we knew someone who might fill in short notice. One thing lead to another, and someone brought up a story I'd told them about our Texas convention and, next thing you know, the producer was talking to you. You're welcome."

Without delay, his ego kicked in to ask, "What story?"

I shook my head and rolled my eyes. "Does it matter? Don't worry, everyone agreed you're nuts."

He gave a fake sigh of relief. "Oh, good. I have a reputation to protect, y'know?"

"Don't I . . ."

The limo's engine came to life, and Ben's voice joined us through the intercom, "Everyone good to go back there?"

I pushed the button to reply, "Yes. Everything's great," and we were off.

Bottle of water in hand, Jack laid back lazily in his seat. "So, you live here, huh?"

"Yep, born and raised."

"Funny, we spent the whole weekend together and I didn't know that."

"Well, we weren't exactly together the entire time. What about you? Where do you live? I get the impression that you're no longer in Texas."

He chuckled, "Nope. Moved back to Erie, Pennsylvania, when we realized I was done playing."

"Realized"? Odd. "Forgive me, I don't know a whole lot about football. What do you mean 'realized you were done'? Most people are just told they no longer have a job."

He sighed. "Yeah, same is true in football, if you know the business. Unfortunately, I got injured and refused to accept the diagnosis." He clenched a fist as he paused in thought. "I was sure I was too valuable for them to let me go without giving me enough time to recover . . . I was wrong." The look on his face suddenly changed to one with more energy. He perked up and continued, "Well, the team did a great job in getting me help. They did all they could and waited for me as long as they could, but there's a point at which their hands are tied. They're awesome and have always supported me," he said, and gave a laugh I didn't recognize; it lacked that Jack "oomph" and I didn't buy it, "so I'll always be a Titan. Go, Titans!" The fist that had by now turned white with pressure shot into the air with a very hollow cheer.

Awkward moments like this have always been especially difficult for me. I wanted to comfort him and searched for the words, but they didn't come. I took a sip of my drink to stall again. If he were a horse, I would have intuitively known exactly the right thing to do, but instead this was Jack. Maybe strong as a horse, or built like one—a Clydesdale, probably—but no such luck. I chuckled at the thought. *Oops.*

He gave me a sideways glance.

Now I laughed.

"You are a strange one, Miss Helena Bliss."

"Thanks?"

A bit of laughter told me he had made it to the other side of the odd spot.

"And you can just call me Helen. I—"

He jumped in his seat like his butt had been bit. "Oh! 'Helena', like Helena, Montana, your state capital!"

I felt heat in my cheeks. "Not all of us are lucky enough to have a built-in household name. Some of us have to invent them."

He shook his head vigorously. "Come on, Jack is pretty darn generic. If not for people trying to market me under my own name since childhood, I would've switched to something much more fancy ages ago." His hands snapped up between us to halt all action. "Wait, that's it. Ohhh, yeah. I could have been Harrisburg Smith." he said, and he fell back in his seat laughing.

I couldn't tell if he was laughing at me or at himself. It felt like he was making fun of my name, one I had been proud to create and had put a great amount of time into establishing. When he finally settled down, it was time to let him know. "I'm already regretting mentioning your name for you to come here.

How can you—"

The laughter stopped and a serious look came over his face. "Why? Did I do something wrong?"

"You sit here making fun of me, my name, and by extension, my career. By all social standards, you know you did more than 'something wrong'."

He sat forward, a look of concern on his face. "Sorry. I swear, I thought we were just having fun. It's the same as I would've done to any of the guys."

I'm one of "the guys"?

"Truthfully, I'm jealous that you got to pick your name. I'm proud of mine, and wear it like a badge, but let's face it, I could've conjured up something more exciting. 'Helena Bliss' is so perfectly suited to you and your writing that I never blinked or thought for a moment that it may have been a pen name."

All I could do at this point was give him the benefit of the doubt and politely move on. "Thanks," I said. And changed the subject. "I'm sure you've done several roundtable things like this before, but KTAL is pretty local and the other authors on the panel are all from Montana. As Sam kept saying, 'Jack Smith will put us on the map. Biggest show ever', and it's not too far from the truth—"

Jack shook his head. "Ouch. Not cool. Honored, but not cool to say to the guests who helped build his station up or kept it afloat all this time. Kind of a belittling comment."

Sam and I went way back, so I knew not to take offense, but Jack wasn't wrong, "He means well. Just don't let it get your head any bigger."

He grinned, "No worries there."

And, as someone who had been a guest on the show three times before, I proceeded to fill Jack in on the rest of the details. He would know what he was getting into, but would the other guests and the producer? I had a feeling this show was going to be far bigger than Sam had ever imagined.

CHAPTER TWENTY-THREE

Jack

*L*OOK AT THAT *smile. That light in her eyes. She's loving this.* The passion Helen radiated was contagious. From the moment she ambushed me at the airport, to her giving me the rundown of what to expect on the show, and then riding up the elevator with me to introduce me to everyone—she glowed. She was in her element and it helped set the tone and get me ready for what was about to come.

Ding! The elevator came to a stop. Helen grabbed my arm and gave it an excited shake. "Are you ready to meet Montana's finest?"

"You know I—"

"Oh!" she said with a shocked look on her face, "I forgot to warn you about Vikki. She—"

The doors slid open and Helen's mouth snapped shut. We stepped off the elevator as two women in business casual outfits took our places inside.

Against the far wall behind a reception desk were blue under-lit block letters: KTAL-AM. Soft pastel colors and the current voice of talk radio delivered by an overhead intercom created a quiet ambiance.

"Jack Smith," called a young guy who looked to be wearing his father's oversized suit, bouncing up from his seat behind the reception desk, the calm disturbed. "Welcome to KTAL, Montana's finest talk radio."

Does he know me, or is he just doing his job? "Thank you very much, I'm happy to be here," I replied.

He didn't hear my response; he was already talking into his headset. "Jack Smith has arrived."

I gave Helen a glance before turning my focus back to him. Nodding my head, I let him know, "*Ms. Helena Bliss*—and Jack Smith—here for today's show."

He glanced quickly at Helen and then back to me. "Yes, sir. We're glad to have you. It's going to be a great show." He came out from behind his desk, smile on his face, hand outstretched.

I flirted with the idea of letting him hang but thought better of it. *No need to get in trouble already.* I shook his hand.

"My name's Roger. How was your trip?" he asked.

"Thanks to Helena here," I gave her a smile, "it was great."

"So good to hear—"

A door off the reception area swung open, and a guy in a shirt and tie that looked like they had been bought off a $5.99 combo rack came through, grinning ear-to-ear.

That's gotta be Sam Proctor.

"Sam, this is—" Roger tried to move ahead of us and take the lead, but I, in my most subtle of ways, tucked in beside Helen to effectively box Roger out and leave him behind.

"This is Helena Bliss," I said, introducing the two of them as if I didn't know they were already acquainted, "and I'm Jack Smith."

"Yes, Helena," Sam said with a smile, as he shook her hand. "Good to see you. Thanks so much for coming," he said, then shaking my hand. *That's the way it should be done. Give the lady her respect.*

"My pleasure. I appreciate the call."

Then the door opened again, and this time the real-life embodiment of a brunette Jessica Rabbit wrapped in a skintight, red, low-cut dress glided into the room.

My jaw hit the floor. *If she's a fellow author . . .*

Roger had made his way around on Helen's side. "Vikki," he said to the brunette, "I was just going to bring them to see you and Sam."

She looks like that, and yet she works in radio? What's the story there?

Vikki ignored Roger, as was becoming the trend, and came right for me.

"Jack Smith," Roger said, fighting to stay relevant. "Please meet the host of your show today, Vikki Lassiter."

Her spicy scent with floral undertones made my senses tingle. "Pleased to meet you, ma'am."

She stopped, barely two feet away, and her eyes ran freely up and down my body, a move so uncommonly brazen outside of meet-and-greets with fans that I was a bit surprised, especially in a professional environment. "I think the pleasure," she paused, her hands now on her hips, moved as if smoothing her dress but purely serving to accentuate her gorgeous curves, "may be all mine."

Sam's audible gulp summed up the moment for the rest of us in the aftershock.

Off to my side, I noticed Helen shaking her head. I could sense the rolling of her eyes.

"Sam, is William in his office?" asked Helen.

"Uh, maybe," he said. "Roger?"

Vikki and I stayed focused on each other while the others made small talk.

"Well, no," said Roger, "William left about an hour ago. Pretty much just after you did, Helena."

Helen sighed, and grabbed my arm. "Good to go?"

Vikki made her way back to the door. "Follow me into the studio. I'll introduce you to the rest of the crowd and we can get ready for the show."

"I'll join you guys in a minute. I need to speak with Roger for a moment first," said Sam.

"Me? Oh, okay," said Roger.

Vikki left us in her dust. As we got through the door and out of earshot of the two men, I slowed the pace to whisper to Helen, "Yep, she's definitely worth a warning." I expected a laugh, maybe just a giggle, but I got an entirely different look from Helen that may not have been all that positive.

I'll never understand women.

CHAPTER TWENTY-FOUR

Helen

"**N**OW THAT WE have the introductions out of the way, let's . . . " Vikki Lassiter paused, her voice dropping to a husky tone as she finished the show's name and catchphrase, " . . . *Get Intimate.*"

The woman was good. I had always thought that Vikki's radio persona could be the basis for many characters, and that her real-life exploits would make her a brilliant antagonist with an appetite known to be voracious, one that had no problem taking out competition. My fingers itched for my notebook.

"Today, we'll focus on the two parts that are my favorites, after the hot man-candy," she said with a throaty chuckle, "the 'heat' and 'the heart'. Let's find out how these romance authors find ways to both get us off and make us fall in love. We want to find out: is there a kinky, voyeuristic side to you people that drives you to write these stories? I want to know . . . " Vikki crooned, her eyes glimmering with excitement as she locked in on Jack, " . . . is that your kink? Does it turn you on knowing you're making your readers so aroused?"

Most of us chuckled awkwardly. We knew from experience that Vikki Lassiter often danced across the border between appropriate and inappropriate. My stomach turned, and I looked at Jack to give him a silent apology, but he was clearly engaged and fully into it.

"Are you, 'my reader', Miss Lassiter?" Jack asked with a grin.

She adjusted her headphones and ran her finger suggestively over the meshed tip of her mic. "Oh, yeah. Right from your 'Scouting Reports' series to this very moment."

"Then, yes, that is my kink, and I—" he said.

We had barely started and it was already time for me to cut in. "It's safe to say, Vikki, that we all write for a variety of reasons, but want to be sure our readers enjoy every beat." Neither Vikki nor Jack bothered to look my way, still making eyes at each other as if the rest of us had ceased to exist.

"I'm told your books are based on real life experiences. Lucky ladies, who received a night with a Titan," Vikki continued.

Jack sat forward, removed his jacket, and patted down his shirt with the appearance of trying to settle the fine material but it was clearly just to draw attention to the contoured frame it highlighted rather than simply covered. We sat waiting. All of us, including those I could see in the sound booth, acutely aware of the dead air. I knew they had to be prompting Vikki to keep the show moving but she just sat there, jaw dangling low over the desktop and on its way to dripping disgusting drool.

Jack cleared his throat, "Well, I can only hope that's true, and I want my readers, your listeners—and you, Miss Lassiter—to know that I'm always looking to create the next great fantasy."

Vikki purred into the microphone.

Come on! She's purring, *for God's sake!* I jumped in again, "Yes, the 'Jack Smith, I write fantasies' spiel. I've heard it already, and let me tell—"

That got her attention. Vikki's head swung my way. "That's right . . . you two just spent the weekend together in Texas, didn't you?" she said.

I felt all eyes in the room, and Sam Proctor's in the production booth, snap my way. *This, Helen, is why you should just blend in.* But this time, I refused to submit to that old voice saying, *Laugh and deflect, so we can move on. Wrong.* They all needed to see a new side of Helena Bliss for once. I did my best imitation of a purr back at Vikki, "Yes, we did, and it was incredible." I glanced at Jack with a smirk, and the look on his face was priceless. *Don't like it when someone else tries to steal the ringleader hat, Jack?*

"Oh, I just bet it was," said Vikki, turning green with envy.

"You want to talk about heart and heat," I said, "I'll tell you something. The first time I met Jack, I walked in on he and another woman going at it right there on the conference room floor. She was screaming—"

Thomas, one of the other panel members chimed in with a dirty laugh and, "I bet she was," before offering Jack a high-five. Jack was staring at me with curiosity, oblivious. The other author's hand fell limply to his side.

I continued, "She was screaming *at* him, calling his name, inviting others to join in. I fell to the ground in surprise as a used rubber came flying my way."

The room cringed, gasped, and gagged.

A large smile took control of my face as I casually looked around the room at everyone, while nodding at their disbelief. "Yep. Hit me square between the eyes. Little did I know, that was then moment which would set me up to spend the rest of the weekend sharing a booth with the infamous Jack Smith."

Jack's expression now changed to one of amusement, and he started to chuckle.

"All because of one piece of grab bag swag, a little rubber heart-shaped eraser, flung carelessly around the room by its namesake, Nancy *Coeur*." *Ha! I kill me!* Inside, I was laughing hysterically and doing a victory dance. Outside, I played it straight, and looked around the room innocently.

"And, without missing a beat," Jack seized the opportunity to pick up the baton, "Helena says to all of us, as straight-faced as she is right this moment, 'Anyone else order the conference facial?'" And he burst into red-faced laughter, sending Sam into fits in the production booth as he frantically adjusted the sound levels.

I couldn't keep my cool any longer and joined Jack in his hysterical laughter, while the rest of the room tried to process the two fools in their midst.

Vikki slowly started to give a throaty laugh, and the rest joined in. "You are a dirty girl, Ms. Helena Bliss. I bet your heat extends beyond your latest book, 'A Long, Hard Road'. And on that note, we'll cut to a commercial. Join us after the break as we 'Get Intimate' at our authors' roundtable, featuring special guest, Jack Smith." She pushed the button in front of her and the green ON AIR light dimmed.

CHAPTER TWENTY-FIVE

Jack

HELEN TAKING THE lead was a surprise. I knew she had it in her, but it was clearly not her usual behavior. It left me wondering if this change was because she was in a more familiar environment, or whether there was something else going on? When she'd started into the conversation about the weekend, a strong wave of anxiety had rolled through me, thinking she was going to blindside me. Instead, she did her thing in impressive style and left me unscathed.

Vikki broke away from talking with the redhead to her right, and put on her headphones and her game face as the ON AIR light started blinking. "Okay, here we go again, everyone," she said, before pushing the button to go back on the airwaves. "And we're back. We're going to continue to 'Get Intimate' with a panel of romance authors who write the hottest stuff around. Let's start out talking about the heat. Here, straight from our local dungeon: Thomas Sheer. Thomas?"

Thomas was my buddy for the day, one of those middle-aged guys who had played high-school football, and retained his stories of what he "coulda" and "woulda" done that kept him clinging to the dream. Guys like him were usually harmless and served as a great reminder of why I had spent my life making the hard choices and putting in the work. I'd never wanted to risk that fate if it was in my control. Unlike the usual guys though, he was one of those who was convinced that he was still "The Man", who wanted to arm wrestle, do sprints, have people punch him in the stomach, and every other cliché that led to him sitting far too close for comfort. Harmless, but his presence could take a toll.

He had the face for radio, but, lucky for him, he also had the voice, a deep bass sound that he used to his advantage. "Yes, Vikki?" he said.

She gave him a big smile and asked, "What's hot to you?"

"I'm so glad you asked. In my newest book, 'The—"

She stopped him there. "No, not in your books. In the world of Thomas Sheer, what's hot?"

"Oh . . . Well, that's also a good question," he said, then coughed and cleared his throat, buying time. "I like candles. A room lit by candlelight, with soft music, rose petals on the floor in front of the fire where we would make love and—"

It was a reflex. I didn't mean to laugh, but it happened. A small one, maybe what others might call a titter if the word didn't sound so ridiculous. I hoped my outburst would stop right there. I tried forcing it to quiet down, but when they all looked at me, aghast, it rebelled and grew. Helen's face went from eyes-widening surprise, to fascinated curiosity, and it egged me on. "I'm sorry, Thomas," I said.

"Uh, no problem, Jack," Thomas offered, "I get it."

I laughed again, "Do you, though? Roses are beautiful, don't get me wrong, but when you get hot, sweaty, and nasty, do you know what happens to those roses?"

"Oh yeah," he was still in the game, or so he thought, laying it on thick with that voice, "once we get going those roses succumb to our passion and create an aromatic—"

That did it. Not only was I laughing harder but louder again. "Man, they get wedged into your ass and any other orifice! They bind up into little piles in your armpits, under breasts, and between cheeks . . . "

Vikki and a few others chuckled as Thomas ground his teeth in frustration. It was then that I realized he had still been going for romantic fiction rather than reality, and a tinge of guilt cut my merriment down to size. "Hey, man," I said to him, "maybe I've been doing it wrong or need some tips." I gave him a friendly slap on the shoulder, "Help a brother out."

He grinned half-heartedly.

"So, no roses for the infamous king of debauchery, Jack Smith," started Vikki. "Then what is it? What turns up the heat for you?"

Silence overtook the room. *There's that spotlight you're always asking for. Only you can take an ensemble piece and turn it into a one-man show.* "Mmm, oh so many things," I said, choosing my words. "A woman who looks you in the eye and says, 'Fu—'" *Drive time radio, Jack, keep it PG,* "'take me like an animal', and then meets you stroke for stroke." Once again, when I surveyed the room I landed on Helen. I had her attention but couldn't get a good read on her expression to even guess what she was thinking. *Frustrating and intriguing, a dangerous combination.* "Decisive, she demands what she wants while being sure to blow your mind, as well. The location doesn't matter to me and wouldn't matter to her, it's about that lustful urgency that can't be fought."

"'Lustful urgency'..." was an echoed whisper by one or two of the other panelists with an "oh," and an "aw", their faces lost to me as I got lost in the moment.

I tried hard to continue reading the crowd, but was drawn back to Helen and a focused look I could not read. "And rain, pouring down hard on us, maybe as I lay her back on the hood of an old Camaro, still rumbling and hot below us . . . " I shifted slightly in my seat, now aroused and aching for release, either through writing, or something far more primal and direct.

"Yes. Oh God, yes," Vikki panted into the microphone. "Any listeners out there with a Camaro?"

CHAPTER TWENTY-SIX

Jack

THE REST OF the segment played out well. They were a good bunch of people. The show and my fellow authors went out of their way to make me feel welcome, and I thoroughly enjoyed getting a front row seat to see Helen in action on her turf. *An intriguing and complicated woman.*

"And with that, I'm Vikki Lassiter, wishing you sweet sensations and reminding you to . . . *Get Intimate.*"

Show over, we were eager to ditch the headsets. The difference between us was that this was the other authors' chance to socialize, but for me, it was my chance to run. Thomas dropped his headset like it was hot, or that was the intent behind his all-too-casual move. His chair spun my way as I was jumping to escape, but he caught me. "So, Titan, what's the strategy for taking over Billings tonight?"

I shook my head, and said, "No strategy here. Just going with the flow tonight. It's been a long run and I'm looking forward to getting some rest." I inched my way to the exit.

He winked. "Oh, yeah, I get it. Lone wolfing it tonight. Nice." Thomas stood up and bodied up on me like we were on the field and he was going for press coverage. "You know, if you want a wingman, I work on an all-pro level," he said, puffing up his chest to match the girth of his belly.

I put my hand on his shoulder. It gave me the chance to look him in the eye and address him respectfully, but, most important-ly, it bought me some personal space. "If I decide to go out 'lone wolfing it' and need a partner to join me on the prowl, I'll look you up. Honestly, though, it'll be a simple night for me, waiting for my flight home to get into my own bed for the first time in far too long." *Especially since I spent last night in a bathtub.*

Everyone else milled around the room, engaged in conversa-tion. I had to imagine each of them had more interesting dialogue to offer than I did. I had only one thought, and it wasn't really about getting home. *Where was Helen?*

Vikki kept giving me the eyes I knew too well, the intensity kicking up a notch when I saw her break free from talking to the young and hefty paranormal romance author, June, and head my way.

Thomas was still stuck to me like glue. *This guy must've been a defensive back with this type of coverage.* "Jack, if you're just looking to chill until you leave, then let me take care of you. I know the perfect place to go and—"

Delicate fingers that sent a ripple of energy through my body slid around my arm. I didn't need to look to see who they belonged to. "Sorry, Thomas," Helen cut in, "I called him in, so I'm the one on the hook to get him squared away and safely out of here." *Helen to the rescue.*

Vikki joined the party at Thomas' side. "Lucky girl," Vikki crooned, the words hanging with a practiced pause, "need a third?"

This was getting out of hand. If I didn't hurry, we were on our way to having some kind of weird writers' orgy right here in the studio.

I didn't say a word. Let's see Helen handle this. We looked her way, the spotlight shining bright.

She grinned, looked each of us in the eyes, and said, "No thanks, not since college."

Bam! Shots fired. Each of us took a blow to the dome, shocked by those simple, yet tantalizingly-teasing words. Before any of them could react, Helen had spun me around and we were flying out the door.

She squeezed my arm tight. I could feel her hands trembling slightly as she whispered, "Don't look back. Keep walking."

I had just been taken hostage, and I loved it. "You're crazy," I said, trying to match her hushed tones.

She giggled, "Maybe."

As we neared the elevators, Roger popped up again from his chair. "Great show, Mr. Smith."

I laughed. *He had no idea the best part happened off mic.* "Thanks, but Helena was the real star in there."

She gave me a swat on the arm.

Ding! The elevator arrived just as Roger was making his way around the desk.

"Helena did what?" he asked, trying to stall us.

We hustled into the elevator.

I shook my head. "No worries. Great to meet you. Take care, Roger."

"Thanks. Great to meet you—" and the doors slid closed.

The silence of our descent was short-lived as we went from

watching the numbers above the door to falling back against the opposite wall in relief.

"Poor Roger," said Helen.

"That guy needs a lesson in manners, respect, and professionalism," I said. "'Poor Roger', my ass."

"Well, that was one way to do it. The look on his face as the doors closed . . . "

"Talk about looks," I said, my laughter rising again, "the look on Thomas' and Vikki's faces when you said, 'not since college', . . . "

Her laughter stopped immediately. "Why was that funny?"

"I, uh . . . " *Oh-kay, this was awkward.* "Because they believ— uh, they were left speechless."

"Yeah, they were, weren't they?"

"Wait, are you saying . . . did you—"

Ding! The elevator cut in, saving one of us by the bell. I'm just not sure who.

I zipped my lips and followed Helen out of the elevator into the underground parking lot.

CHAPTER TWENTY-SEVEN

Jack

"HELENA BLISS DRIVES a big blue pickup truck? Ha! I never in a million years saw that coming," I said, busting a gut and slapping my knee.

She flipped me a scowl. "Helena Bliss doesn't; Helen does. And what's wrong with a pickup?"

"Oh, nothing. It's just new to me."

"Isn't most of my life here in Montana new to you?"

"Yeah, I just meant that I don't know many women—" I started to say.

We stopped at a red light and the deeper tone of her voice made it clear I was already wandering into trouble. "Careful how you choose your next words, Mr. Smith."

"Okay, okay. I think it's great. It's just different than I'm used to."

"Then I guess you haven't met many true country girls."

The light turned green and we slowly moved again with the traffic. *You're not winning this one, Jack. You stepped in it, suffer with the smell.* I turned my attention back to the city. There was something strangely familiar about the place, with its streets upon streets of low-rise homes and businesses. With its smaller community feel, I realized this was a lot like being home, right down to the same cool spring weather that had us putting on jackets as the sun went down. The biggest difference was that where we in Erie had a Great Lake as our backdrop and foundation, this place had gorgeous mountain terrain on the horizon.

A few minutes later, Helen re-opened the doors of communication. "Am I driving you to your hotel or somewhere else?"

"Honestly, with how fast this all happened, I didn't really make any plans. I thought it would be great to pop in on my brother while I'm here and—"

"You have family here? And you've never been here before?"

"Yep. Well, not family like you're thinking. One of the guys I played with lives out here and got a great gig at one of the local high schools. I've often dreamed about coming out here, meeting his wife and kids, and maybe guest-coaching with him for a day."

"Ahh, that kind of brother. Like the driver in Texas, Ed, is your brother."

"Yeah. You spend enough time with people, sharing life and danger, and you get close."

"I get that. It's kind of sweet."

"Uh, you said that, not me," I said with a chuckle. "It's really kind of crazy. You get a group of guys from every part of the world who would otherwise never meet or get along, but you throw them into a blender together and you get family. I'm a very lucky man in that regard."

"I've mostly gone solo."

"Which is probably how the writing started, right?"

"Hmm." She paused a moment, deep in thought. "Probably."

You finally got one right. "Excellent."

"Your brother's place it is."

I opened my phone, scrolled through the contact list, and found his address. "Okay, Waggle lives at 32—"

"Wait . . . 'Waggle'?" she said, giggling.

"Yeah, he was our QB. He lives at—"

"But his name: *Waggle*. Is he from Montana? Because I've never met anyone—"

I shook my head and snickered, "It's a nickname."

"Oh! Of course, I should have known. All right, hit me with that address."

I gave it to her and she pulled over to the side of the road. "I'm not really sure where that is," she said, punching it into the GPS. "Oh, that's out of town. Not too far, but out there."

"Oops. Okay, well, that kills that. I can—"

"Wait, it isn't a problem. One condition though."

"Oh no, what's that?" I said.

"I need to meet him. I need to be able to say I met someone named Waggle," she said, with a grin.

"Deal!"

And we set off.

About five minutes later, as we were leaving city limits, I noticed the time. *Clearly, it was too late to help out at a practice. The family will have already had dinner, and you know you can't do any more drinking.* "Helen, I think I made a mistake. It would be great to see him and his family, but it's too late, especially to show up unannounced."

"Oh, okay. Where to, then?"

"Good question. Any recommendations? If not, or if you're short on time, I could just go to the hotel."

Her head lifted high and she lit up like a kid at Christmas. "Of course I have a recommendation. Especially since we're out this way. I know just the place." She kicked it into high gear with a smile blazing across her face. Only moments later, I watched that smile sink like I was watching a second sunset. "Big question I should have asked you first," she said. "Do you like nature?"

"In what way? I like Yogi Bear and Boo-Boo, if that's what you mean." *That'll get her going.*

The back of her hand slapped hard against my bicep. "No, funny man. Nature. The outdoors, trails, hiking, camping, maybe even rock-climbing. I can find that stuff for us anytime, day or night, we have the most amazing parks. Tourists love them. I was going to show you that kind of stuff . . . unless you prefer something in the city?"

"I'm a guest in your state. Show me what you've got. Give it to me," I replied.

The sun rose again. "Oh, good. There's so much to show you!" She started quietly singing some song I didn't recognize. Every once in a while, I caught a part that may have been the chorus: "Montana, Montana, Glory of the West . . . "

I listened, enjoying every beat. The girl had passion and pride. *Me, I have sarcasm.* "You tired of living here yet?"

Caught up in the moment, she raised her voice louder. "M-O-N-T-A-N-A, Montana, I love you!"

I laughed.

Her smilin' eyes stayed fixed on the road ahead as the street lights began to disappear behind us. My eyes continued to lean more toward her than the tree-lined street.

Helen slowed down as we approached the end of the line. A

tall worn post covered with vertically stacked signs provided an exhaustive list of places whose names were absolutely foreign to me.

"Your call," I said, staring at the crossroads.

As the seconds ticked by, I was grateful that there weren't any cars sitting behind us to blast their horns. Helen was looking at the signs as if she was just discovering them and trying to process their meaning. She took a long look to the right, then to the left, before quietly muttering, "I'll give you something even bet-ter . . . " She suddenly wrenched the steering wheel to the right, sending me lurching into the center console as the tires and road screamed in angry confusion.

"Uh, Helen?"

She stared ahead, the road narrowing to two lanes and then one.

"Is everything okay?" I asked.

She glanced at me, a look of conflict and confusion in her eyes that made me double-check my seatbelt. "I don't know. But if you've never been to Montana and want to see what's good about it and why it's the place for me—I'm going to show you."

Swallowing hard on her words, her focus returned to the road. The distant city was a fading postcard in the rear-view mirror.

CHAPTER TWENTY-EIGHT

Jack

TWENTY MINUTES HAD passed since we saw the last house, and we were now climbing a gravel road in the darkness, heading toward a yellow beacon. As we drew closer to the light, the look on Helen's face continued to soften and a smile grew.

"We're almost there," she said, in a voice barely above a whisper.

The late night wisp we had been chasing evolved into a large lamppost rising high overhead at the crest of the hill. Passing it brought us to the wide double gates of the "Last Chance Ranch".

Helen hit the brakes, and jumped out of the truck. Punching in a code on a small panel jutting out from one of the posts had the gates swinging open for us as she looked back at me through the gleam of the headlights with a childlike grin. Racing to the truck and leaping back into the driver's seat, she squeezed my arm. "You ready?"

I believed success came when passion met commitment. Helen had become a big ball of passion, and whatever was about to happen next meant a great deal to her. That excitement drew me in. A big smile had spread over my face, too, and I nodded enthusiastically. "I am ready. I truly am."

We entered the ranch and the gates glided closed behind us. The road split into three from this point, one going up toward a large ranch house with a wraparound deck to the right, while the other two rolled off into darkness. We swung left, and in no time an enormous two-storey building emerged from the night. I would have called it a barn if it weren't nicer than the average home.

Helen began to hum a beautifully melodic tune as we approached.

The gravel crunching under our feet sounded its displeasure at our late night disruption as we left the parked truck and cut through the otherwise silent night. The distinct smell and taste of hay, dust, and livestock wound their way into my senses, a strong odor that brought back great childhood memories of visiting the county fair.

I watched as Helen punched another code into a box inset beside the large barn doors and then looked back at me, a ball of energy vibrating with impatience, shifting from foot to foot.

The door slid open to reveal a wide, dimly-lit hallway lined with some rubber grid-type flooring.

There's no question that my technical knowledge of barns was extremely limited, but, when compared to others I'd seen over the years, this one was near the top-end and would make many proud Texans want to eat their hats.

Once we were inside, Helen slid the door closed behind us, and, with a voice straining to contain her excitement, said in a hushed tone, "I've got someone for you to meet."

She speedwalked her way down the main aisle toward the rear of the facility.

CHAPTER TWENTY-NINE

Helen

I WRAPPED MY arms around her chestnut-colored neck while Jack stood at the stall door, quietly waiting and watching. She snuggled into my grasp, the hair from her mane tickling my nose. "Hey, gorgeous," I whispered, her ears already at full alert, "I missed you, my queen."

After doling out a heavy dose of kisses, praise, and much more cuddling, I stepped away slightly while continuing to rub her neck just in front of her withers. As always, she began doing a small dance on the spot, alternating from her right to her left foreleg while curling her lips. *I love this girl.*

"So, Jack, you being a Texan—"

"Adopted Texan. I know where this is going," he said, with a chuckle.

I giggled. "Fair enough. My point is, I'm sure you've spent your fair share of time with horses, right?"

He nodded his head, "Yeah . . . " In the dim light, I watched as he looked around the barn, everywhere but at me. "I spent time with them, that's true, but not much closer than this with the exception of photo ops and other promotions."

Okay, this might be a problem in this friendship. "Wait, you don't like horses? How can that be?" I said. The moment I stopped rubbing my mare's neck, she spun her head toward me, looking for more, and I snuggled in again. "They're so fantastic. Both loving and lovely."

Staring at the ground, Jack began to shift lightly back-and-forth before his jaw clenched and he looked at me. "I'll admit, they make me uncomfortable. They're too unpredictable. Scare too easy. You can't trust them and—"

No way! "You're scared of horses?" I asked.

"Hey! Who said anything about being scared?"

I kept my eyes locked on him.

He stood, unflinching, under my stare.

I waited.

"Okay, I guess you could say something like that. I wouldn't," he shrugged, "but you could. Though I'd deny it anywhere else."

"Really . . . "

He shrugged, comfortable with the words he'd set free. "Yeah, but don't get me wrong. They are gorgeous and, of course, like people, the ones bred for competition are crazy impressive, but you can't count on them not to turn on you."

"Turn on you?"

"Okay, maybe not turn on you, but they're fight-or-flight to the core, and the moment the wind changes they'll bolt. And I don't handle that kind of personality all that well, y'know?"

"Oh, really! I know I'd like to hear a shrink's thoughts about that statement," I said, taking advantage of the opportunity to give him a ribbing.

"Yeah, I hear that a lot," he said.

"Well, then, maybe this was a better choice for an activity than I realized."

He smirked in that smart ass, Jack Smith way. "The night's still young. I'll be the judge of that."

"Funny guy. So, can I convince you to come into the stall and say hi to my girl here? I know you don't shy away from females."

He chuckled, "If you're saying it's safe, okay." Closing the stall door behind him, he approached, arm stretched out toward her as if meeting a dog.

Sure enough, she turned her head away and gave him the sideways stare. I continued rubbing her neck and jokingly said, "I know. So rude, right?"

He dropped his arm to his side. "What?"

"Come around here to her side. Remember that fight-or-flight stuff? Treat her like a lady. Don't just rush right in and stick your hand in her face."

This time, he moved much more slowly, but the mare watched him every step of the way until he was by my side.

"Here," I said, patting her shoulder. "Rub here."

As he did, it became time for introductions. "Jack, I am pleased to introduce you to my one and only, Cleopatra."

Like the silly person he is, Jack gave a cautious but grandiose bow. "Most honored to meet Your Majesty."

Somehow I wound up laughing at his silliness. "And, Cleopatra, please meet my friend, Jack Smith."

I guess between my laughter and the gesturing introductions, we had stopped giving Cleo enough attention. She gave a couple of perfectly-timed snorts and sent a look my way. "Yes, I know, but I tolerate him," I said, and returned to giving her love.

"See, now that's why I avoid horses," he said. "Such critics."

"They are, and they're right!"

He chuckled, "Well, yeah. Maybe," he said, and began rubbing her neck while I ran my hands over her body and gave her a full inspection. Between Texas and the chaotic days around the trip, it had been more than a week since I last saw Cleopatra. It felt like ages.

Coming around front, I gave her a gentle rub on her forehead. *How do we take this to the next level?*

The two were getting along well and Jack now had both hands on her, stroking her gently.

"Uh, not too far, Jack. Not too near her legs or her butt yet."

A sudden laugh burst out of him, and Cleopatra's eyes shot my way. "Oh, you've heard the stories about me, have you?" he said.

"Funny. And yes." *That's the answer. He's used to hanging with the boys.* "Wait. I have an idea." I gave Cleo another little nuzzle, "Be right back, beautiful," I said, and headed out of the stall. "Jack, follow me."

He responded by letting his shoulders sag and giving a big pout. "But she likes me."

Truth is, he was right. She did seem to like him, and that was a huge plus, but I chuckled while shaking my head. "Just come on," I said, and, reluctantly, he followed.

We went two stalls down to find the beautiful chocolate lad that Cleopatra and I love so much. Naturally, he was already standing at the ready and looking for some attention, too. "Jack, the queen and I would like to introduce you to our champion. This is Sir Lancelot." Right on cue, Lancelot's muzzle popped over the rail looking for affection or treats.

"Wow. He's gorgeous," said Jack, his hand immediately going into the flax-colored mane.

I did a double-take. Sir Lancelot is notoriously friendly, so it was only a small surprise that he didn't flinch, but Jack going for it—*Yeah . . .*

I smiled. "Yep, he's quite the ladies' man. Want to take him for a ride?"

That was it. Jack stepped back, Lancelot's head swung away, and they both looked at me like I was crazy.

"Uh, it's nighttime," said Jack, his face now pale.

"I'm sorry, we don't have to—"

"Too dark to see, right?"

"Actually, horses have great night vision and we do enough tours of the land that these two know the trails well," I said.

"Right. Oh. Well, I've never ridden before and wouldn't it be—"

"Honestly, Jack, it's okay." *Yep, Helen, you misread the moment. This is why I never make the first move.* I felt my cheeks begin to heat up. "I just kind of got caught up in the fun. It's been too long since I've been out and—"

"No, it was a great idea and I love that you'd share it with me. Can I, uh, maybe get a raincheck—for the next time I'm back in Montana?" he said, smiling.

"Yeah, when's that? Next week?" I said, before giving him a shove as I hustled by, eager to escape his gaze and return to my girl.

When I got to Cleopatra's stall, I was surprised to see Jack wasn't right behind me. I looked back and found he had stayed a little longer to share words I couldn't hear with Lancelot and take the opportunity to pat the horse's forelock.

I looked at Cleopatra and muttered, "Boys," and she huffed a response that I believe meant she knew exactly what I was talking about. "They complicate everything!"

CHAPTER THIRTY

Jack

W̱E ENTERED A room at the rear of the barn where bales of hay and straw were stacked to ridiculous heights, and I was immediately glad I wore jeans today. *This might get messy.* Helen grabbed an electric lantern from a nearby shelf and, turning it on, led the way up a wooden ladder to the second floor.

"You probably noticed the main stairs by the entry leading up to the second floor . . . "

She was right, I had.

Helen continued, " . . . which might make using a ladder seem kind of odd."

It does, though the kid in me appreciates it.

"Truth is, this part of the loft wasn't really intended to be an area for people to hang out, but I like it," said Helen.

We got to the top and now stood in a space that could rightly be described as a nook. It was too small to be a room, and had no furniture. A single light bulb dangled from a wire in the corner.

"I often come to the stable at night. Sometimes to ride," she said, placing the lantern on a wooden beam along the far wall, "and sometimes to write." A few bales of hay were tucked into another corner, she grabbed one from the top and began dragging it to the middle of the floor.

With the two of us each taking a side, it moved easily and dropped with a soft thud.

Helen surprised me when she pulled a wood-handled lock blade from the inside pocket of her coat and cut the binding on the straw bale. I followed her lead, beginning to spread it over the floor of the loft. She slid into the pile like a plow to push it in a soft mound where she wanted it, which had her landing on her own little straw bed.

"O-kay," I said.

"What? You afraid of getting dirty, cowboy?" She looked at me and I saw a look of recognition on her face. She sat up. "I'm sorry, I got carried away. I forgot that you—"

Jeans, no matter the price, are meant for playing rough, and maybe I shouldn't wear such fancy, frilly Western shirts to radio shows . . . "Watch out!" I hooted, and I slid into the pile myself, joining her. I had tried to avoid crashing into Helen, but wound up bumping her off to one side, starting a romp back into being kids again. "Yeah," I said, "these may not be my standard play clothes, but how often does a person get to do this? By my count, for me, just about never." Goofing off, I pushed her over again, and began waving my arms and legs in an effort to make straw angels on the ground.

She grabbed a bunch of straw with both hands and threw it at me, covering my head and chest, a few pieces poking into my mouth and nose.

She flopped down beside me, and we both started coughing from the dust—still laughing in between gasps for breath—until our energy finally wore off. Lying back, I noticed a large skylight above us, a frame for the clear night sky, now jam-packed with brilliant stars.

"Whoa . . . " was all I could muster.

"Uh-huh," she said softly.

We'd lain there, staring up at the heavens, for what had felt like an immeasurable amount of time, maybe seconds, maybe an hour, before feeling any need to speak. We were just two souls marveling at the unmitigated awesomeness that is the universe.

The quiet had become part of our being, so I now spoke in hushed tones, "You know, I can't remember the last time I saw a sky like this." I rolled over to look at Helen's tranquil face. "Thank you. This is far more than I could have asked for, or expected."

She sat up and turned my way. "I'm glad you like it."

"Oh no," I whispered, "'like' doesn't even begin to touch it. This is the stuff that makes us realize who we are as people. It lets us know nature. It lets us . . . "

She smiled before giving me a poke in the ribs. "Is this how Jack Smith writes a story?"

"No." The moment changed and I sat up, moving back into my own space. "You don't want to know about that."

"Why not? Are all Jack Smith stories created in fantasy brothels of the world, and written in permanent ink on the flesh of buxom beauties, then photographed and printed off for mass consumption?"

"That," I said, through bursts of laughter, "is quite the inspiring image. I'll have to try that sometime, funny person. No, but since you've gone there, I actually write on a laptop or, when on the road, a phablet that—"

"Wait. A what?" she asked.

"One of those devices that's too big to be a phone, but too small to be a tablet," I shrugged. "I don't know, that's what they told me to call it. Anyway, like the writing geek I really am, I carry it with me pretty much everywhere to write whenever I find something fun or interesting to make notes about, or in case I get inspired. Truth is, looking at this view, I wish I had it with me now."

An amused look came over her face with a glint in her eye. "I get it. Where is it?"

"I did some writing on the plane and tucked it in my bag when I met you. Haven't had chance to dig it out yet. How about you?"

She stuck her hand into her jacket and pulled out a blue spiral-bound notebook, small enough to fit in the palm of her hand. "I, too, am a geeky writer. Maybe worse than you, even, because I'm still a pen-and-paper person."

"That's awesome. I miss pen and paper. Unfortunately, between my trips to brothels around the world and my newfound career of straw-diving, notebooks don't survive all that well. Plus, I hate to say it, but I wound up getting a few of them stolen by fans, so something had to change. Lucky for me, one of the promos I did was for a tech company. They end up sending me a new phablet at least once a year."

"I would think people would be more inclined to steal those, rather than pen and paper."

"Me too, but it didn't work out that way. I don't know if it's the size difference—"

"Size does matter," she said, with a silly wink.

"But, also, when one of my phablets did go missing, I knew it was at least password-protected, and everything was on the cloud, so I didn't lose any work."

"Hmm, good point," said Helen, returning her notebook to her jacket.

Then it dawned on me. "Hey . . . your fantasy!"

"What's that now?" she asked.

I leaned forward, elbows on knees, staring at her intently. "We were talking about fantasies at the station, and you didn't give us one."

She began buttoning up her jacket. "True. The question didn't come my way."

"Okay. But if it did?"

"It didn't."

"You know that just takes my curiosity to another level, right?"

Her shoulders bounced with a shrug. She tried to play it cool, but I could see by the way her brow had begun to furrow that she was considering her next move to change the subject. "Maybe," she said. "Sorry about your luck."

"You heard mine. Now show me yours," I teased.

She threw another handful of straw my way. "Nope, no chance. Plus, your story was vague and I didn't buy it. At least . . . well, it seemed rehearsed, like you had said or written it before."

She's good! "Okay, you got me. Then give me something like that—Oh! I know. Do you have something there in your handy-dandy notebook? That can't be so bad, if it's stuff you'd publish. I'll take it simply as a story."

"I don't know . . ."

"And just imagine that it's you," I said. That earned me a smack on the knee.

"Okay, fine. I have one I've recently been working on. But you have to know that it's very rough, just a first draft, and I don't even know for sure if it'll end up in the new book."

"Sure, sure. Let it rip."

When the notebook reappeared, I noticed the way her fingers clutched it hard enough to begin to bend the edges. "Helen, I'm just being a jerk. If you don't want to share right now, that's okay."

In the faded light, I could see her thinking it through. "You know what? I'm going to do it. You did this," she waved her hand over the straw, "and we're both writers, so what would be the harm—unless you're one of those writers looking to pilfer the material of others."

Funny. "No worries there, you know how my stories are written . . . " I laid back in the straw and closed my eyes to focus on her forthcoming words. "No harm at all. Hit me with some Helena Bliss action."

CHAPTER THIRTY-ONE

Helen

I FOUGHT THE butterflies fluttering in my stomach, working up the nerve for a full scale mutiny on silence. *One, two, three.* I drew air deeply into my lungs through my nose. *Four, five, six.* And gave a long exhale through my mouth. *Okay, Helen. It's going to be okay.* "Again, rough draft, random stuff, and all that . . ."

"Absolutely. No problem. Understood," Jack said, settling himself deeper into his bed of straw.

Then I began to read:

There was a sense about him of a hidden past, of secrets well-hidden and disguised. He had a side to him few knew, and that was okay, because so did I.

I knew he had a history of debauchery, scores of women littering his past, but it didn't matter. I was his tonight.

"Get on your knees," I said.

The raised eyebrows, the head tilt, and the sudden lack of witty comebacks said it all.

Yeah, I'm taking mine tonight.

Slowly, he dropped to his knees.

I stepped in to aid his progress. My hands on his head shoved him to the floor.

He looked up at me with a grin. "So, there's another side to you—"

"Shut up and put that mouth to work," I said.

With a smile growing beyond its limits, he placed his hands on my thighs and his face under my short skirt, onto the naked flesh he had glimpsed earlier in the night on the dance floor. He stared at me, eyes lit with passion, before making another attempt to talk that was one too many.

Looks like I'll be teaching some lessons tonight. *My fingers went from resting comfortably on his head to seizing his hair. Pulling him toward me, I straddled his face.*

He got the hint. His tongue dove for home and I felt a wave of energy roll through me. That great feeling of expectation rising with the realization that the tension we built from the moment we had crossed paths at work to tonight's chance encounter on the dance floor was nearing release.

A deep sound rumbled up from my soul as he inserted a finger and his tongue began to pick up pace.

"Yes, own it. Make it hum, baby," I said. It was just the random sex-talk that sometimes comes out in the heat of the moment, but he seemed to take it as another order and went to work.

His lips began to hum slightly, a strange and wonderful vibration I had never felt before. He slipped in a second finger, stretching me slightly. My legs wobbled. I moaned.

He groaned.

My nails dug hard into his skull and we shared a deep shiver through our bodies.

His hand began to work faster, his mouth moved to suck on

me—

A familiar deep voice suddenly called up to the loft from the stable below: "Hey! Everything okay up there?"

Jack and I almost jumped out of our skins.

I stuffed my dirty notebook back into my pocket as fast as I could, and peered down the ladder.

CHAPTER THIRTY-TWO

Jack

"**H**EY, EVERYTHING OKAY up there?" Some old guy's voice destroyed the moment.

Helen raced to close her notebook and stick it back in her pocket. "Uh, yes, Clay. It's me, Helen—"

"I saw your truck out there. When I got the buzz from the gate being opened, I figured it had to be you." The voice didn't lie, I saw, as a man poked his head up into our loft from the top of the ladder. Clay was an older fellow. His close-cropped silver hair showed an age only surpassed by his hat, fit so snugly it was just as much a part of his person as the nose on his face. He had a wind-worn face that had seen more sun than dark days, but it was the clear sky blue of his eyes that held a surprising youthful energy that was most striking. "I just wanted say—" and that's when he saw me, "*hello.*"

I waved.

Helen jumped to her feet with a mess of straw fighting to cling to her clothes. "Hello, Clay. This is my colleague, er . . . friend," she said, glancing at me as I got to my feet.

Party's done, Jack. Parents are here.

She continued. "This is Jack—"

I leaned forward to shake Clay's hand. "Jack Smith, sir. Pleased to meet you."

He took my hand as he finished his climb and gave me a true look-over, and then threw a curious stare at Helen.

"Jack's an author. He came to join us on a radio show today, and since he had time to kill before heading home, I dragged him out here to meet Cleopatra," said Helen.

"And Sir Lancelot," I added, but really didn't know why. *Real adults still make you nervous, Jack?*

Clay returned to sizing me up. My instincts quickly ruled out any romantic feelings between them, and I assumed he was some type of close friend, or maybe even had a paternal relationship with her as he spoke. "Yeah, Cleo missed you something fierce. You know how Her Majesty gets when she's not getting her way." He removed his worn-out beige cowboy hat to dust it off.

That was the way into the conversation for me. "Nice hat. Classic Cattleman. I learned early on in life that you can tell a lot about a person by the hat they wear."

"Oh, really?" he said, leveling a critical gaze my way. "What's my hat say about me?"

"That color: a man who's serious about life, and confident. You don't feel the need to draw attention to yourself through any kind of flash. And the style: the Cattleman is both functional and traditional."

Clay's subconscious began kicking in as he nodded his head, though with his expressionless face I couldn't tell just how close to the mark I was.

"The Cattleman's designed to be there for the long-haul, and will get the job done. It's well-worn, yet in good condition for its age. That shows loyalty and care for things worthy of respect. I—"

"Hmm. You're not from around here, are you, son?"

"No, sir, but I do know that every hat has a story."

"Where'd you learn that? You look *pretty . . .*" the emphasis on the word wasn't lost on me, " . . . well-dressed to know about workin' hats. You spend some time on a fancy little dude ranch?"

"'Clay', was it?" I asked with a laugh.

He nodded, "It is."

"Clay, I can't even begin to claim being any kind of cowboy, but I have spent many long days working in the hot sun, and been around enough good ranchers to learn a little somethin' about somethin'."

"Jack spent most of his career in Texas," said Helen.

Some of the tension eased from Clay's body when Helen spoke, and a small smile began to appear. "Some nice ranches and great horses down that way, too," he said.

"Yes, there are," I said.

"Jack was there to play football. He's a bit of a star," added Helen.

"Eh? He did?"

"Yes, sir. I did play some football. As for 'star', I think that depends on who you talk to."

He chuckled, "Some wise words there." He shook my hand again, finally accepting me. "I don't know who you are, but if you're some kind of friend—"

"Colleague," Helen cut in.

A wry smile appeared on his face. "—a friend of Helen's, then you're okay with me. Come by any time."

"Thank you, sir. That's most generous, but I head back to

Pennsylvania—where I live—in the morning."

"Good man," he nodded, the look in his eyes saying there were deeper thoughts going on than were showing on his face. "Right way to go. Have a safe trip."

"Thanks."

"Now you, missy," he said, shuffling over to Helen. "Miss Big Time Author." Clay looked back at me. "She is, y'know? Since she was a little girl, she was always runnin' around with a notebook, writing stories. We knew she'd be famous, and now she is. Best one to come out of Montana in . . . well, I don't even know."

"Oh, Clay," she said, and gave him a little swat, embarrassment coloring her cheeks. "It's not at all like that."

"Don't be so modest. It's true, and you deserve it. Now, give me a hug before I head back to the house."

They shared a warm hug, and it got me thinking of my family. The times that were happy and great with hugs overflowing, to days where I couldn't buy a hug with any amount of cash. *Don't get pushed backward. Life is good, here and now.*

When he was done, Clay made his way back down the ladder. "Do you need anything while I'm here?" he asked Helen.

"We're all good, thanks. Heading out in a few minutes."

Before disappearing completely, he stopped his descent with just his hat and head poking up through the hatch. "Oh, before I forget. One of the reasons I had come up here was to let you know that there's a big deal of rain rolling this way. If you're thinkin' about a night ride, please be extra careful, or maybe think about doin' it another day. Okay?"

"You know me too well. I was thinking about it, but will take a pass tonight. Thanks again. So great to see you. I'll be back out again in a day or two."

"Good girl. And if you have time—I know you're busy—but if you do, come up to the house a minute and say hi to Mother. That'll make her day. She's been asking about you."

"Give her my love, Clay. I'll be sure to stop in."

"That's great," he said, giving me one more look and a wave. "Good to meet you, Helen's friend. I'll be expecting to see your hat next time. I'll let you know what I think of it." He slipped away, leaving a snickering trail behind him.

I looked at Helen.

She shrugged her shoulders. "So, now you've met Clay. Don't let that old worn cowboy act fool you. He's sharper than—well, insert witty country saying here."

"That's pretty clear. Also clear he thinks the world of you, the famous author and country girl. Great to see."

She looked down, scuffed her boot across the ground, and broke out an old-time rural accent, "Aww, shucks, Mr. Smith. You're too kind."

I chuckled. "So did you want to pick up reading where you left off, or should we get out of here and try to beat the rain?"

Helen made her way slowly to the ladder. "I love the rain. Especially in the country, and at night. There were times where I'd crash right here in this very spot to enjoy the storm—"

"That sounds incredible."

"It was, and it's the only reason this space wasn't converted to a utility room like the others. Clay lets me keep it for myself for as long as I'll be coming up here." She looked around at the simple space one more time with a light sigh. "Oh, the good times." Then she slid down the ladder like a sailor in a submarine.

I raced to the top, and looked down at her smug, upturned face. "How'd you do that?"

"Spend enough time somewhere and you learn some things."

"Yeah, well, excuse me while I get down like normal people," I said, shaking my head, taking each rung one at a time. *I need to learn how to do that!*

We meandered slowly through the barn, saying goodbye to Cleopatra, Sir Lancelot, and the rest of the herd as Helen stalled the inevitable departure.

When we finally made it back to the truck, she stowed her coat and boots back in their place behind her seat. We sat in silence for a moment as she stared back at the barn.

A faint flash of lightning sparked across the distant horizon.

"Looks like Clay was right, and we're leaving just in time," I said.

"Just in time," she nodded. "Where to?"

That was a loaded question if ever there was one. Care for some trouble, Jack-O? "How about my hotel?"

I waited as Helen kept looking off into the distance. Another wave of lightning rolled across the sky, much closer than the last, and came with a jolt of thunder. "Okay," she said, "your hotel."

The truck's engine roared to life. She kicked it into gear, and we raced off just as the first large drops of rain began to fall. The storm had arrived and we were making our escape.

If only I could read her mind. Are we on the same page? Most would consider it pretty obvious when a guy like me invites a girl to his hotel. I only hope this won't be awkward.

CHAPTER THIRTY-THREE

Helen

CROSSING THE THRESHOLD of the hotel changed everything. At this time of night, all the activity would be in the restaurant and lounge area, yet I felt like a yoke had been fastened around my neck to bow me down in front of each person we passed. They stared with the eyes of the Spanish Inquisition, and I bathed in the guilt heaped upon me, each of them so acutely aware of the wanton thoughts that I had been wrestling with the whole drive here. *Maybe since the day Jack and I first met.*

Part of me felt alive, invigorated, and loved being the center of attention, and with an opportunity to do something so out of character and completely taboo with a man of Jack Smith's reputation, success, and strength. The rest of me struggled greatly with every step we took across the lobby, making an effort to keep up with Jack's confident and bouncy stride. *Of course he's happy. This is what he does. Was probably his plan from the start, and now I'm going to be like every other one of his floozies.*

"Welcome to the Billings' Bounty Hotel," the impeccably-dressed woman behind the desk said, sporting the hotel's standard burgundy blazer and a fun series of rainbow ribbons woven through her auburn braid. I wanted to compliment her hair, but instead found an impossible familiarity in her eyes. I knew it was unlikely that she knew me, yet I could almost hear her voice in my head, asking, *"What are you doing here, Helen? And who is this man?"*

I looked at Jack, who was smiling away, the epitome of cool. *How can this be so easy for you?*

He turned my way and raised an eyebrow as if he had heard me and was confused by the question.

Politely, the desk clerk tried again, "Good evening. Do you have a reservation?"

"Uh, yes," I said, torn between trying to understand Jack's look and wanting to get this done as fast as possible. "It will be under 'Buchman', for KTAL Radio."

The clerk punched it in, smiled, and checked us in. "Room 404. That's a good one. You'll have no problem finding that." She hit a few more keys and popped a big smile. "I'm happy to tell you that we were able to upgrade your room to a suite, along with a complimentary executive package. Trust me," she said, putting the key cards on the counter, "you two will love it."

I took a key, handed it to Jack, and pushed the other one back across the counter. "Thank you, we'll only need the one."

"Okay, great. If you change your mind, just let us know."

The plan had been to get out of here before Jack opened his mouth and made this even more awkward. I had no such luck as he pulled up close beside me.

"Thank you, Tiffany, you've been incredibly helpful," Jack said.

"My pleasure, sir."

Trying to run interference to get us away from the desk, I

jumped in with, "Yep, everyone here is fantastic. That's why this is our hotel of choice. Thanks again." I turned away, hoping Jack would take the hint and follow. Much to my surprise he did. *Conversation done. We're on our way—*

Jack stopped, looked back, and said, "Oh, and please let me compliment you on that fantastic braid. It's great to see someone bring some pizazz to the party."

Sure enough, Tiffany was beaming from the compliment.

See? You should have mentioned it. "Yep, I love it, too," I said.

"Thanks, Mrs. Buchman," said Tiffany, sending a sick shudder through my body. Not because of the name, but because she seemed to assume we were a married couple. "Have a great night."

"Oh, you can bet we will," said Jack with a smirk.

I shook my head and rolled my eyes at him as we headed for the elevators.

"Look at that, dear. She thinks we're married," he said.

"You are something else."

Encouraged, he twisted it into some form of flattery, "Yes, my wife. Yes, I am."

As we crossed the tiles, the room seemed to grow in front of my eyes. It appeared to stretch on forever, and the elevators began to feel like they were an insurmountable distance away. My stomach rumbled and made me jump. "Food!" I blurted out.

"You okay?" asked Jack.

It took all my restraint not to bolt for the lounge. Instead, I bounced like a child getting ready for a surprise party. "I'm great. Really. We just haven't eaten. How could I have forgotten dinner? How rude of me. How—" *Helen, you're rambling.* I took a breath to compose myself as the sour look returned to his face that I had seen for a moment earlier when I decided to take us to the ranch.

"Oh yeah, wow," he said, and took a look at his watch. "We really are late. Let me toss my bag in the room and we—"

"Oh no, it's just one little bag, let's just—" I stammered.

Jack began to shake his head with a counterargument.

"It's fine," I said. "I can keep it on my side of the table, it's no bother. I'm used to having a bag with me anyway." I patted my purse. "If we—"

He smiled and shrugged. "How can I say no? It's been years since I've seen someone get this excited about dinner. Let's go find out where—"

"Follow me," I said, and now I was the one dragging him (and his bag) across the lobby and down the hall to the restaurant.

CHAPTER THIRTY-FOUR

Helen

THE RESTAURANT WAS timeless. It had been quite a while—maybe even too long—since I'd been here, yet walking through the rustic wooden doorway brought me a feeling of comfort and strength. *You can do this, Helen.*

We followed our host across a floor of the natural stone reminiscent of so much of Montana, and were treated to a table barely ten feet away from a large open hearth. The fire crackled and embraced us with that real wood campfire scent that I loved so much.

"Oh, yeah, I could get really comfortable here," said Jack, settling into his chair. "Now I see why you were so anxious to get a table."

"Please enjoy your evening. Your server will be with you in a moment," said the host as she disappeared into her work.

We sat quietly, Jack taking in the warm ambiance of the restaurant, while I took in Jack to help me make a decision on where tonight would go after we left the comfort and security of this place.

"Good evening, my name's Bruce, I'll be your server this evening. What can I get you to drink?"

"Uh . . . I . . . um, orange juice for me, please," I said. With everything else, even that decision felt a little overwhelming.

Jack laughed, "Still playing safe, Helen? Okay, Bruce, make that two OJ's, please."

"Excellent. Here are your menus. I'll be right back with your drinks and to take your orders."

Bruce was five feet away when the smile on Jack's face changed. He looked at me with his brow wrinkled into a look of concern. "After all this time, you're still scared of me? Still don't know what I'm about?"

"It's not you, it's me." *Oh, Helen, really? Yeah, stress sends me to autopilot. And autopilot always lands me on an airstrip of clichés and alliteration.*

He slapped his knee and sat back, his face beaming. "I'm not sure how to take that, but I've used that line myself often enough, and had it used on me enough times to know it means that it's time for me to shut my hole, or at least change the topic. So . . ." He cast his gaze about the room while I waited anxiously to see what was next.

If there ever was a night that I could use a real drink . . .

"I love these old wooden crossbeams. The whole place, with this fireplace," he stopped to inhale deeply, "the stone floors, and even these small wood-framed windows. It feels like we're in a lodge somewhere up in the mountains. The Alps, maybe, or somewhere like that—not that I've ever been to the Alps."

"How about the Rockies? You are in Montana."

"Nope never been. Yep, oops, not sure how I missed that. I was think—"

"Here are your drinks," interrupted Bruce, appearing out of

nowhere. "An orange juice for you, ma'am," he said, placing a large frosty glass in front of me, "and one for you, sir." "Are you two ready to order or would you like more time?"

"Well, I'm ready but I'm not sure about the lady," said Jack. "I'm just going to leave it as the chef's choice, unless you have another recommendation. Helen, Do you need more time?"

I folded my hands in front of me, sat up straight, and said, "That works for me. Two, please."

Bruce took both menus from the table. "Excellent. Our chef is fantastic and loves to create special dishes for our guests. May I ask if there is a special occasion being celebrated tonight?"

"Oh," said Jack, sitting forward, his eyes squinting as he focused on me. "Hmm, what do you think, Helen? Something special tonight?"

I met his stare and glared. *The nerve. He wants to see me be the one to back down? No chance.* I pulled on a big smile, raised my drink (with Jack smirking and following suit), and said to Bruce, "Yes, we're celebrating first times." Jack's eyebrows raised, and a look I didn't recognize sprang upon his face, one that said his swagger had been shook. *Was he having doubts?* I touched my glass to his, said "Cheers," and took a big drink while his glass hung a moment longer. "Oh, and, Bruce, could you grab us another drink? I'll take a rum and Coke."

"Excellent, will do," said Bruce.

"Jack?" I asked, "How about you?"

He put his glass down on the table, still looking at me. "Uh, no, the juice is good for me, thanks."

I grinned and sat back in my chair.

"Terrific. I'll be off to put in your orders," and again Bruce was gone. This time leaving me and Jack on equal footing.

Dinner was fabulous. We wound up with a chicken-and-rib combo that was as good as it was messy. The conversation flowed well, most of the time, until we started to get too personal. I was surprised to see how well Jack was behaving. No sexual innuendos. No checking out waitresses or other guests. His attention was focused on me the entire night and it felt great—and thus my continued internal conflict. Food done, I was still nursing my first rum and Coke. The writing was on the wall: it was time to break the ice and figure out where the rest of the night would lead.

It looks like you're going to have to be the one to take charge, Helen. You can do this. You are a strong, capable, and accomplished woman.

I decided playing it cool would be the way to handle him tonight. "Jack, how are you feeling?"

"Good," he patted his stomach, "and full. You?"

"I'm really glad you asked. Dinner was amazing but I feel like we've found ourselves in a troubling situation."

"Oh?" He sat up and looked me over. "You okay?"

Here we go! "Jack, I have never been so inspired, so motivated, as I have since we talked that first night in Austin. In just these past few days, I have written more than 20,000 words—all of which lead me right back to thinking about you."

He nodded, and with a sheepish grin said, "Yeah, me too. And 18K."

"See, but here's the thing. I have someone." *Not just "someone"!* I jumped to my feet. "No, that's not right, or fair, either. I have a *husband.* I'm happily married to an absolutely amazing and incredible guy who loves me with all his heart!"

Jack's jaw hung slightly open, maybe its weight was the cause of his head slowly bobbing up and down.

"And I love him . . . "

"Oh. Okay, well, I—"

"So that means I can't do . . . " My shoulders shrugged as my eyes searched desperately for inspiration, for the appropriate words. " . . . I just can't do *anything*. I'm sorry if I led you to think otherwise, okay?"

A wry little grin slowly overtook Jack's face and sent the pit of my stomach fluttering. "Uh, would you mind sitting back down, or is that the 'anything' you were referring to?"

I felt my face flush as I slunk back into my chair. "Sorry," I kind of mumble-whispered.

"Don't be. I understand."

"I hope so, because this has been—"

Jack's tone was flat when he cut me off. "I have a wife, too. She's amazing and I'm very much in love with her."

"You what? But your stories? The women . . . "

CHAPTER THIRTY-FIVE

Jack

I COULD ONLY imagine what the look on her face had meant, and everything I came up with was terrible. She could call me a fake, a phony, a sell-out, all those things I spent my life trying to avoid being called, and yet being those things was what had actually helped me achieve my level of success. They had been a big part of my public superstar "Titan" persona, but now it was true. I was a caricature of Jack Smith.

"Wait, what was all that dramatic stuff back in Austin, in the dining room, about providing a fantasy?" Her face wrinkled up in disgust and her eyes were lit with a smoldering fire that was burning a hole in me. "The way you and Sandra were all over each other?"

I felt the air in my lungs leave me. I sat there trying to figure out a way to explain to Helen all of the things that had troubled me since day one, when Angelina and I had decided on this career move. "Please understand, this is not me being flippant about the points you make, because they're valid, but that speech I gave that evening was true. Everything I do and am in the public eye is to provide a fantasy, including that show with Sandra. If you remember, I didn't touch her, I—"

She gasped, shock striking her face, "You—"

I shook my head vigorously. I knew I had made a mistake, and had to stop the train there. "I'm not saying that makes any of it okay, but it's the fine nuances that allow me to sleep at night. A very specific set of rules that I follow, like 'no touching me below the waist', 'always redirect them at the earliest opportunity', and 'smile', which, through it all, is usually the hardest part."

"Hard? Yeah, right, having women swooning after you is hard?"

I felt the hairs on the back of my neck prick up. Too many of these moments had come during my career, and I'd had to keep silent. Usually because the person making the point didn't matter, but this was different. "Everyone thinks the spotlight is great. Life is easy and fun. Again, that's the fantasy. I can't begin to tell you the effort it takes me to get ready for those moments. The self-talk fighting with self-doubt, and worst of all, the voice that increasingly often prays for me to be found out."

Helen's head tipped slightly to the side, as though a different perspective might help her to better deal with me.

"It's true, I swear it," I continued. "Don't get me wrong. There's a part of me that loves it. I need the pressure, the rush, the adrenaline pumping through my veins, fueled by fear. I love it and it fuels that ego that helps me survive. But what started off as a great idea has twisted into something entirely different."

"Oh yeah?" She grabbed her napkin and wiped her already spotless mouth again, as she leaned into the table to ask, "Then why do it?"

My thoughts had now been delivered through her voice. I felt my head shaking slowly side-to-side, still unable to find an answer. Then it hit me. I pushed back my chair, which screeched across the floor at the sudden jolt. I stood, threw my foot onto the chair, and tried to roll up my pant leg. I could feel Helen's eyes fixed on me and knew she had to be thinking about leaving. Jeans weren't meant to be rolled high enough to reveal my scars, so I lost that fight, but—"This," I said, and my index finger stabbed at my knee, thrusting deep into the ACL that had already been surgically repaired and had been the catalyst for other lower extremity issues, "this is why I do it. Why I take the injections. Take the shots, go under the knife. To make this work. To make the rest of me work."

I could feel those terribly dark emotions creeping up, and knew that tonight wasn't a night where I had the strength to fully suppress them.

"Your whole family counts on you to get on that field. Your team, your parents, agents, sponsors, and even all those creditors you were too young to understand or resist when you came into the League. Everyone. They need you to do your part but they don't realize just how enormous that part has become and what a constant weight it is on your shoulders."

I gently sat back down in my chair, amazed that Helen was still here, even though she was staring at me with a look. *And what* was *that look? Disgust? Shame? Embarrassment? All fully justified.* "And then how does it end? You get used to it all and somehow you begin to know this as your life. The only life you know." I couldn't look at her anymore. My head drooped, the table all I could see. "And when you stop producing, it all goes away. They go away. They lose what they know as life and you wind up getting tossed aside, just some former star looking fat in a bathing suit stuck on the cover of some gossip rag or becoming a joke meme on-line as you wind up in the gutter, jail, a cycle of rehab clinics, or dead. Doing this is all I have and all I can do. I made the choice, and I live with it."

I took a deep breath and watched as Helen processed everything, gave her time to digest it all and hoped that somehow we could be okay. *Where're your jokes now, Jack?*

The ball was now in her court.

CHAPTER THIRTY-SIX

Helen

I FELT THE urge to reach out to Jack. To help him with his burden. To thank him for sharing what I know had to be incredibly tough. But I knew that one touch, no matter its intent, would lead us on a path neither of us could tread.

Staring at that beautiful man who had trusted me so deeply gave me butterflies. Yet, just as the feeling started, the fluttering in my stomach turned to acid, my heart a weight sinking down into that terrible pool. I hated myself for it, but I had to be strong. No possible fling, or whatever this could be, was worth risking what I had—Oh! *have*—with William. "Okay, then," I said, "that makes things easier. We're in agreement that nothing's going to happen here—or ever."

A smile began to appear on his face as he chuckled.

It was the wrong time for that, and I could only assume he was laughing at me, or masking the discomfort we both felt.

"Guess so. We don't want to be a clichéd romance like in one of your stories," he said, baiting me in the playful way I had come to enjoy.

"Or like the trite tropes you pander to trollops."

"Eww, she fires back with the Dr. Seuss-for-adults alliteration. Well played."

I tipped my imaginary fedora his way. "Yep, never been much of a fan of the cheater romances, or the love triangles."

"Or love rectangles, as the case may be."

"I can see the book title now," I said, and created a frame with the thumb and index fingers of both hands for the marquee, "Love Squared."

He snapped his head back and rubbed his neck to act out whiplash.

Despite myself, a silly schoolgirl-style laugh escaped that brought me right back to my earliest crush on Bobby Addelbaum in 8th-grade.

"Whoa . . . that's a good one," he said with an appreciative sigh. "Or . . . " and as he leaned forward conspiratorially and began drawing a misshapen rectangle, I found my body mirroring his, " . . . *Parallel Amour.*"

"Holy shi—!" My hand clapped over my mouth as the letter "t" started to escape my lips, "That's brilliant—but don't let your ego know that I said that."

He let out a full-on belly-busting unabashed howl that sucked me into his ridiculousness until I was sure the whole place was looking at us—but I didn't care. *Let 'em stare!*

Our laughter eventually lost some of its momentum. As it continued to flicker, it was clear we were just stalling to figure out the right thing to say or do.

I opened this can o' worms, guess it's on me to take the next step.

Swallowing hard, I gathered any willpower I could summon to at least stop my hands from shaking, my knees from knocking, and my teeth from rocking out of my skull. Jack sat forward. He could sense a moment was coming and the look on his face was one I couldn't place.

I stood, took my purse from the table, and slung it over my shoulder before grabbing my jacket. "I would think this must then be goodbye." I nodded to the waiter who quickly hustled over to bring the check. I fought impossibly to avoid Jack's hazel-colored stare, "Thank you for everything. All the best to you."

This was the first time I had seen Jack Smith speechless, and there was something unsettling, even heartbreaking, about that defeat. I don't know if it's because most girls want a guy to leap to his feet, grab her up, and refuse to let her go, or that I knew he wouldn't because he respected me too much and it left him powerless.

I took the check, gave it a blind glance, and smiled at Jack. "I've got this." Covering the bill just seemed right, even if it was the least I could do.

He sprang to his feet. "Oh, no!" and tried to snatch it from my hands. I held firm, and a tug of war ensued whose awkwardness was only surpassed by the side-to-side fidgeting of Bruce, who was trying to figure out if he should bolt.

Eventually, I released my grasp. Apparently, paying the bill wasn't the least I could do.

Jack sat down triumphantly. "Thank you."

I pressed my lips together to stop myself from saying anything. It had to end here. I nodded, spun quickly on my heel, and hustled across the room and out the door as fast as my feet would take me without causing too much more of a ruckus. The words, *You did the right thing,* were a murmuring, repeated chant as I escaped into the night.

I would need to walk this one off for a while before I could go home and face William. Hopefully, he would be sound asleep, none the wiser about the near catastrophe I almost caused, and we could start fresh in the morning.

MY HEAD FELT too frazzled to drive so I left my truck for the night to do the winding walk to peace and back home. Now, standing in the dining room of our apartment with a smile on my face, I could enjoy reading a note left for me on the table: *Welcome home, Mrs. Buchman. Cocoa and cookies are on the counter.*

The warm-and-fuzzies ran through me and came out as a blissful sigh. Sure enough, a plateful of my favorite cookies was laid out in the shape of a heart, beside a cup of Godiva cocoa waiting to be reheated. Beside the food stood a stack of the latest celebrity gossip rags that were my guilty pleasure.

Helen, you are one lucky girl. Dodged disaster, and came home to a dream.

CHAPTER THIRTY-SEVEN

Jack

UNDER THE COVERS, razor-sharp fingernails nipping at my calves roused my attention.

Dreaming or awake, I couldn't be sure, but it felt good as they continued to work their way up, splaying wide with soft and delicate hands, cool against the warmth of my body.

She changed her mind. Even if this was a dream—it was a good one. I smiled. My dick throbbed. A sweet and floral scent drifted into the scene.

Deliciously gentle lips began sprinkling kisses on my legs.

This is wrong . . . yet right.

She began to nip gently as she made her way to my inner thighs.

"Oh yes," I said, the sound barely a whisper as it became clear this was much more than a dream.

I shivered deeply as her tongue took over. Making its way up, closing the distance.

Nope. I can't. It's still wrong. "Sorry, no," I said, and my hands went down to her head to push her away. "I can't let you."

At the same time, the silky feeling of her hair clicked as being all too familiar.

"But, baby, I've missed you so much," said Angelina, and I nearly jumped out of my skin.

I flipped the covers back to reveal her grinning face.

"Are you sure I can't offer you a little bit of good morning fun? Even if it's just for me?" she said, with the sexy look that had won me over back in the day and continued to wind me up now.

"Well, I—Hey, wait! How did you even get in here?"

She giggled, "Really, you can ask that of me? After all these years? Not only am I the wife of Jack Smith, but I'm one hell of an agent, too. Who can say no to this face?" She delivered her trademark smile that had been the feature face of her website, business cards, and billboards for quite a while even before we got together. "Which is why I know you aren't saying no now," she said, taking my fully-erect shaft in hand and beginning to stroke.

She was right. There was no way I was even considering saying no, not after the build-up of this past week. *Giddy up!*

Once fully spent and overly-indulged in Angelina's affection and room service, I laid back in bed with a smile. "Baby, I've missed you so damn much. Y'know?"

She rolled over to cuddle in close, and her hands aimlessly wandered across my body. "Ditto. Though I know it couldn't have been all bad, having all those screaming, desperately panting, panty-soaked women fawning all over you."

I chuckled, "Yes, there are worse jobs, and I'm not planning to go back to them anytime soon."

Her fingers began walking their way down the middle of my chest. "No chance of that, not with me by your side." She gave a little nip at my nipple that sent a ripple of pleasure through my body. "Did you indulge at all this time?" Her fingers continued their path to find me ready and waiting. "Find some extra-special cutie to inspire your next story?"

I jumped to sit upright. *Does she know about Helen?* "What do you mean?"

She giggled, "Always so jumpy. You know I trust you. Lay back down with me, I liked where we were heading."

I slid back down, my anxiety still ticking away.

"But, the last couple times you did one of these trips, I did tell you that if you wanted to, it'd be okay with me as long as you followed some ground rules."

"Yeah, but I'm not interested."

"Not even the slightest bit interested?" she said, her hand now at home and stroking my cock again. "You're on the road so much, with the insatiable appetite of the Titan. Working so," she gave me a firm squeeze, "so hard all the time."

Oh God, this amazing woman. "Depends how you define 'interested'. I did meet one woman who was pretty interesting, another writer, but while that bully in your hand may have had a few passing thoughts to share, I wasn't interested enough to take that kind of step or risk." Brushing Angelina's hair aside, I placed a gentle kiss on her forehead. "I love what we have so much more."

She began stroking me, from balls to tip, a slow rhythm that never failed.

"Besides, she already has someone, and I was sure to let her know I was happily married, as well. She understands me, and our business, so we're all good." With that off my chest, I could finally relax and let things take their course.

Angelina began to slowly pick up the pace while adding a

small twist that sent sparks down my legs and had them involuntarily flexing in response.

The building excitement and need for release had my mouth feeling desperately dry, but another thought popped into my head which had to be shared first. "Oh! Speaking of working hard, you won't believe how many words I wrote in Texas and since the convention. It's been—"

Words were forgotten. They abandoned my brain as her mouth engulfed me. *Talk about a way to handle the Titan!* Grinning, I laid back and enjoyed the preparations for Round Two.

CHAPTER THIRTY-EIGHT

Helen

THE SUNCATCHER DANGLING in the window cast a beautiful rainbow mosaic across the room. Smiling, I rolled over to begin the debate of whether to wake William, or to cuddle up and head back to sleep.

"Well, that fun was short-lived," I said to the pillow that was my abandoned partner. Scooping it up, I pulled it in close to my breasts. William's wonderful manly smell still lingered and I inhaled deeply. *I sure have missed that man of mine.* Easy decision to make, I closed my eyes to see if I could catch up on any of the interesting dreams that had played through my mind last night.

"Morning, gorgeous," William said quietly. It was his way of checking to see if I was sleeping without the risk of waking me up.

I decided I would play possum, and wait to see his next move.

Sadly, there was just silence. I waited, trying hard to do that awkward trick of controlling my breathing to look like I was sleeping, without looking like someone trying to pretend to be sleeping. *Oh, Helen.*

Movement, a rustle of some sort at the end of the bed, and then hands on my right foot that sent a small wave of heat up my leg. William's whiskers brushed the inside of my foot just before his lips landed on my instep.

Yes, baby.

"I missed you," he whispered, and delivered another delicate kiss on the top of my foot and then a second one above my ankle.

That's it, moving in the right direction.

Another quiet whisper, barely audible, which left me unsure as to whether I was actually hearing it or simply feeling it carried by his warm breath on my calf.

Despite my attempts to play it cool, a small moan rippled up from my chest.

"Good morning, sweetheart," his tone louder now and with an excited quiver. "Roll over." Without waiting for a response, he turned me onto my stomach. "Tell me you missed me," he said, and his mouth came down on the back of my knee, his hot breath, his silky tongue.

I was already wet and a deep quiver answered with a voice he couldn't yet hear. "Desperately," I said with a groan.

He knew he had one of my sweet spots, and continued to deliver the attention that had my arms now stretching back across the bed, feeling the sensation of the cool cotton sheets against my skin. With one hand on each thigh, grabbing and groping, he began nibbling and nipping the back of my thighs before reaching my butt.

I moaned again, deeper. The need in me reaching out for the need in him.

His right hand now traveled up and under me, and his fingers felt so hot against my swollen wet lips.

"William, ple—" Before I could finish begging, he delivered a finger inside me and his teeth bit deep into my ass cheek.

I bucked hard against his face, his finger quickly engulfed by me. "Yesss," I said. "God, yes."

Just when I thought we were on the right track, he removed his finger to leave me feeling desperately empty, until I heard the sound of his mouth sucking on his fingers. Butterflies raced in my stomach. I held my breath in anticipation.

One finger, no, *Oh God!, two* fingers dove in all the way to his knuckles, and had me rocking at a nice pace with each motion.

"Yeah, you missed me. I feel it," he took a painfully nice deep bite out of the other cheek.

I missed him. I was his. Each moment slipped by, fantastically slowly and fully-savored.

Gently, he removed his fingers and teeth from my body. "Do you know that I missed you too? I thought about you constantly." He pushed my legs open a little wider and slid in between my legs, his hands on my butt before delivering a cool breath on my pussy.

I pushed back toward his face and he dove in, his fingers lapping at my lips. I raised up higher to bring my clit toward his loving mouth. His tongue greeted it with a gentle flick. I buried my face in the pillow to stifle the moans and screams I knew were on their way as I prepared to release the build up from the past week. *Ride me, baby!*

I FELT GREAT. This was home. This was the life that was meant for me. This was also the first time I had spent more than a few hours lately without Jack Smith entering my brain, but even this brief thought of him disappeared quickly as I stood up from the bath to be greeted by William, carrying a freshly-warmed full-body bath towel. Smiling, I stepped into his arms and reveled in the pampering of him drying me off.

"Feel good?" he asked.

"Incredible."

"Good. I know how tough those road trips can be and I love helping you recharge." He took my hand and led me out to the living room, where a covered platter of food and a fresh pitcher of orange juice waited on the coffee table.

I sat down on the couch and had a chuckle, thinking back to that night where it was my drink of choice when first meeting with Jack.

Rightfully so, William gave me a look of curiosity. "What's up?"

"Oh, just that orange juice and Jack Smith," I said, acutely aware of the smile on my face. *Of course you're smiling, you're with the man you love and being spoiled like a princess.*

"How's that again?"

"Remember me telling you about him and the big show he made in the hotel dining room at the convention, with everyone being so catty? Well, we wound up ducking away to one of the other tables away from the group and I decided then that orange juice would be my drink of choice for—"

William's hand was now on my thigh slowly sliding its way up under the towel. "So he wouldn't get you drunk and take advantage of all this delicious goodness?"

I laughed, maybe more loudly than was appropriate, at how accurate he was. "Kind of, yeah. He has a reputation of sorts."

He guffawed, mocking me with his turn to be louder than appropriate, "Believe me, don't I know it. Superstar jocks and their conquests. A steady diet of hot and easy women."

"But not me!"

"No?" His hand resumed its climb up my thigh. "Not at all? You had to at least be a little bit tempted, right?"

I stared at him, trying to figure out where this was coming from. *Was he crazy? He couldn't be serious. Did he know about last night?*

He took his hand back and gave me a big hug. "I'm just kidding. I know my sweet and innocent Helen was unlikely to be interested in a guy like that."

"A guy like what?"

"Well, you know . . . the football player type."

I wasn't sure what he was trying to say—and whether it was about me or Jack—but somehow the tone just rubbed me wrong. "He's actually very handsome and physically fit. He's not just the stereotype or whatever you may have heard about him. There's much more to Jack than—"

He cut me off with a passionate kiss. "Baby, I'm just teasing. Actually, from what I hear, he really is a great guy. I was just playing with you a little bit, knowing full well you'd feel compelled to defend him, as you always do for the underdogs. Or, in this case, those unable to defend themselves." He chuckled again, "You should've heard the way Vikki Lassiter was carrying on about him when I got back to the station yesterday and asked how things had gone on her show. I'm sure he got some of that last night."

I smiled and shook my head. "Nope. I defended the underdog there, as well, and kept him safe from her claws by taking him out to see the city and getting him checked in at the hotel."

"Oh," he said, with a dirty little smirk, "and that's when he made his move?"

I gave an exhausted sigh. "No. In fact, you'll be happy to know that from minute one I told him I wasn't going to do anything with him and reinforced that point with him last night, letting him know I was married to an amazing man." I could tell by the look on William's face that his mind was beginning to wander elsewhere. "When we were at the station, I was looking for you so you two could be introduced, but they said you'd already left."

His attention came back my way. He thought about it for a moment, and said, "Hmm, maybe she wound up going to visit him at the hotel after you left?" His dirty grin returned once again. "Yeah . . . I bet that was it."

Jack. Could he? Did he? Even after our talk? I sat up and shrugged, "You know what? I've had about enough of Jack over the past few days. I just want to spend the day with my man. Let's eat!"

As my hand reached down to lift the lid from the tray, William's hand came over mine and held it in place. His other hand gently brought my chin around his way. Staring deeply into my eyes, he said softly, "I love you. Thank you, we'll leave work behind. I have a wonderfully romantic day planned for us to catch up." He gave me a kiss and removed my hand from the lid. "Allow me to serve you."

I sat back and prepared to enjoy being spoiled.

CHAPTER THIRTY-NINE

Jack

"COME ON, JACK. Three more," Angelina ordered.

I stood up again, the weight across my shoulders making my legs shake.

"You got it. Two more."

Slowly, I dropped down for another rep.

"Push it. Don't you quit!" she said, willing me to rise again.

I hit the top, paused one beat, and went back down for the last rep.

"That's it. There's only one Titan."

I felt the burn in my quads. I heard my legs begging to quit. Threatening me with days of pain and agony. *Bring it!*

Her arms slid in place at my sides ready for a spot and she whispered, "Show me why you're the baddest motherfucker in this place."

With a desperate grunt, I drove hard, shaking the whole way up, my head ready to explode, until I hit the top and let out a big exhale.

Angelina kept me steady as I racked the weights, my legs wobbling. Grabbing my face, she gave me a deep kiss before drooling on me with, "You are so fucking hot. No man in here compares to you. That's why I belong to you." Again her tongue returned to my mouth.

There had been a long period of time where training and sucking face were awkward workout partners, but it had been a good problem to solve. With the work schedules we maintained, including all the travel, we had to find opportunities together where we could. Few couples can spend time like we do and with the same intensity, but when we were around each other, it was always heavy duty. It's what made us click on day one.

"Finish up with a few more laps in the pool?" she asked.

I chuckled, "If I can handle the walk there, sure."

She giggled and as I watched her wiggle away, I miraculously found the motivation.

"THAT WAS GREAT," I said, using the napkin to give my face a quick swipe.

Angelina nodded with a smile, "They do make such great food here. I think I'm already beginning to like Montana."

"Well, don't fall in love too hard. We're out of here in a few hours and finally back to good ol' PA"

"Oh yeah." She folded her napkin and placed it beside her plate. "Your flight leaves at five, doesn't it?"

"Uh, yeah, assuming you booked it as planned and you're not leaving me behind?"

She giggled, "No. You're all booked and good to go. Unfortunately, I didn't know how everything would time out and wound up with another meeting with a potential client tonight. So I won't be able to leave until tomorrow morning."

Bah. Just our luck. "That sucks."

We held hands and shared a baleful stare.

"I know," she said, "but after this, I think we should both be home for about a week."

"Hey! I could check into moving my flight."

"Kind of like you did in Texas?" she said with a grin.

"Uh, kind of." A strange twinge of guilt sparked in me. "But this will be for us."

I could see her weighing the options before shaking her head. "I love it. That's very sweet, but doesn't make much sense, especially when we'll be getting a week together anyway. Let's get you home, settled in, and maybe you could have a little something special waiting for me when I get there."

Grinning, I said, "Never little, baby. Never that when it comes to you."

"Don't I know it," she said, leaning in to give me a big kiss, "and that's one more reason this plan seems like a good one." She giggled before continuing, "It'll give my body another day to recover from this morning."

My ego puffed up its chest. I smiled. She had won us over. The anticipation of tomorrow really would make it all that more sweet, and I knew I could think of a few fun surprises and treats to throw her way. "Okay, then. Deal."

"Great! Now let's get out of here and make the most of our last few hours. I saw a park nearby with bike rentals. Looks like it would be a great chance to see more of Montana's beauty. You game?"

"Always, baby."

CHAPTER FORTY

Helen

*T*HE CITY REACHED *out from the rocky world as a bastion of strength and security. In it, thousands loved, died, sang, and cried. All on their own little journeys alone, parallel to strangers that life may never let them meet.* Smiling, I closed my notebook, and clicked my pen closed. "This view…" I said, staring in awe from the boulders to the city below in the distance.

"I know," said William, slinging his arm over my shoulder and planting a kiss on my cheek.

Snuggling into him, I melted into the moment. *Every love story could be written with the moments spent with him.*

A young boy's voice screamed through our peace, "I'm going to be first!" Sure enough, from the path we had just traveled, three kids came scratching and scrambling to where we stood. A woman who looked more worn out from life than from the climb trailed behind.

William sighed and shook his head.

Swatting him in the chest, I said, "See, if we had rented those horses for the other trail, you wouldn't be up here grumbling about the kids and 'those damn tourists'.

A sudden exhale of derision made his shoulders shrug. "Yeah, you know I won't get anywhere near those fleabags." Bumping me with his hip and adding in a chuckle did nothing to mask his words being rooted in truth. "That's why I let that be your own private time. You can go do that stuff and not have it ruined by me."

"First of all, Cleopatra is not a fleabag. She—"

He shook his head and laughed. "That name kills me every time. Somewhere in the world, Egyptian royalty is rolling in her grave, that a horse has her name."

I wound up to give him a swat and he countered with a kiss. *You each have your own thing, that's what makes it work. He's just teasing you and you always fall for it.* I resisted briefly before getting a grip.

"Oh, sweetheart," he said, "you know I'm just playing with you. It's a nice name and I'm sure she's beautiful. You deserve nothing but the best."

I cuddled into him and went back to enjoying the view.

"Stop!" the woman's voice screeched, as the boy slammed into our legs and began pushing his way between us with a girl in close pursuit, while the third child made his way more slowly toward us.

"You two better stop. Don't get so close to the edge, Jack and Helen. It's dangerous."

Who? What? I gasped and my eyes flashed to William, whose face was going red with anger at the interruption.

"We know, Mom," yelled the boy, as the two of them hit their air brakes just in front of us.

"You know," she grabbed the boy and girl by the ear, "but you still do it."

The third child seized the opportunity for trouble and chimed in with, "Mom, does this mean Pat and Ellen are going to be in trouble and only I get ice cream after? You said—"

Her head snapped his way. "You just worry about yourself!"

Ohh, Pat and Ellen. I need to get out of the sun.

William took my hand. "You okay?"

I smiled, "With you I am."

"Great, let's get away from here."

I nodded and followed his lead back down the path.

"Are you enjoying Helen Day?" he said, with that little head sway that showed he was proud of himself.

"Yes, though you may need to work on that name," I said with a giggle, "I'm glad you do better with that kind of stuff at the station."

He chuckled, "Hey, they pay me well for that. Anyway, I think it's the perfect name. Clear, to the point, and there's no mistaking who deserves all the attention."

"Thank you." I stopped our walk to pull him in for another kiss. "I don't know what I did to deserve you, or any of this, but I'm so very grateful." I gave him another peck. "Let's face it, after all that time apart, it would have been good enough just to wake up the way I did. Add to that the breakfast, the shopping, the spa, this hike, and whatever else you have in—"

"Uh-oh."

"Huh?"

"I feel bad and hate to say this, but the hike was the last thing on my list for today besides a nice drive home, and maybe a quick ice cream. Then I have to head back into the office."

"What? Why?" I tried hard to hide the disappointment in my

voice. Everything had been so amazing and while my schedule had some flexibility, I know William probably had to jump through hoops to get the time off today that he got.

"We're trying to land a new client, a big one, and are doing some game-planning tonight." Once again, he took my hand and began leading the way down the path. "I know it sucks, but you know my schedule—"

"I know, I know. I'm sorry."

"Don't be sorry, I'm sorry. I'll make it up to you."

He stopped, I bumped into him, and he spun around with a devilish grin on his face. "Don't worry, though, I did take care of dinner and have a movie and a book waiting, your choice, to keep you company."

"You really are the best." My hands reached up behind his head and pulled him down to my waiting mouth. My tongue pierced his lips to find home. We kissed deeply and I felt a twinge of deep and passionate excitement . . . until I heard kids racing down the hill behind us. *Oh, come on.*

Breaking our kiss, he gave an exaggerated catch of his breath. "You always did make it hard. This is not easy."

"This situation may not be, but when it comes to you," I said, grabbing his hand and placing it on my inner thigh and moving it up to where I ached for him so desperately, "*I* am."

"Helen," he said, and jumped back. His cheeks flushed but his hand lingered.

Yep, you still got it, Helen.

The kids were almost on top of us when he took my hand again. "Now I remember why I married you," he said with a chuckle. "Let's get out of here before you get us arrested or make me change my mind about tonight."

"Pat!" I looked back over my shoulder at the mother calling after the boy racing toward us again. "Wait for us at the bottom."

Then the boy, who'd barely slowed his pace, yelled back to his mother, with a resolute look much older than his age: "I'll wait for Ellen, but not him. Only Ellen."

Oh man, is that what I have to look forward to? I giggled, and began to drag William skipping along with me.

CHAPTER FORTY-ONE

Jack

WELCOME TO THE JUNGLE screeched as the front door swung open, just missing me for a bell-ringer. I stumbled back, and yanked my earbuds out as Angelina waltzed through the door. The big smile on her face dropped in surprise.

"What the hell?" I yelled.

" . . . Surprise!" she yelled back.

Wrapping her up, I scooped her off her feet and we both laughed.

"You're a nut," I said, putting her back on the ground, "but I love it. I didn't expect you home until later."

"I wanted to join you for your workout. Some yoga at 7 a.m., right?"

I chuckled. *One of the benefits of keeping to a schedule is your wife being able to surprise you.*

"Great! Give me a minute to grab my gear," she said, "and I'm coming with you."

"Awesome. I'll bring in your bags."

She stopped in her tracks, her face frozen, and she stared at me like she was trying to figure out the words.

"Oh no, you didn't leave your bags at the airport again, did you?" I asked.

She chuckled a little before dropping into a proper laugh, "No, not this time. Don't worry about my stuff. Grab me a drink while I get ready?"

"Got you covered." I went to the kitchen, threw together a quick post-workout drink, and by the time I got back to the door, Angelina was packed and ready.

When we got to the street, I was boxed in by her car sitting double-parked.

I shook my head in disbelief. "Looking to get another ticket?"

"Hey, they threw that ticket out, remember? I've never had a ticket stick to me."

"You are the teflon agent, no question there," I said with a chuckle. "That mean we're taking your car?"

"You wish. You're not sweating up my baby."

With a sharp crack, my hand swatted her ass to cause a skip in her step. "Now you've got a problem with my sweat?"

She giggled, "Save the foreplay, it's not going to work. No yucky man-stink today."

This girl and her car. "Okay, my car it is."

"How about I race you there?" she said, bolting for her door.

"Cheater. I can't even get out until—"

"I hear a lot of talk and excuses," she said, then slammed her door and began to drive as I slipped in behind the wheel of my matte black Escalade.

I took every shortcut I could think of. Our rules on these things, because they happened more than one might imagine, were very clear: No breaking the law. Nothing that puts anyone else at risk.

"Lucky day!" A spot right in front of the studio, and her nowhere in sight. "Oh, it is going to be a good day."

Standing on the stoop to gloat became less exciting as every minute ticked by. Two minutes became five, which became ten. When she finally arrived, I jogged to her door and opened it. "You okay? I was starting to get worried?"

Whoa. There was something about the look on her face, or the vibe she had, that felt really wrong.

Angelina waited a moment or two in silence before finally getting out.

I gave her a big hug. "You okay?"

She looked at me with eyes so crystal clear. "Yeah, I think so. Or will be."

"We don't have to do this workout. What can I do?"

Her tiny arms were like a vice as she squeezed me. "No, I need this. I just saw something on the way that kind of freaked me out."

"Kind of like when that deer was bouncing around the streets into traffic?"

She nodded. "Kind of, but worse."

"Okay, no need to talk about it unless you decide you want to."

She gave me a nice little kiss on the cheek. "You are such a good man."

"Why, thank you. Now, this good man needs to get his stinky sweat on, so get your butt in gear."

She gave me a salute, and grabbed her bag from the car. We rushed in quietly to unroll our mats and join the class just as it was about to start.

After the hour-long stretching session, we met in the lobby, showered, fresh, and feeling limber and fine.

"You rock my world," I said, my eyes working their way around Angelina from those fantastic muscular thighs that "could crack walnuts" as they say, to those hips that made the earth shake, and that ass that was like "pow!".

"You perv, stop that," she said.

I shook my head no and continued my journey to that amazing little tummy that rippled just right when she giggled or, if I hit the spot just right, when she came. *Oh, when she comes . . .*

She gave me a tiny flick on the cheek. "I know that look. Not here."

"Oh? You have other plans?"

"Don't I always?" she said. "For now, let's eat. Time for breakfast."

As we headed out, I tried, in the most subtle of ways, to adjust the bulge her delicious frame had inspired. *And I hadn't even got to that knockout chest and those killer eyes. Okay, down boy.*

I opened the door to her car. "I already beat you handily today. How about I follow you this time?"

"Sounds good. I already made us reservations."

More surprises. My woman! "Nice. Okay, I'll be on that sweet ass."

She jumped in, I closed her door, and by the time I was ready to go she was already on the road and busting my balls, honking her horn to get me to rush. I rolled down my window so she could see me and kicked it down to slow motion. Angelina laughed and flipped me off.

Chuckling I pulled in behind her and we were on our way.

CHAPTER FORTY-TWO

Jack

MOANING DEEPLY, I let my teeth sink slowly into the soft-as-butter filet mignon. Three bites left, and my stomach was still begging for more.

Angelina chuckled. "It always amazes me how much you get into your meals."

"You know me, appreciate it, now that you've got it."

"I've always loved that about you," she said, a small smile on her face as she stared off into the distance.

The true depth of the quote, "There's no place like home", is lost on most people, especially those kinds of people who go on a vacation and feel dread when its over and it's time to return home. For me, it's the opposite. I was born and raised in this city, but so much of my life was spent away at school, various football camps, try-outs, and games—and now all the meetings and appearances that go along with my writing—that when I finally get a few days in a row here in Erie . . . well, there's nothing like it. I get a chance to recharge. The colors are brighter, the sounds clearer, and everything tastes better. Probably a big reason why I'm feeling so aroused following Angelina home. Hotel sex just doesn't cut it. It eases the pain, no question, but at home, in your own bed, with your own toys and whatever extra accoutrements, it can't be beat.

"Yeah . . ." I muttered, nodding my head as we each pulled up in front of our house, my palms getting sweaty and my heart beginning to race. I parked behind Angelina and was out the door before she had even turned off the ignition. But when I got to her car, the door handle didn't budge, and she just sat there staring at me with an odd look on her face.

I knocked on the window. "You coming?" I said, drooling heavy with double entendre.

Angelina swallowed hard, and it delivered a strange sick feeling into my stomach. She rolled her window down, took a deep breath, and said, "Jack. I need you to listen to me carefully because I'm not going to repeat this or get into a long discussion about it. Okay?"

"Uh, yeah. I guess. Though I have to admit, you're beginning to make me a little nervous." I gently cupped her shoulder. "Are you okay?"

"Not yet. But I will be."

Oh shit. A stalker? Worse, cancer? So many—"Whatever it is, we'll get through it together. Don't worry, I'm here for you. Whatever you need."

Nodding in agreement, she said, "Good to hear," and looked at my hand still on her shoulder.

I got the hint and removed it.

"Okay, you need to go in the house. I will not be coming with you."

"Oh?"

"Here's the thing, Jack. I'm leaving you."

My legs went weak and I could feel the world beginning to tilt. *No . . .*

"Yes. While we were out, I had some movers come and get my stuff—" She paused and I found an emptiness in her eyes that I had never seen before. A look that reminded me of Shark Week, that lifeless look of death and destruction. "Nod if you understand me."

Dazed, I responded with a slow, deliberate nod.

"Good. See, Jack? You'll get through this just fine. I know you will," she said, with that smile I'd seen her practice in the mirror a million times. "I didn't take much. Just the stuff that is specifically mine. Considering the circumstances, I feel you are fully entitled to keep most everything—"

Oh, God. No. I tried to talk; she didn't have to silence me, my brain was AWOL trying to find words.

"Please know you've been an amazing partner. You're an incredible and inspiring man. I just feel—"

No! No! No! Don't say it. There's still time for this to be a dream, to change our minds—

"—that it's best I end things. This isn't right for me anymore."

The ground dropped and I fell to my knees, my hands gripping the window ledge of her car door. I didn't feel it coming, and the deep sob sounded like it must've come from someone else, but I knew, as my chest heaved, that it was me. "Why? Is there someone else? Did I do something wrong?"

"I told you, I don't want to get into a discussion about this. I'll be working on making sure my mail and other items get forwarded to my parents' place—"

"Is that where you'll be staying?"

"No. So please don't bother them with this, it's between you and I. I would also ask that you redirect anyone who's asking to reach me by text or email—"

We had been through so much. We had come so far. We were so perfect together . . . Then it hit me. I dragged myself back up and began laughing. "Oh, good one. This is a joke, right? Okay. Haha, you got me." The laughter started to pick up momentum, then headed into hysterics as she continued to stare at me with that look I've seen her give in so many other negotiations. Her "end-of-the-line" look, one that should never have come my way—yet, here it was, and like all the rest, I was powerless. *Worst of all, she knew it.*

"I hope you can understand. We both know you'll be okay. I swear I did everything I could to make this as easy as possible, but unfortunately I feel like I've been forced to make this move." She placed her hand on mine, but what I thought was heat, some sort of warmth, was actually just an icy sting as it became clear that she was merely trying to clear me away from her vehicle.

My hand fell away, hanging awkwardly adrift in the wind.

"I thank you for everything. It's been a great ride. Best of luck to you." She drove off while I stood in place and swayed, lost and confused.

Please, God, let her turn around. Make her stop.

He didn't.

She didn't.

Her car raced away and I watched until it was a faded blur in the distance. I continued to stand for what felt like an eternity. The words, "The End", flickered before my eyes like some old black-and-white movie where the sun should be fading to black but there I stood, just in case.

Finally, something clicked. I began to move. My legs ached nearly as much as my heart, but I began to move. The greatest woman I had ever met was now gone, and I had a choice: win her back, or, for the first time in my life, become a quitter.

Not a chance. Never that. Time to step up and be the man you pretend to be in all those romance stories. Time to win back the love of your life. Those thoughts, that goal, gave me the strength to move again.

CHAPTER FORTY-THREE

Helen

*T*HE DOOR EXPLODED *inward, startling me from the dizzying stack of number-riddled papers.*

He entered the room with his eyes blazing, chest bare and glistening.

I gasped and thought, Accounting can wait!

His eyes locked on me as he crossed the room.

"Jacques," I said.

"Oui madame?" In his left hand, the buckle holding his belt jumped open and with a flick of his right wrist, the entire belt came free from the waist of his pants, which, free at last, now slid down his muscular thighs as I ached to do.

I could not move. My heart raced. My breath was shallow. I could not move . . .

He stopped, and with his eyes still boring holes into my soul, he removed his boxers, setting his rapidly-rising cock free.

I felt my pussy ache in wanton anticipation.

Jacques began wrapping the belt around his right fist and with every motion, he reeled me in. I don't know when I stood up. I didn't feel my legs moving, yet, powerless, I was drifting his way—

"Hey, Helen, you ready to go?" asked William, popping his

head through the bedroom door. "We have reservations I would hate to lose and—Oh, you're in your notebook again," he said with a chuckle.

I blushed, a mix of embarrassment at being the cause of us being late and also at the recognition of the heat between my legs that my writing had fueled rather than cured. "Sorry, sweetie. I just had to get a few words down while it was in my head."

He smiled and nodded, "I know. It's one of the things I fell in love with, but we've got to scoot. Please, either bring it with you or put it away."

You're a lucky girl, Helen. While other authors struggle to find balance, your man loves it and encourages your writing. I put the pen in my notebook, closed it up and put it in the drawer of my desk before grabbing a thin sweater to go.

"You sure this dress will be warm enough for where we're going?"

Eating me up with his eyes, William smiled and said, "Absolutely. In fact, I'm betting you'll be hot by the time all is said and done."

"Oh really?" My fingers ran over the collar on his shirt, and followed his thin blue tie down to circle his belt buckle. "Mmm, I was just writing something so fitting for this moment."

"Yeah?"

Both of my hands gripped his belt, waiting for the green light. "Oh yeah. I could show you."

He took my hands in his, raised them to his mouth, and gave each a kiss. "You know how much I love your stories, and even acting them out, but we don't want to miss this. Raincheck?"

Yanking him close, I nipped his bottom lip, kept it between

my teeth, and nodded.

Once free, he pulled back, shaking his head in shock. "Helen, you are one crazy girl."

"And you love it."

Hand-in-hand, we left for our adventure.

TWINKLE TOES DANCE STUDIO. The big white letters painted stylishly above a dancing couple's silhouette hung above an entirely foreign door but, judging by the look on William's face, it had to be our destination.

He broke the silence. "Okay. You don't get it, right?"

"Right. I get that it's a dance studio, but—"

"All those years we talked about doing some dance classes are now suddenly forgotten?" he asked.

My eyes jumped from him, to the couple, and back to him again. "Really? But you said so many times—"

"How else was I going to surprise you?"

"Wow," I giggled, "Yes, I am surprised. Let's go!" In a flash, I was flying across the sidewalk to wait in the doorway. "Come on, slowpoke. Get some speed." I did an awkward but big spin, arms outstretched. "We're dancing!"

He giggled, and followed me up the stairs two at a time.

We climbed into silence. The feeling a mistake had been made slowly crept through me until the beautiful sounds of Buenos Aires suddenly wafted out of a door at the top of the stairs to greet us. Before I knew, it I was jumping up and down, clapping my hands with a smile on my face. "William! The tango. It's a tango!"

"You know it," he said, shoulders popping up. "Through that door is our private instructor, and the beginning of the next step in our journey."

It was everything I had pictured. Wooden floors, mirrored walls, old, large speakers perched above us in the corners, and a piano behind the sound system. In the middle of it all, a gorgeous man, his dark hair pulled back to reveal a gleaming smile, moved like no-one I had ever seen before.

Our presence did nothing to slow him down. Clearly, he could see us, but he was caught in the flow of the music, and I was in awe. I knew that feeling well from my writing but had never been able to translate it to movement. *In my wildest dreams, never like that.* The urge to reach for my notebook fought with my desire to be present, to go with that 1-2-3-4 beat that flirted so lasciviously with me.

William's hands on my shoulders tipped the scale, and I had begun slowly swaying along to the music whie trying not to do the impossible and intrude on the private spectacle we were witnessing.

The song ended and that gleaming smile turned our way. "Welcome, dancers," the man said as he moved with a flourish to grab a bottle of water by the sound system.

"Thank you, I'm William, and this here is my wife, Helen."

"I am so glad you both have decided to join me tonight," he said. He put his bottle down, and grabbed a towel to give his heated brow a quick swipe.

Now I really need my notebook, I thought, then sadly remembered I'd left it in my bedroom dresser. His look was so perfect, so everything I would hope to write. The hair, that smile, the loose-fitting floral shirt that could only convey such strong alpha-masculinity in a man like this, and then there were those pants. Those incredibly tight pants that seemed impossible for dancing as they clutched his ass and presented his package, but had been made exactly for this purpose.

William broke into my thoughts, whispering in my ear, "I know that look. You want to write right now, but I'm not letting you, that will have to wait. This is a special moment for you, for us."

I shuddered with the excitement, feeling somehow hot and bothered again.

William chuckled, "Please excuse her, my wife is a writer. An amazing writer, in part, because she always makes notes about everything then transforms them into stories that people love but tonight is about trying something new, different, and much more freeing."

CHAPTER FORTY-FOUR

Helen

"OH NO," THE dancer said, with a sweet Spanish accent that had to serve him well with the ladies. "No. Never apologize for passion. It must be nurtured, respected." He extended his hand, I assumed for a handshake, but it was palm down and at chest height.

I began to miss the music as we all stood wrapped in the quiet of this odd moment. *Do I take his hand? Kiss it? Aren't you only supposed to do that with women and royalty? Oh, and also the Pope and the Godfather! Do it. Take his hand—*My fingers wrapped around his and as I pulled it toward me he took a large step to his right, lifted our hands, and next thing I knew I was twirling. *Me, twirling like a dancer!*

"Passion must be loved," he continued, "and, most importantly—worshiped." He finished by bringing me in close, my hips to his, and dipping me backward.

I was dizzy with excitement, from more than just the spin. And, like a kid experiencing a roller coaster for the first time, I was immediately hooked and needed more.

"I do adore Helen and her passions," said an upside-down William.

My instructor raised me back up, and looked me in the eye. "My name is Raul. I am honored to have been chosen to share this evening with you, and promise to help unleash the passion I can see in your eyes. In your soul."

There was a heat in my cheeks that was only surpassed by my growing awareness of his accentuated pelvis pressing firmly against me. *I hope he's wearing a condom, because those pants are too thin to count as protection.* A giggle escaped, but I quickly turned it into a cough to salvage the moment as I stepped away.

"Thank you, Raul. How do we get started?" asked William.

The next thirty minutes were an adventure I would never forget. Raul had a grace and style that reminded me of the old-school foreign romance novels from my mother's collection, and the TV shows I grew up with. He was Erik Estrada and Ricardo Montalbán, wrapped in the dreamy body of Ricky Martin or William Levy. *Oh, those hypnotic smoky brown eyes!*

After a small break to talk and have some water, we were ready to learn the next set of sexy steps. I took my place on the floor and William followed. From behind me, William's hands gripped my hips and pulled me back into him. His breath was hot on my ear, and his voice made me quiver, "You move like a goddess." He felt so hard that I could feel him throbbing as he pressed himself against my ass. His hips started swaying, and mine followed.

The music came on, now just a distant rhythm, faint in my ears, as I became engrossed in the sensation of the softness of his lips on my neck.

I felt so hot. So ready for him. I opened my eyes, embarrassed, and glanced at Raul. If only William and I were somewhere else right now. I turned my head around to whisper in William's ear, "You will get one heck of a thank-you for this when we get home."

His teeth nipped my neck and I felt my pussy quiver, begging to be taken now.

Raul quietly cleared his throat. "Are you ready?"

Oh God, yes.

William stepped back. "Yes, I think she is."

I looked back at William, trying to beg him with my eyes to continue the dance.

"I think I'll sit this one out and let you two get going. I'll join in soon," William said, sitting down on the floor against the mirrored wall.

"That is perfectly fine with me," said Raul. He took my hand, ready to go. "How about you, Helen? My turn?"

William nodded encouragement and I went with the flow.

I gave Raul a big smile. "Okay. Yes, I am. Teach me to dance."

"Excellent. Now we tango."

The dance started well with something called the invite, him taking my other hand and then pulling me close. We moved well together. I felt awkward and natural all at the same time. We danced, Raul corrected, then we danced some more. Much to my surprise, William soon stepped back on the dance floor and returned to his place at my back.

Rock hard, his cock pressed against my ass again, causing me to jump slightly in surprise. It had been a long time since I had felt that level of arousal from him.

I smiled nervously, but sank back into him as we somehow

continued dancing, the three of us having become and exotic tango sandwich.

There was no denying how hot it felt to be in this empty studio, late at night, learning the sexiest dance on the planet, stuffed between two gorgeous men. But when I felt Raul's little dancer (which felt far from little right then) push and throb into my hip, I felt overwhelmed. Almost dizzy.

What's happening? Do I want this? What would William think if he knew Raul was also experiencing this in a sexual way?

Just thinking William's name brought my focus back to how wonderfully hard he was against me. How much he wanted me.

Wait, maybe he does know? Maybe he wants this to happen?

William's hands slid up from my hips to cup the sides of my breasts.

He does! Do I? It was all happening so quickly and unexpectedly that I didn't quite know what to think.

The look in Raul's eyes as the three of us continued dancing was mesmerizing, and when he leaned in for a kiss—

This isn't cheating. William is here William wants this. I moved to meet Raul's hot and sensuous lips. I pressed my ass hard against William, and I went for it.

Raul moaned. William's hands began aggressively exploring my breasts as Raul's tongue entered my mouth—and that's where I drew the line.

I disengaged from the kiss and pulled away from both men. "I'm sorry, I—"

"Just go with it," said William, coming up close behind me again and nuzzling my ear. "Don't worry, I'm here. This is for you."

Raul had stopped dancing. He tipped his head slightly to look me in the eyes. "Are you okay, Helen?"

I shook my head, slowly at first, then vigorously. "No, Raul. Thank you, but no I'm not."

"She'll be fine," said William, still pressing against me, trying to get my hips to move with him again.

Raul stepped away and went to turn off the music while I turned to confront William. "I said no. I will not be fine. This is not happening."

As the music went off, so did William. A side of him I had never seen. "What the fuck is wrong with you, Helen?"

I felt tears leap to the corners of my eyes. "What?"

"You write about this shit but you aren't ever willing to try anything. You—"

"But I only want you, William. My husband. Just you." I fought to keep the tears at bay. Fought to stay upright against a weight I felt was crushing me.

"Just want me? But I want more," he said sharply.

A sudden pain in my heart came out as a sob, and then tears raced one another for freedom. I stumbled toward William, hoping that if I could just wrap my arms around him I could bring us back to the perfect relationship we always had. But as I reached out, he pushed me away.

Raul's gentle hand touched my shoulder. "William, this is not what you said to me. You said she was interested. This is wrong."

William's lips curled, and a raw and rough voice I'd never heard from him before appeared. "Fuck you, Rico Suave. I did everything I could for her, and this is what I get . . . "

"Why?" I cried, "Why are you saying this?"

"I did all I could to be considerate, but you wouldn't take it. You were too high and mighty. Have to always be better than the rest of us." And that's when I noticed tears in his eyes. "I didn't want to hurt you, Helen. But you've left me no choice."

Once again, I reached out to hug him, but he turned his back on me and walked to the top of the stairs. "I'm sorry, Helen. Hopefully, you can find someone else. But we're done."

"No," I whimpered, my body wracked with pain, convulsing endlessly.

"Don't worry, I won't be coming home. You'll never see me again."

Crushed, I fell to the floor as I listened to William stomp down the stairs, slam the door, and walk out of my life.

CHAPTER FORTY-FIVE

Helen

M Y KEY FROZE in the lock. I couldn't make it turn. *Once I go through this door, I'm no longer going home. I'll be going to something entirely new. A place that will look familiar and have my stuff, but will not be my life. If I go through*—Open the door, Helen.

And I did. The bolt clicked over, and I stepped into the darkness.

The door slammed shut behind me. Surprised, I didn't flinch. My nerves were too far gone for that. I stood waiting for my eyes to adjust to the dark. It took time that I couldn't measure and only revealed the smallest hints of my surroundings. Finally, I moved forward, dropping my keys, purse, and then my clothes as I stumbled across the living room and did a slow zombie-shuffle into my bed, and fell into the deeper darkness of sleep.

Eventually, I stirred. The morning sun scorched my eyes. Rolling over, even with my eyelids shut tight and a pillow pulled across my face, did little to stop the pain. "William? You left the blinds open. Can you please come close them?"

I gave him a minute. Nothing, so I yelled a little louder, "William. Blinds. Please."

What felt like five minutes passed. I threw my pillow against the wall, and stomped out of bed. "Never mind, I got them . . . " And then it hit me. *William's gone.*

The ground hit my knees hard as I collapsed. I sobbed. I cried. I wailed. I felt my heart tearing apart, a soul-wrenching pain William and I had promised never to inflict upon one another. "You lied to me," I said, through blubbering tears. "You said forever," I screeched, the shrill volume shredding my throat. The carpet did nothing to soften the blows as my fists pounded the floor. Tears drained freely as my voice reemerged with a whisper, "William, you promised . . . "

In time, I ran out of tears. My throat had become raw and my full-body pain found focus in my lower back. Standing up, I realized my naked form was directly in front of the window. *Fuck it, who cares?* The warm sun embraced me as I stood, arms stretching up to close the curtains on each side of me. In six years of living on the fourteenth floor of this building, I had never experienced this sensation. Before this day I would have hid or covered up. Now I felt the warmth of the sun's rays on my face, my cheeks, and no longer did it burn my eyes, it was just a new light. I shuddered slightly when I became acutely aware of the heat on my breasts, feeling my nipples perk slightly and goose-flesh race across my back. The heat of this new day was exquisite.

Self-indulgence done, I slammed the curtains shut and went to find a tissue for my eyes and runny nose. *You may feel a bit better, but you look a mess.*

William smiled a big fucking grin.

"Oh hell, no, you don't." I grabbed our wedding picture from the top of the dresser, took it with me into the kitchen, and threw the frame into the sink where the glass shattered. I sifted through the debris to remove the photograph. I took it over to the blender, opened the lid, ripped the picture in two, and threw his fake fucking face into the blending jar, then hit "Crush". "Oh, yeah. *Crush,*" I said, wiping my tears on my hand before moving up to nose on arm. "Take that, you useless little prick." I pushed the button again. It did nothing new, but it made me feel good. I mashed it again, then again, then repeatedly until the button became stuck in the base of the blender. I pulled the plug, grabbed the blending jar by its glass handle, stormed my way to the bathroom, filled the jar with water, swished it around, and emptied the whole mess into the toilet. The sound of flushing had never been so grand. "Bye-bye, you waste of human excrement!" I said with a maniacal laugh.

I stood there, jar in hand, looking in the bowl and waiting for the water to settle just to be sure none of him had survived. When satisfied, I grabbed some more tissues, blew my nose heartily, washed up, and started the purge.

First, the closet. Every jacket of his, every scarf, sweater, pair of shoes and boots, and his favorite old khaki raincoat, were thrown into garbage bags. "Those'll burn well. Trip to the ranch today for sure."

As I moved into the living room, I found my stuff trailing across the floor from last night, in particular, my purse which contained my notebook. "Oh, you could write some angsty shit in there right now, Helen." I flung the bag of his stuff behind me; it splattered against the wall, his clothes tumbling out of the bag.

Purse in hand, I started to race to the couch but stopped when I glimpsed myself in the hall mirror. There I stood, still naked, a smile like the gates of Hell had spilled open, clutching my little purple handbag. *Yeah, bitches!* For the first time in my life, or at least my adult life, I flexed at my reflection, a big two-gun salute, then continued to the couch, cackling hysterically.

Pen on paper, my hand filled with energy, I went for it.

I mashed his skull with the wooden mallet—he would talk. "Why did you do it?" I asked.

"Because I'm a low-life piece of scum—"

I swung again, his shoulder cracked under the pressure.

"Yes, you are. Now come here."

He got on his feet, stumbled my way.

"I can't trust you, can I?"

He shook his head, tears rolling down his face.

"I know," and this time I swung the mallet low—

I ripped out the page, crumpled it up, and threw it across the floor. "No, let's really write something. If we're going to write about that part of anatomy, let's make it a positive." I hit the next page running.

His massive cock waited desperately for me, its only salvation. It flexed, it danced, it begged. It needed me, and—though I would never let him know—I needed it just as badly.

I let my finger gently graze the tip. He shuddered with a full-body moan. "Please," he begged, "I ache only for you."

My smile widened, canines glistening, "Of course you do."

I was jolted from my writing to notice that my left finger had been delicately grazing my clit, that the feelings I had been experiencing while writing this had started right there. I closed my notebook, put the pen away, and kicked my feet onto the coffee table. As I began to work on rubbing out the frustrations that had been building since my last writing session, I noticed that the window in this room was also uncovered. The sun was now barging its way across the floor in my direction, and the thought of its heat soon caressing my body drove me onward to start my day in a way I hadn't in many years.

After my living room release, and then once more in the shower for good measure, and some breakfast in my belly, I stood in the kitchen looking out at the rest of the apartment trying to figure out my next move.

"Well, Helen, this would be the time in the movies where you're supposed to call up your girls, go out drinking, find a man, and party the pain away. 'Best way to get over a man is to get under a new one'. But I don't have a set of girls like that, and I'm not really into drinking or random hook-ups. So how does this film end?" *If I were writing this story, where would it go—without me burning down this apartment building to rid the world of all traces of William's existence?*

I found inspiration in the form of William's pride and joy sitting on his dresser: a 14k gold watch he'd received two years ago as "Top Radio Ad Exec—Montana" (per the engraving on the back). It became the basis of a pile that included his other watches and jewelry, his laptop, autographed photos of celebrities and politicians he'd met over the years, and anything else of potential value. I would donate a variety of the items to a local charity, and sell the rest at the flea market.

"This girl's about to get some party money."

CHAPTER FORTY-SIX

Jack

TO THE CASUAL eye, the house looked the same. You couldn't tell that someone had just broken in and stolen my life. But the absence of Angelina's shoes in the closet, the football she'd had autographed by her first ever pro client that she'd always proudly displayed on the mantle—and of course her juicer—screamed a story I couldn't misunderstand. Surprisingly, the movers missed her cushion on the couch. To most it would look too ratty to matter, but it was the one thing she'd cuddle with while watching a scary movie.

It was small comfort to find that our wedding picture was still untouched above the mantle. "Look how happy we were," I muttered. Picking up the frame and running my fingers around the edges, I traced the outlines of her dress. Landing on her beautiful face sent tears trickling down my cheeks. I gave her picture a kiss, clutched it to my chest, and made my way upstairs to flop, fully clothed, onto the bed.

"Don't worry, sweetheart. I'll make it right," I said, staring into her gorgeous blue eyes.

I had stayed like that, staring at her, trying to figure out what I could do to salvage our relationship, when my phone rang.

Pulling it out of my pocket, I saw Troy's name. *Oh, great. It gets worse.*

I hit talk, and tried to sound normal. "What's up, Missing Link?"

"About nine inches. Where's your mom?"

"Fuck you. I think she's out pegging your dad."

"Ouch!"

"Damn right. Now, what's up?" I asked, eager to get off the phone and back to my sulking.

"Um, I don't know, really . . . "

Oh great, it's going to be one of those *calls. Not tonight, man.*

"I just felt like giving you a call," he said. "What are you up to?"

"Nada. Just hanging."

"Hey, uhhh . . . " Troy cleared his throat, loudly and repeatedly, right into the phone, "You okay?"

"You mean besides the fact that I'm here alone at the house, after having just gotten ditched by Angelina?" *Oh, shit. Why did you tell him that?*

"Shit. Dude . . . I'm on my way," he said, and the phone went dead.

"Fuck." I called him right back.

The phone rang three times before he answered. "What? Need me to bring something?"

"No, I need you to stay put."

"But, Jack—"

"Look, I'm okay. I just need some time alone to—I *will* find her and win her back."

"Jack?"

"Uh . . . yeah?"

"No, you aren't okay," he said, in his most certain tone.

"Hell, yeah, I am. I'll do a couple online searches, call her parents, all that. It's just a—"

"We both know her well enough to know that if she's done with you and doesn't wanna be found, she won't be. The only way you're seeing her again is on her terms."

The sickness in my stomach did flips. Tears began to silently roll down my face once again.

"Jack?"

I wiped my cheeks.

"You know I'm right, don't you?" Troy said.

I nodded. "Yeah . . . "

"So that brings us back to 'do you want some company'? Because my schedule is free, and I'm just sitting here all alone staring at the walls going a little crazy anyway."

"Dude," I said with a chuckle, "'a little'? You passed 'a little crazy' years ago."

Troy paused a moment before joining in on the laugh. "I guess that means you're okay?"

"Yeah, thanks, buddy. You always show up at the right time and know the stupidest things to say to set me straight."

"Cool. Glad I could help."

We hung up the phone. I threw it on the desk, jogged downstairs, grabbed Angelina's cushion from the couch in a bear-hug, came back up and laid back down on the bed. In minutes, I was asleep.

I slept hard, passed out until nearly eleven the next morning, when I was awakened by an alert from my phone that I prayed was Angelina. But it was only my calendar app, telling me I had another convention next weekend. "Fuck!" I threw my phone against the wall. Much to my disappointment, it bounced off with a happy little thud and fell to the carpet, waiting for more. I made a quick trip to the restroom, then was face down on the bed again.

About nine p.m., I woke again, feeling exhausted but still managing to stumble up and out in spite of the howling protests of every part of my body. The parts of me that needed another trip to the restroom, the parts that always begged for food, the part that said "time to do some thinking about the shit you're in and what you're going to do about it". In my past, this would be the point where I would throw out a heavy dose of self-talk. Or when a coach would scream and yell about how worthless I was, or when Angelina would—*Well, it didn't matter what she would have done, anymore, did it? She's fucked off.*

A race to the rest room was won by me, barely, as bile from my stomach heaved forward at the sudden remembrance of her absence and my new reality. I would have to find a way to see her again and salvage things. Whatever had caused her to leave, I could fix it.

The sound of another phone alert called to me again from the bedroom. Washing up quickly, I went out to find it. There it was, that little annoying light, flashing away. A look at the screen showed it was an email about the convention. *To throw this fucker again, or not to throw?* "How very Shakespearean of you, Jack," I said aloud. Rolling my eyes, I went in search of food while scrolling through the event info. The big splashy landing page faded behind one of the author names displayed: "Helena Bliss".

"Oh, great. Add *that* to my already complicated life, and a convention I don't remember booking and really don't want to attend." That was the tipping point. The phone took flight again and laughed at me as it skidded across the kitchen floor. *I wonder if she knows?*

CHAPTER FORTY-SEVEN

Helen

S ITTING ON MY balcony, wrapped in a light blanket on my comfortable chaise, I watched the sky as it played, washes of amber and crimson rolling across the horizon as the day's last escapades settled down into night. This was a perfect time for reflection.

The last twenty-four hours had been a roller coaster of emotions that saw me gleefully smashing more pictures of William, shredding his underwear, and falling asleep with his sweater, in tears. I managed a brief reprieve from the turmoil with a trip to Clay's ranch. Cleopatra and I rode hard, strolled in the creek, and had a small picnic before I returned to my disaster. Alcohol was consumed (mostly wine), as were cake, chocolate, far too many unanswered questions, and guilt.

Had I really become such a bad partner?

Do I really come across as "high and mighty"?

If I had engaged in William's fantasy—whatever it was—at the dance studio, would we still be together?

The thoughts made my stomach churn, made my head spin and turn. It was more than I could handle right now and any answers wouldn't really change things. *Time to move forward,*

Helen.

I unwrapped, and went inside for a bowl of Rocky Road ice cream. "What do they say on all those talk shows and advice columns? 'Drop that zero and get yourself a hero'? Yeah, something like that . . . " I said, giving myself a peptalk, and made my way back out to the balcony with my bowl, where the last rays of sunset and my laptop waited.

As I covered up again, the red and burnt-orange of the sky blurred with blue and then purple. I felt a moment of peace as I found the bottom of the bowl. I gave it a last scrape with my spoon—just in case—and then swapped it for my laptop.

Writing today had been difficult, with the exception of a few terrible tirades that couldn't see print without me being locked up. Yesterday's sexual sidetrack was an isolated incident that I still didn't understand, but had at least been momentarily satisfying.

A new email appeared with a ping, with the heading: "Ten Days to Go. The Countdown Has Begun." I opened it to find the info for the annual Rose City Romance Convention in Portland, Oregon.

"Oh, yeah. I don't remember booking that . . . " I mumbled.

But I loved that event. It would be my third time attending, and the chance to see both ocean and mountains in the same weekend was incredible. But did I really want to go anywhere right now, no matter how tempting the place? Would I be up to doing the work? *You have a better plan, Helen? You're going to run out of things to throw in the blender by then.*

Following the link to look at the event details and get the itinerary took me on an unexpected turn. Suddenly, filling the screen in front of me, was Jack Smith and his trademark smile. "Is

245

this conference still the best plan? Or just more trouble?" *I wonder if he knows?*

Staring at the screen didn't change anything, so I went inside and grabbed one of the already open wine bottles littering the counter. Pulling the cork, I took a big drink and wandered back over to the hall mirror to toast my still-naked self once again, then returned to the balcony.

"Let's find out." Huddled under my blanket, I reached for my phone, then remembered it had disappeared during last night's debate of whether to call William or not. *There's a chance it also wound up in the blender.* Before a pout could crease my face, I took decisive action, opening Skype and hitting Jack's name on my contacts list to send a text. "Hmm. What to say to the guy you told yourself you should never see again?" I took another sip of the Moscato and typed.

Me: Going to Oregon?

I slapped my forehead so hard it made me dizzy, and let out a groan. *Did I really just do that?* I took another drink and discovered Rocky Road and white wine didn't go together as well as one might think. Dropping everything onto the chaise, I ran for the bathroom.

Much heaving followed, in the most unladylike fashion imaginable. I washed up, shivering, and put on my robe to officially end Naked Helen Day. *Maybe he won't get my message. Yeah, good luck with that. Okay, maybe he will get it, but won't respond.* "Get real. This is Jack we're talking about. Either his ego or curiosity are going to make him answer, maybe both," I argued with myself. "But it's like ten or later there; maybe he's sleeping already and I'll be sober by the time he—" As I crossed the living room, I heard a text alert on my laptop.

I bolted for the toilet once again, and heaved up whatever had somehow survived the last visit.

Three messages awaited me when I finally got the courage to look at the screen.

> **Jack:** *Next week?*
>
> **Jack:** *Yeah*
>
> **Jack:** *You?*

The bottle hit my lips, the wine snaked across my tongue, and my stomach immediately sent up warnings of revolt. I took the hint, grabbed the former ice cream bowl, and spit out the wine, hoping I had averted disaster. *Not my finest moment.*

> **Jack:** *Hello?*
>
> **Me:** *Hi*
>
> **Me:** *I am.*

"Oh, Helen. You'd better figure out your next move now, because this conversation is happening. If it gets out of control you could just be heaping on more regrets . . . " I hissed at myself.

> **Jack:** *Oh. I can cancel, if that helps?*

I tried to rationalize my way to an answer. *Who had the bigger fan base? Who had more to lose?* Clearly, it wouldn't work out. Could we share the same venue but maintain distance? *Again, this is Jack we're talking about.* A movie montage, maybe more like a slideshow, of Jack memories flipped through my head. He wanted me. *Yeah, and so did Raul—and William—and look where that got you.*

> **Jack:** *Should I cancel?*
> **Me:** *Hold on! Thinking.*

"Great, Helen. Great response," I muttered.

> **Me:** *Sorry. Please hold on.*

I shook my head and rolled my eyes. "Yeah, that's much better." *Run, Helen. Just lose link.* "Wait, no. I'm done being the one to run."

> **Me:** *Listen. I'm going through some stuff right now. I'm going to go.*
> **Me:** *If you're going, that's okay. I don't see us hanging out, though, and I can't be your cover this time.*

My heart was racing. *What a rush. I could get used to just letting go.*

"Incoming Call" popped up on the screen.

"Oh, no. I can't," I moaned.

That distinct Skype ringtone continued to play with Jack's far-too-perfect headshot icon—the one that I just saw on the conference website—front and center. *Why was he calling? We had text.*

My fingers ran through my hair hopelessly. I gritted my teeth, quickly wiped under my eyes to clear away any lingering smudges of eyeliner or mascara, and hit "Accept Video Call".

Jack's face appeared on the screen.

"'Going through some stuff'? You okay?" said Jack.

"Um, hello to you, too, Jack."

"Sorry. Hi . . . "

"I know it's late. I didn't expect you to—"

Jack's face tightened, his jaw more rigid than I remembered, almost sharp.

I learned about that look when he had last come to Billings. *He's embarrassed about something.*

"No problem. I was awake, just, uh, trying to do some writing," he said.

"Oh yeah? Me too."

He nodded. Silence followed.

I went first, "Okay, so about Oregon . . . "

"Yeah, all good there," he said, and then that look came across his face, a warning of incoming sarcasm, "although it's going to be hard to find another person to be my cover who can drink orange juice like you and won't expect sex."

"Don't worry, I'm sure there are ample people in Oregon who would rather avoid 'The Titan Experience'," I said with a wink.

He blinked in surprise. "Ouch. My ego."

Change the topic. "Your writing is going well?" I asked.

"I've had better days. You?"

"There's been nonstop material recently. Just a matter of sifting through it and keeping focused." *Technically not a lie.*

"Oh!" His face lit up the screen. "I've got an idea."

I would've expected a feeling of dread at those words, yet surprised myself with a twinge of excitement that was immediately followed by guilt. *Remember who he is and what happened last time, Helen.* "Uh-oh . . . "

"Read for me," he said.

"What?"

"Recently, I lost one of my readers—my beta readers. Would you read for me?"

Do I really need to read about Jack's debaucheries right now? Wait, I know it's fiction. It would at least be a distraction. And it could be fun. "Okay, I'll do it, but there's a catch."

"Good. What is it?"

"Read for me. I also happen to be in need of a new reader. Will—"

The excitement in his eyes and his voice, even through the screen, was contagious. It tested my resolve to stay in my current funk. "Done," he said. "I'll get something ready and send it in about five minutes, okay?"

"Uh . . . "

He was already in full motion, apparently jumping out of bed.

See? It really was too late.

"Sorry, am I moving too fast? Is that too soon?" he asked, the background swinging by in a nauseous way as he carried his laptop to another room.

I chuckled and shook my head in disbelief. "You're something else, Jack. Send when ready, and I'll get something together ASAP."

It was hard to make him out, his image a blur as he raced around. "That's great. I'm looking forward to it," he said.

A smile was winning its way across my face.

"Okay, bug you later," he said.

"I know you will."

His laugh was sudden and large. "You're too much. Oh, and

Helen . . . " his face came clearly into focus, " . . . thank you."

The call ended. I closed the lid on my laptop.

"Helen, what did you get yourself into?" A small charge of giddy energy was rolling through me. My hands were shaking. I needed to write. "Oh, shit, you *do* need to write. He'll be expecting something."

But I cheated. I sent him some stuff I had worked on about a week ago. *We didn't say that it had to be fresh off the press.*

It did feel good to be in contact with someone again, and Jack's energy was pretty contagious after my past couple days of self-imposed solitude. And we would handle this conference better than the last one. We knew each other now and would be on good footing—and safe.

Question is, can I keep my heart safe when I'm around Jack Smith?

CHAPTER FORTY-EIGHT

Jack

A S THE BAGGAGE carousel circled, my focus split. One part of me kept searching for my bag, and the other part was hoping against odds that Helen might be in the vicinity and kept looking for her. I knew her flight was scheduled to arrive hours ago, but with the way airlines work, anything was possible.

When my bag finally came around, I grabbed it and made a mad dash out to the waiting car. Oregon was one of those places where the greenery, while beautiful, always felt like more of a distraction. Like the curtain at the theater where you knew the real awe-inspiring show laid just beyond its barrier. I ached for a chance to see the nearby river, climb into the mountains, or get out on the Pacific in a zodiac. But, once again, I was running late and in a race to the hotel.

It was hard to believe I was here, on my way to a convention, when almost two weeks ago, Angelina—the driving force behind my writing career—had bailed on me.

Troy had been right, she wouldn't be found. I'd made multiple attempts and failed miserably. Her parents, as wonderful as they were, were no help at all out of respect for their daughter's wishes.

Thankfully, at least I had a good distraction. I'd managed to get a little writing in, more than I would have expected, and even did some reading for Helen. We had begun to build a better friendship. An understanding was formed, this was not something romantic, or physical, we were going to keep it as friends. It was one of the few times in my life that I was friend-zoned and was happy about it.

I'd learned that her guy was a fool and had just ditched her, too. Even though she'd broken down and cried when she told me, from the sounds of it she was better off, and it was good she got away from him when she did with the way he was trying to force her into the situation with that dancer guy. We were now talking on the phone almost every night and had become critique partners, which led to some interesting debates as we were both very protective of our writing, but I believe my writing was better for her criticism and hope she would say the same.

I exited the cab, tipped the driver, and wheeled my bag into the hotel lobby.

Now, isn't that some luck?

Helen stood at a magazine rack, buried nose-deep in some shiny paperback that should've been mine—except I don't do shiny covers. I dropped my bag and ran across the lobby as light-footedly as possible, trying not to draw too much attention to myself or scare anyone. Helen didn't see me as I snuck up behind her and yelled, "Boo!"

She flinched slightly—far less than I would've expected—and gave me a two-handed shove in the chest. "What's wrong with you?"

With a hangdog expression, I lowered my head. "I just don't

know, ma'am. Please save me from my sorry self."

"No chance of that, at this point," she said, and stepped in for a hug that I was more than happy to deliver, and that I enjoyed more than I wanted to. "I guess we'll just have to keep in you tied up in the yard. They say you can't teach an old dog new tricks."

I gave her a squeeze, lifted her up and gave a half-spin. "'Old dog'? I thought we were on peaceful ground."

"Suck it up. There's likely going to be much more where that came from."

Oh, yeah. Something about Helen had definitely changed since last I'd last seen her. There were glimpses of it in our calls, and an edge to her writing, but now, seeing her in person, it was clear— she had found some sort of new confidence. I might have to ask her secret, because Angelina's effect was still weighing pretty heavily on me.

I couldn't shake the feeling that maybe all those years where Angelina had encouraged me to play the ladies' man to sell books had actually been hurting her. *All the secrets, having to keep our marriage so private*—once again my stomach was sinking and I wondered why I was here.

"Hey, what's going on with you?" Helen asked. "First of all, put me back down. But where did you just go? I saw it in your face. Somewhere dark."

"Angelina . . . "

"I understand," she said, and gave me another big squeeze. "But let's not do that this weekend. Let's live it up the way we're supposed to," she leaned in to whisper, "*the way people believe Jack Smith really does*—but without all the sordid and douche-y debauchery." She stood up and gave me a shot in the shoulder.

"Okay, friend?"

My spirits lifted. She was right.

"In fact, how about we make a pact?" she continued. "Any time either of us starts to think about those . . . uh . . . *losers*— because they did lose by letting us go—" her smile was big, her eyes blazing "—when we think about them, we say . . ." She looked around the room.

I joined her, not knowing our objective.

"Oh, I know," she said, staring at the nearby restaurant, "melon balls!"

"Absolutely, yes. That's perfect." The words bounced around in my head, crashing into imagery of Bob in the dining room of the Grand Hotel, and the story Helen told about her crazy 'bad convention' experience, and had me laughing.

"Good. Let's get you checked in," she said, and took a quick glance around. "Where's your stuff?"

"Over there." I pointed at the lonely bag in the middle of the lobby that everyone was giving a wide berth. "I had to drop it for stealth."

She rolled her eyes. "Of course you did. But where's the rest? No books or anything?"

"No, whenever possible I get them sent to the venue in advance. Makes travel a whole lot easier."

"Hmm, I'll have to look into that."

"Any questions, I'm your guy."

Bag in hand, heading for check-in, Helen suddenly yanked my arm, stopping me in my tracks.

"What?"

"Look. There, at the desk. In the pink dress."

Any doubt who it was immediately disappeared when I saw the desk clerk's exhausted face struggling to get through the exchange. "No. *Nancy Coeur.* Here?"

"Hey, you know the circuit. It was bound to happen," Helen whispered.

"Admittedly," I whined, more in fun than anything, "but so soon?" I let go of the handle of my suitcase. "You know I'm waiting until she's gone, right?"

"Oh, Nancy? Hello," Helen called. Her face was full of mischief as she dragged me by the arm toward the clerk.

All I could do was grab my bag and go with the flow. "You're nuts. I miss the old Helen," I hissed.

Funny enough, I think the only one enjoying this new Helen trick was the desk clerk, because Nancy shot a glance our way, her jaw dropped, and she snatched up her stuff from the desk and was off like a shot. I'd say she was acting like she didn't hear or see us, but that would be foolish. We all knew she was trying to avoid us and make the weekend plans pretty clear: we would not be doing any suntanning or shots together.

"Okay, then, sweetie. See you later," called Helen the Instigator, before she and I started howling with laughter.

"You are freaking horrible," I said. "I love it."

My turn at the desk went far better and faster than Nancy's, and in a flash we were in the elevators heading to my floor.

Helen pushed sixteen for me, and then twelve.

"Twelve?" I asked.

"Yeah, my room. 1203. Call down when you're ready."

"Oh, okay. Just lucky I caught you down in the lobby when I did, right?"

Ding! The elevator stopped on the twelfth floor, and the doors slid open.

"Lucky? You told me when your flight was scheduled to arrive. You had to know it wasn't coincidence and that I was waiting for you, no?"

Helen stepped out and the doors slid closed between my surprised face and her taunting grin.

Looks like you've met your match, Jack-O. Hold on tight.

CHAPTER FORTY-NINE

Helen

THE ELEVATOR DOOR closed, leaving me standing in the hallway all alone, giggling like the crazy person I felt I had recently become. Gathering myself, I took a deep breath, walked with slow, determined poise to my door, unlocked it, entered, closed the door, then squealed and bounced around like a kid set free in a toy store.

"'You're nuts'!" I said, in my best imitation of Jack's deep voice. "'I miss the old Helen'!" I bounced around the room, tickled pink. "Yeah, well, I don't. Buckle up, baby, this is who the world is going to get this weekend." I flipped on the little nightstand radio beside my bed and some song I had never heard before became the backbeat to my dance party while I searched for another outfit to wear.

Changed, my book boxes moved and organized, my clothes sorted (and after a minor raid on the bar fridge for snacks), I sat on my bed and twiddled my thumbs, waiting for Jack to call.

Turning on the TV, I began flipping through the channels. "Nope." I jumped up, threw my shoes on, and was out the door.

The elevator slid open, and there was Jack in a nice pair of jeans and a charcoal grey button-up shirt, smiling like one of the male models who were always smiling back at me from the cover of my books.

"Good evening, Miss Bliss."

For whatever reason, the term "Miss" struck a nerve. It was a common greeting at these events, and meant respectfully in many areas I travel, but right now it was like a direct shot about my marital status and the way things had, or rather had not, worked out with William—and I sunk.

As the elevator door began to close, Jack jumped off and took me gently by the shoulders. "No. No, you don't."

I felt it welling up through me from the base of my throat, the corners of my mouth beginning to twitch, my eyes building tears. "Why couldn't I make it work, Jack?"

"Oh, sweetheart, it wasn't you. He made a mistake. He's the one—" His sudden pause caught my emotions by surprise and somehow put them on hold.

I looked at him, ready to unleash my tsunami of tears.

He grinned. "Hey. Melon balls."

Oh, come on.

"I said, melon balls!"

Such a fool.

"Don't make me say it again. Because, by God, I will." Jack's focused stare challenged me.

"You better not," I replied.

"If I don't see some sort of smile in 3 . . . "

"Don't do it."

"2 . . . "

"I swear. You're such a fool," I said, and fought to keep my mouth from turning up for him.

"1 . . . "

That did it. I shoved my way past him, looking to push the button for the elevator but mostly to hide my smile.

"Oh, yeah," he said, and I could hear some type of shuffling on the hallway carpet behind me.

Don't look, Helen. He's like a kid, it will only encourage him.

"But I won. I. Got. You. To. Smi-ile." To add extra oomph, he stretched the word smile to the point where I was powerless and had to look back at him.

I regretted it the moment I did, because he started moving like he had bigger problems than I realized. He was jumping, spinning, and flailing his arms, all at the same time. "What in the world are you doing?" I snapped.

"My touchdown dance. Love it?"

"No! I don't. You look like you're fighting off a swarm of hornets."

He didn't care, and continued to butcher the concept of "dance" with his moves.

"I'm guessing you didn't score many touchdowns, did you?"

He stopped abruptly, facing the other way. "Why, Helen? Why ya gotta hurt me?" He jumped up and spun around. "That's right, you can't. It's my touchdown dance!"

Ding! The elevator doors finally opened to admit us and apparently the gods of romance, parties, or touchdown dances—I don't know which—must have decided they needed to get in on the fun because, lo and behold, the elevator was filled with Nancy Coeur and her cronies, now staring at Jack and I with upturned noses and sour pusses.

Jack didn't see, he was in the backward portion of his routine, but I saw enough for both of us and nearly peed myself with laughter. I had never played pro football, never even thought about it, but right there on the spot I created my own little touchdown dance to show those snooty party poopers what for.

As the door began to close, Jack came around again and saw the last of their faces and joined me in my hysterics until we lay in a heap of red-faced humor against the hallway wall.

Comfortably, we sat in that uncomfortable position for a few minutes.

"Thank you, Jack. I needed that."

"We're a good team," he said. "Can you imagine what they're saying right now? I can already tell this is going to be an amazing weekend." Just then, his phone rang. "Bah, always at the worst times," he said, with a chuckle. Taking it out of his pocket, he looked at the screen. "Uh-oh, it's my brother, Troy. You think I'm a fool, you should see the two of us together. Oh, that's it! You should come to Cleveland sometime and meet him—"

"Ah, another 'brother'," I said. "I see."

The phone rang again; apparently, this brother was impatient.

Jack pushed a button on the phone, held it to his ear, and said, "Your dime, fucker. Use it or lose it." Then he looked at me with an expression I couldn't place. "Yes, I'm his brother, Jack Smith. Who's this?"

He listened for a moment and then dropped the phone. A "Noooo . . . " slowly slid out of his mouth. A violent torrent of tears rushed from his eyes. His face was pale. His body shook.

A wave of panic went over me. "Jack? Talk to me."

"No," he shook his head once, then twice, and then in rapid succession.

261

I picked up the phone. "Hello?"

A man's voice answered on the other line, "Hello? Is this the wife?"

"No, a friend. What's going on?"

"I hate to be making this call," the man said, then paused, apparently searching for words, "but I'm going through Troy's phone to try to reach his family and let them know . . . to let them know that he has passed."

Whoa . . . Take care of this, Helen. "Can you tell me what—"

"No! God fucking no!" screamed Jack, now back on his feet.

"Thank you for calling—I gotta go!"

Jack had found the strength not only to stand, but to start hammering the walls, booming out his anger. The pictures rattled, and his roaring filled the hall.

I pressed "End Call" and went to him.

Suddenly, he pulled a picture and threw it across the hallway, where it shattered against the opposite wall. Fragments of glass leapt at him and impaled themselves in his shirt, his hands, and his face. He grabbed another framed picture, gave it the same treatment, and received the same result.

I wanted to break through, to help him, but felt entirely lost. "Jack?"

He turned my way, agony and rage mixed with the blood and tears sweeping across his face. "He can't be, Helen. He can't! I won't let it—" He took off in a full sprint.

I chased after him, quickly falling behind.

He reached the end of the hall and ran into the door to the stairwell, shoulder first, with a fantastic crash.

I prayed that most of that sound was the door, but the damage being done to his body was racing to catch up with the pain inside him.

Jack flung open the door and disappeared down the stairs at an astonishing pace I could never dream of achieving, his screams echoing in his wake.

I made my way down after him as fast as I could.

Another loud bang, followed quickly by a second one that made me believe that this next door tried to put up a bigger fight.

The trail of blood led me to him. I got to the bottom of the stairs, and sure enough, there was another blown-out door. I hurried into the parking lot where Jack stood, arms spread wide, screaming up at the early evening sky, "Why?"

As he demanded, "How could you?"

As he begged, "Please, no, just take me . . . "

And he collapsed face down on the concrete, as nervous hotel security guards and other concerned guests showed up on scene.

Out of breath, I forced myself to push through the onlookers, afraid of what I might find. Jack was a blood-speckled wreck whose arm now hung at a wrong angle from his shoulder. A new wave of panic hit me as I realized he was now silent. I couldn't see breathing. Kneeling beside him, I put my hand on his sweat-soaked back. "Jack, I'm here for you." I got nothing. I began to shake him gently, trying to rouse him, now sending up my own prayers to whomever might be listening. *Please. He's a good man . . .*

"Helen," Jack finally sobbed.

"I'm here."

"They took Troy."

"I know."

"I can't do this."

"You can. I've got you," I said, and he lost consciousness again as sirens cried in the distance.

CHAPTER FIFTY

Helen

PRIOR TO MEETING Jack Smith, limousines were an oddity. One did not simply travel in limos on a whim. They were for big events only. I had only been in two of them before meeting Jack: one for my high school graduation, and the other for my wedding. Right now, I would give anything to reduce my total by one as the two of us rode in the long black car in the funeral procession for Jack's friend, Troy.

Passing through the gates of the cemetery delivered a shock. Looking out my window, I could see dozens of other black limos mixed in with countless cars, many of them exotic and right off a showroom floor or a magazine cover.

Jack leaned into me to look out the window. "I know, right? Cleveland may never be the same." His attempt at humor lacked the usual punch.

As we drew closer, our driver drifting the limousine slowly down the narrow road looking for a place to park, I saw the others attendees gathered at the roadside and noticed the way they were dressed. As I began to recognize celebrities in the crowd, my insecurities began to rise. "I don't know if I should be here"

"Why?"

"I . . . I'm not—"

"You're a good person. A kind person. Every occasion needs people like you," said Jack, his hand patting my knee.

My fears retreated as I saw his smile. Today, he wore sunglasses. They would hide some of the damage he had suffered: his fractured nose, the black eyes, and the tears that continued to flow frequently. It had taken some fast talking, and a number of autographs and plans for future appearances, to get Jack out of trouble with both the hotel and police. He was lucky that the officer on the scene was a big football fan with another former pro on the force, and that the owner of the Portland hotel happened to have some sort connection to the Grand Hotel chain, which of course, took care of Jack.

"On top of it all," he said, "you're here for me. *With* me—I just wish Troy had been able to meet you." He tried to sniffle, and winced in pain. Jack was fighting every step of the way not to take the pain pills the doctor had prescribed, and I couldn't blame him. I didn't know the full story, but I knew that pain pills were somehow related to Troy's death.

We sat back again, me observing the gathering crowd out the window and Jack in his own world—until he started talking again.

"He'd called me."

"But you couldn't have known—" I said.

"Troy called me. He was looking for help, and I was too self-absorbed to listen."

"Jack—"

"You know this is part of who we are, right? We play the

game. We take the pain and this is our life. It's what we do."

I could feel him spiraling and wanted desperately to stop him before he got too deep. "Jack, no—"

"Yes. If you want to know me—be friends with me—you should know this. Because the next time you end up in a place like this, it could be me, or one of my other brothers. This—"

If this was one of the stages of grief, I didn't recognize it and wanted it to stop, the way Jack was leaning forward, his body tense, talking anywhere but at me, his head swaying slightly side-to-side.

"It's the nature of things. The game we played. Who we are. It's us."

Jack's whole body snapped my way so fast it startled me. I gasped, and without thinking, leaned back slightly against the door.

"So many athletes, so many football players, we all go through a tough transition, even between seasons. Anxiety, depression, pain. Troy had been out of the league for years, and yet they still kept feeding him those goddamn pills so he could get out of bed." A small sound, kind of like a chuckle, bounced from him as his shoulders shrugged. "When we even get out of bed. You know how often you hear of guys stuck in their beds, or their houses, for weeks or even months after a season?"

"No, I don't. I—"

"Most never hear about it. Wouldn't be good for the image, but it's the life. Today, one of my football brothers is being buried. This one due to the shotgun he turned on himself. And there have been so many others, as a result of drugs, booze, crime, or otherwise. But if you want to know what really put them there—it was this life, this sport."

"I'm so sorry, Jack . . . " I had spent my life weaving words to suit various moments, but had nothing for a scenario like this, nothing for something so real and in person.

"Don't get me wrong," Jack said. "I'm not necessarily jumping in with the whole post-concussion syndrome thing, or the chronic traumatic encephalopathy debate—"

I didn't want to interrupt him, but I needed to understand. "I'm sorry, Jack . . . chronic traumatic *what*? I don't know what that is."

"CTE. It's the big hot-button topic right now. The reason everything in the game is starting to change. The rules, how teams practice. And, now, some of the big leagues are getting sued for even bigger bucks. Essentially, the more we bang our heads . . . " Suddenly, Jack struck his forehead with his palm, hard. The hit startled me, but what truly made me uncomfortable was that he was so caught up in his thoughts that he didn't seem to feel the pain that should go along with such a blow. " . . . there's a cumulative toll." He struck his head again. "And it screws up the way we function, the way we think, what we think about, our emotions, stress, and—you know the kicker? The craziest part of all? Right now, the docs don't even have a definitive way to diagnose CTE until you're dead!" He fell back into his seat laughing. It was an odd, slow sound laced with sadness and frustration.

I gave him his moment.

He sat forward again, head in his hands, for a few minutes before looking back at me, "Don't get me wrong. I'm no doctor. I'm just saying it's more than just damn concussions. There's the meds. The depression. All that stuff left without help. It's not just us football guys, but that's my world and it's what I know best. I just know we keep losing great guys to boxes. Either wooden ones like today, or ones with metal bars for doors."

I moved over to give Jack a hug, but realized he was no longer seeing me.

He leaned back in his seat. "Troy called me. Maybe I am the narcissist they all say I am. I didn't take the time to listen."

Two minutes later, the limo finally stopped. The engine went silent and I waited. This was Jack's time. I was here to give him what he needed.

CHAPTER FIFTY-ONE

Jack

I T WAS A struggle getting out of the limo. Helen had taken care of me with kid gloves. I couldn't have been luckier than having her with me to face this.

When we made our way through the crowd, there were so many faces from my past. Some were family, others I had hoped to never see again, but nonetheless I was grateful they were here to pay respects.

Space was limited, so Helen excused herself to stay with the crowd while I made my way to the front to stand with a group of guys from our playing days. Having showed up late, I gave only a small nod and wave to Troy's family, with the intent to speak to them after the service.

While we stood there, the ringing in my ears began to return. It had been there since the news about Troy. It was uncomfortable at first, but then became soothing. Before I knew it, my mind was wandering somewhere else, into a colorless void that was so peaceful.

After a short time, I came back to the scene, and the pain. *My heart feels so heavy.*

The minister was speaking, the words a useless monotone

filling the silence that used to be owned by the man in that fucking box, now poised so precariously above a black pit.

The tingling in my nose returned. I adjusted my glasses, and what had to be a camera flash popped in the distance. *Fucking vultures.*

"And as we gather here to share in this moment of respect and gratitude . . . " said the minister.

I leaned in toward Rolly, who was standing beside me, stoic and strong, and knew a huge bender was in his immediate future. The guy never had a thought that didn't escape, the odd times one didn't meant there was trouble brewing. Rolly's drinking was generally proportionate to his silence. Tonight, some bottles were going to turn up empty.

"Just like the old days, huh, Rol?" I whispered. "Huddled up together while some old dude drones on and on?"

Rolly refused to bite, but turned to me with glazed eyes, anger and hatred running wild in their depths. It was a look I had seen so many times when we got him going before a game. The list of the memories he would channel from his childhood and life outside the painted lines was long and terrible. He had said those three hours on the field were the most peaceful times he had ever found, the only time he could try and unload some of his pain, legally. There were times where I had literally been afraid for our opponents, especially when we faced Los Angeles. I knew the look but had never had it turned my way, until now. Rolly's lips curled in a snarl, ready to rip a new hole in my hide.

I would've flinched if I didn't know better.

Rolly's cheeks were flushed, his forehead cut with lines as if from an iron chisel.

I wrapped my arms around him, and he sobbed. Loud, desperate sobs, that we all felt deep in our souls. And I joined him. Releasing my pain. Arms surrounded me, surrounded him, and together we let it all out.

"It's not right, Cap," he said. I would always be Rolly's unit captain. I took him in after he was traded twice in his first season and wound up with us, but it had been so long since I had been called that name.

"I know, man. I know."

"I would've saved him. Whatever he needed, I would've done it. He—" Another big sob wracked his body and shook our huddle.

Another voice. Sammy, our stand-out wide receiver added, "Me too. It should be me in there, not him. Never him."

I heard the signature smack we all knew had to be Waggle's hand landing on the back of Sammy's skull. The same smack we had all heard so many times in practice, the one we called the Montana Smackdown. Quickly, Waggle's presence was confirmed by that distinctive drawl, "Fuck you, ya twat."

For some reason, that familiar ridiculousness snapped something in me, and a little laugh burped out that surprised all of us. Rolly's bloodshot eyes looked my way, a tear clinging to the corner of his eye. We stood there a moment, the cries and sobs had been put on hold. Another laugh jumped out and was joined by someone else in our group, then another until the wave finally came back and hit Rolly and he broke. His big gap-toothed smile ran roughshod across his face.

A few more giggles began in the crowd around us. Maybe at our ridiculousness, or out of discomfort for us, it's hard to say. In an effort to maintain some type of decorum, the minister cleared his throat to continue. This pushed one of our guys into deeper laughter. We had grown up with coaches smacking us with clipboards, baseball bats, thirty-pound tackling pads, and anything else they could get their hands on to keep us focused. The mere clearing of a throat showed the minister he was presiding the wrong way at the wrong gathering. And if he didn't already know it, we were good at making it clear.

Breaking away from us with a long slide-step forward, Rolly peered down at the minister, and said, "You don't know him."

Refusing to give up his sworn duty so easily, the minister responded with, "I know we are all God's creatures and—"

Rolly cut him off, "'Creatures'?"

"Uh, yes. We—"

Rolly's swat on his arm sent the older man teetering a little. To his credit, however, he stayed upright and somehow maintained his dignity and that look of conviction. "Reverend? Father? Sir? Whatever," said Rolly, "that was the first thing you said right about our brother, Troy, all day." Rolly now positioned himself in the place of the minister who had, without choice, accepted a backup role close by. "That overexcited, rowdy motherfucker—" Rolly said, his face flashing red as he peeked over at Troy's mother standing nearby. "Sorry, ma'am," he muttered, "but he was a 'creature', all right."

A small smile appeared on her face that hit home. It was Troy's smile, and it made fresh tears drop down my cheeks. An arm slid around mine from the left, and grasped it firmly with delicate fingers. Without looking, I knew it was Helen, and a warm wave of strength flowed through me.

Rolly continued, "That rowdy M.F.—" he took another quick peek at Troy's mom who nodded approvingly "—he was everything anyone could have ever wanted in a friend, teammate, brother . . . " with each title mentioned, he cast a look at the various members of the crowd that each descriptor fit and received nods and smiles in return, " . . . or son. He would always be there for you. He would give everything he had to be sure you had what you needed and what he felt you deserved, which was often much more than any of us could have imagined, or sometimes, wanted," he said, cracking up slightly. "I remember one time, we were heading to the playoffs and my girl had just dumped me. The moment our team checked into the hotel and the coaches gave us the green light to go—"

Bringing my right hand up to about shoulder level, I waved it to get Rolly's attention. But I got nothing, and he continued.

"—out for the night. Troy grabbed me by the arm and man-handled me out the door saying, 'You know, I've got the cure for your woman troubles', and, wow," Rolly's face was lit with the happy memory as a laugh broke through the players, "he really did. We went to club after club—"

Sammy cut in with, "Yep, Troy loved to dance and hang out with the guys to prep for a game, didn't he?"

Rolly's face went through a twisted process as he was deciding how to proceed, before realizing that Sammy was interrupting to keep him in line before Rolly said something he shouldn't about an epic wild night of women and drinking. "Uh, yup, Sammy. He really did," and we all shared a polite, knowing murmur of approval.

It was then that I saw her—it was just the smallest glimpse, but there was no chance of a mistake. I swear ominous horror movie music played somewhere in the distance as I saw Angelina and some guy slip into the crowd.

Helen's fingers suddenly clamped down sharply into my arm in a way that would've earned both holding and unnecessary roughness calls if we were on the field. Instead, I had to just grin and bear it while trying to figure out why it just happened and how to make it stop.

I looked down at her with a "What the hell?" stare, but Helen didn't see me. Her eyes bulged as they threatened to leap from her skull into the nearby crowd. I didn't know that look, and never want to see it on her face again. Following her eyes, I couldn't see anything that looked like it should draw that kind of reaction. Trying to fake a casual and relaxed demeanor, I leaned in and whispered, "You okay?"

Silence. But once again, Helen squeezed my arm and this time gave an added tug as her head nodded just enough to draw my eyes back to where she was looking. For an instant, barely the blink of an eye, I saw Angelina again, and had an "aha!" moment, but then I remembered that the two had never met, so Angelina showing up here couldn't be Helen's problem. The guy escorting Angelina, however, whom I could now see just as a floating head, bobbed into my line of sight again. Helen's nails amped up the torturous fun they were having with my forearm. My brain rocketed through its files, trying to put a name to this guy's face or a way to tie to him to Helen, but I was drawing a blank. He was no-one I'd ever seen with Angelina before, either. *Who was this guy?*

CHAPTER FIFTY-TWO

Jack

"RIGHT, JACK?" ROLLY'S voice cut through my thoughts. A hand slapped me on the back.

I looked at him, still standing by the grave, almost glowing in the midday sun, then quickly read the room, and answered, "That's right, buddy," and got a smack on the back of the head that had to be from Waggle.

Rolly looked at me with a confused look, shrugged, and continued talking, "Yet Troy never did . . . "

Helen pulled me down, her hissing mouth at my ear, and said, "Jack. That's *him*. That's William."

"Huh? Where?" Once again, I scanned the crowd as I whispered back, "Odd. I just saw Angelina here, too. She was Troy's agent."

The Space Agency could've done a countdown as Helen's and my thoughts went on a collision course. *3 . . . 2 . . .1 . . .*

Oh, shit! That guy! With Angelina. It's Helen's William. And they're here together.

The minister thanked Rolly for his comments and once again took control of Troy's service, providing an opportunity for others to speak as Rolly slipped back into place beside me.

"What's the deal?" he whispered.

I nodded toward Angelina, unable to find words.

Rolly gave a girlish gasp that, any other time, would've made me laugh, but this time underscored my feelings. "Well, I guess you had to know she'd be here. If nothin' else, she's a good agent, and took care of him best she could."

I felt my jaw tighten. Rolly was right, but it didn't make Angelina being here feel any better. Out of the side of my mouth, I managed to whisper to Helen, "Any ideas? What do you want to do?"

Even though she'd remained completely silent, she was in tears. They rushed hard down her face, covering her cheeks, chin, and chest.

I was stunned and began to form new tears, these ones for the pain Helen was so clearly experiencing. I stooped down for us to be eye to eye. "Let's go?"

She sobbed, a loud, deep, from the depths of her soul sob that tore at my heartstrings.

I turned quickly back to Rolly. "Dude. I've got to bolt. Cover me on this."

He gave me that nod and smile I realized I had been missing in all my time away from these guys. *They always had my back.*

Blanketing my arm around Helen, I began to try and gently force our way back out through the crowd, away from the many eulogies which had begun. As we escaped, I felt numerous hands patting my shoulders, folks slowing us down to throw compassionate comments my way, but I was focused solely on getting Helen somewhere private, to a less pain-inducing location. I saw daylight looming ahead, with only a few more people to clear, when Angelina and William blocked our exit.

Helen stopped and locked herself in place, rigid, unable to move or be moved. Her hands snapped up to cover her mouth and its desperate gasp for air.

I tried to gently get her going again, but it was impossible. So I waited.

Angelina and William stared at us with mixed expressions I didn't recognize.

It wasn't until he took a step toward us that Helen moved again, this time with her legs so weak she began to collapse.

I clamped on tight before anyone else could notice and quietly said to her, "Don't give that prick the satisfaction. He lost. He made a mistake and whatever his reason for being here, he has to know that you are the one with the strength. Whatever you don't have, you can get from me. I got you."

Somehow it clicked. I felt Helen's body solidify, her spine straighten, and her chin rise up. A slight trembling could still be felt, but it was buried so deep as to be invisible. She walked forward, and I hung on with my arm still around her, following her lead.

We took two more big steps toward them before the crowd finally parted, and I noticed that Angelina and William were holding hands. It was my turn to falter a moment, but Helen kept pushing us forward until the four of us stood face to face. My eyes were locked with Angelina's, Helen's with her ex's.

Angelina and William offered a broken chorus of an "I'm sorry" from her and a "Listen . . . " from him.

In unison, we replied with a "Save it!" that had both their jaws dangling in shock.

Did they really think this would be cool and friendly?

"I don't know why you're here but it's in really poor taste," Helen snapped at William.

"I . . . " He had nothing in response, except the shakes I could see working their way through his body.

On the other hand, Angelina stepped to it with, "I am . . . er . . . *was* Troy's agent. I'm supposed to be here."

Helen's head bobbed, and she seemed to grow before my eyes. "How sweet. You're here because you're," she did air quotes with her free hand, "'supposed' to be here. You're a sweetheart. That's—"

Angelina's face went ghost-white like I had never it seen before, it was almost unnerving, but her instincts were working at full speed. "I, uh, that's not what I meant. I—"

Helen shrugged. "You know what? I don't care," she said in a quiet hiss, and started to walk again.

William finally found a few words, "Can I explain?"

But Helen didn't flinch, or even slow her pace. "Not likely."

William followed us. "Please let me try. It wasn't supposed to be like this."

Helen turned to me with a look that asked, "Should we?" and I nodded.

"Fine," Helen said. "I'll give you guys five minutes."

William jumped in, unwilling to waste a moment, "Excellent. I—"

She stepped out of my grasp to close in with him, "Not here, you fool. You still have no social sense, and are hogging the attention at someone else's event." Her arm outstretched, she pointed a finger at our waiting limo. "In the car. Get in the car, and we'll give you both five minutes to explain, and then you can disappear."

Angelina had remained uncharacteristically silent for far too long, and now took her cue by responding with an overly sweet, "Thank you, Helen. That is very mature of you."

Helen stifled a laugh as she hustled back to me. She grabbed my hand, casually, the way anyone would when trying to rush off with another, but it was unlike anything I had felt before. *An electricity. A warmth.* A tingling sensation quickly rumbled up my arm from my fingers and made the hairs on the back of my neck stand at attention. A river of energy coursed through my body from my head to my toes that threatened to spill onto the ground around me and catch me in my tracks. Best of all was the look on Helen's face as she froze mid-step and quickly glanced at me, and I could see my own emotions mirrored there due to this new experience. One that would be the subject of our next talk, and likely many stories to come.

But, first, we would deal with "them".

CHAPTER FIFTY-THREE

Helen

I ROLLED INTO the limousine, a seething ball of rage and agony. I wanted to lash out. To scream, to yell, or maybe to find a mallet to introduce to William—my writing made real—but with Jack by my side, I was finding some level of self-control.

The feeling that had run through me when I'd touched Jack's hand was a spark of energy, of life, that I had never felt before. It was part of my current conflict; there was an urgent need to address that feeling—or run away from it—but now was not the time or the occasion. And, first, I had to put my past to rest. So, I took my seat on the plush black leather, holding Jack's hand, while our two lowlife exes slithered in across from us through the doors.

They'll be leaving soon.

"Your five minutes starts now," said Jack. "Say whatever you've gotta say," his hand clenched slightly as his focus turned to William, "and then you better get running."

Angelina looked cool as ice as William sweated buckets.

I always hated that about him. Washing his clothes, the sheets . . . oh, and sex . . . I shuddered thinking back to just how much of his sweat would cover me by the end. *What were you thinking, Helen?*

"Okay. Thank you," said William. His eyes jumped between the three of us. "Okay, well—"

I had thought that I loved him, and that I would spend the rest of my life with him . . .

"I just want you both to know, that this," he bobbed his head sideways gesturing to Angelina, "is about more than just sex."

The ice bucket barely made it up fast enough as a stream vomit made an emergency exit from me.

Jack handed me a couple napkins and a bottle of water. I wiped up, swished with the water, rolled down my window for a bit of air, and regained my composure.

"Yeah," said Jack, "I second that. How fucking disgusting."

"No," said William, "you don't understand. I said it's not just about sex."

"I'm about to lay you out right here if you talk about having sex with my wife one more fucking time. You understand what I'm saying?"

People try to write about terror, to express it through prose, but nothing really compares to seeing your ex tremble in fear of retribution he knows he deserves.

William slid back into his seat, casting small glances toward Angelina without a word.

"Three minutes left," said Jack.

We were making it through this, in spite of my little gastrointestinal rebellion, but we were doing it.

"How long?" I asked.

"Huh?" said William.

Angelina patted William's hand before giving it a quick

squeeze and returning her hands to her own lap, "Helen wants to know how long we've been together."

"Oh. Okay—"

"I've got this," said Angelina. "We met actually working for you two. I was looking for promo opportunities and—"

"Wait," said Jack, "did you say 'promo' or 'porno'? Because that would explain a lot."

Dismissing him, she shook her head and rolled her eyes. "Billy here—"

"'Billy'? Since when have you ever fucking been a 'Billy'?" I shouted. *I don't know why that struck a nerve, but that mother—*

"Yes, I like 'Billy'," William said. "It's a little less pretentious than William, or at least I like the way she says it."

I huffed my disgust. "You are a special piece of work."

"No need for name-calling and insults, Helen," said Angelina in her condescending tone.

My nails bit into the palm of my hand as my fist clenched. *It had been a very long time since I was in a fistfight. Today was feeling like it might be time to come out of retirement.*

"I don't know why we're even doing this," Angelina continued. "The point is, we don't want to be with the two of you anymore."

"It's true," said William.

"Shut up, Billy. Grown-ups are talking," said Jack.

"I . . . " Billy shut up.

Jack asked the million dollar question, "Okay, but why be such hurtful assholes about it?"

"Because, Jack," said Angelina, "we knew you two wouldn't understand. Look, we did our part. We tried to set you two up to soften the blow. It wasn't our fault you two—"

"'Set up'? Shit!" I said. "You two had nothing to do with us—"

"Oh, Helen," said Angelina as she turned to William. "You were right, Billy. She's so naive—"

The ice bucket went flying across the car. Angelina ducked and let out a horrified screech as the rear windshield was spattered with icy vomit, and the mostly empty bucket rolled back across their seat to land on the floor at my feet.

Apparently that did it, or the five minutes was up, because Angelina was now hustling her Billy out the opposite door as she screamed at Jack and me, "You think it's an accident that you two met? That you two happened to be in Austin together, then had that stupid radio interview in Billings, and then coincidentally had another conference booked together in Portland? Give your heads a shake, kiddies."

Her hand pushing on his asscheeks made Billy stumble out his door and land on his knees in the grass.

Now that's what I came to see.

Angelina didn't care, didn't notice him. She was still ranting, "We gave you guys every opportunity at happiness, every chance to get out of this in a good way. We didn't even look for money or anything. At the end of the day, where you are now is thanks to us. We were the good guys. You two were just too stupid to realize—"

I cut in. "Too stupid to realize this conversation was a waste of time. Goodbye," I said, and with both hands, I shoved her bony ass out the door to knock William, once again, into the grass. I slammed the door behind them, then hurled the ice bucket out of my open window.

"Here, this is for you. Consider it a parting gift," I shouted.

Jack's eyes sparkled, his smile radiant. "Helen, you are—"

I jumped into his lap. "Take me," I said, rapidly tearing through the buttons on my blouse.

His hands were on my hips. My head spun. A desperate need roared inside me for Jack and I to be one, to have him—and to be had—by a man who looked at me the way he was looking at me right now.

It was then that I realized it. *This was why I wrote and what I had been chasing all my life.*

CHAPTER FIFTY-FOUR

Jack

SEEING HELEN TAKE control of the situation and get rid of Angelina and William so deftly was pure inspiration. Helen shone with a light so hot it scrambled my senses—and then she was on me.

Her eyes blazed with passion as she tore through the buttons on her powder blue blouse. She straddled my thighs, and my hands clasped her hips as I lay back and pulled her close.

The pain in my damaged face? Secondary.

The ache of my injured shoulders? Irrelevant.

The need to have her? Infinite.

She began to grind on my cock. It rapidly rose to the call. Our breathing was heavy, our hearts beat hard in a single deafening sound.

"Jack—I need you," she said. Her hands gave up wrestling with my tie and ripped open the buttons on my shirt.

"Yes, Helen. All of you . . . " I said, as I slid my hands up under her skirt to pull down her lacy blue panties.

Then I stopped. She continued to move forward.

My lips froze, but she nipped them; once, twice, then a third time that threatened to draw blood.

"Jack?"

I moved slightly to the side to allow her to slide off my hips for better eye contact. "This can't happen, Helen."

The confusion in her eyes quickly turned to hurt. "I . . . I don't understand," she said.

"Me, neither. Well, only barely." I tried hard to focus my thoughts and clarify them to make sharing possible. "Here's the thing, I want you—"

"And I want you."

"But not here, not like this. Not at my friend's funeral in the back of some vomit-splattered limo. And, most of all, not just after having that encounter with those two." I shifted us again so I could move closer, our foreheads touching. "Helen, I don't know where things can go from here, but if it's going to happen, I don't want to have any part of them associated with our life. I want it to be purely us. You know?"

"This *is* us, Jack. I didn't know it, not really, until just a few minutes ago when our hands touched and I felt—something incredible. A connection. You didn't feel it? You don't?"

"I did and I do, and I know, but they're still out there. They've stirred up all this energy. At the end of the day, wherever our relationship might go, I don't want us to ever look back and wonder if Angelina was right, that we owe all of this to them." I gulped hard, the pain in my body now concentrated in my heart, which was trying not to break—again. "Please . . . please tell me you understand."

It was an eternal moment that we shared, wrestling with the strange twist of fate life had presented. Finally Helen spoke, "Thank you, Jack. I do understand. And I agree."

From there, we snuggled in tight. We cried quiet little tears for all that had happened to us over the past several days. We let it all wash out of us, so we were no longer rooted in pain, anger, and fear, but coming from a place of strength and security.

I think we may have eventually drifted off to sleep from exhaustion when the driver's voice cut through on the intercom, "Sir? People are beginning to load into their vehicles. When they leave, should I follow?"

The smile on Helen's face was everything I had wanted to see. I sighed, "What do you think?"

"I think you need to be with your friends."

The words registered as correct, but they went against what I wanted most. "You're right, but . . . "

"I know," she said, and gave me a small kiss on the cheek.

"The driver will take you wherever you want to go. I hope we'll continue to remain in touch," I said.

"Thank you," she said, and a smirk crept across her face, "of course we will. You agreed to read for me."

I shook my head at her silliness. "You're right, I did."

"Okay, now get out there," she said, and gave me one of her trademark swats on the shoulder that delivered a world of pain.

I jumped up, and bumped my sore head on the roof. *More pain.*

"Oh, no! I'm sorry," she said, cringing away, trying not to inflict any more damage.

"I think I need to get away just to survive," I said with a laugh, as I made my way out the limo's rear door to send Troy off right, and rebuild my bond with brothers who clearly needed each other right now.

"Take care, Helen. You deserve only the best," I said, and I left, adjusting my shades so whatever tears slipped out wouldn't be seen.

CHAPTER FIFTY-FIVE

Helen

THERE WAS TOO much going on in Cleveland right then for me to stay a minute longer. When Jack left, I had the driver take me straight to my hotel for my bags and booked the next flight out.

My plane wouldn't be leaving until early evening, but I couldn't risk bumping into Jack again at the hotel, or, worse yet, possibly Angelina and her 'Billy', so I went to the airport to wait.

Everyone knows that airports aren't usually a place you'd want to spend a whole lot of time, but I found an airport bar proudly proclaiming "Now Featuring Karaoke" on a sign beside its doors. I ducked into a booth, flipped on my invisibility shield, and began people watching. It was amazing to see so many others trapped in transition finding ways to pass the time, and even bond with others, through song. I pulled out my notebook and had a field day.

After nursing several glasses of orange juice, it was time for me to leave. An older gentleman with salt-and-pepper hair was up on the little stage belting out the Beastie Boys' classic, "No Sleep Till Brooklyn", with two younger men, and it felt incredibly right even though I was on my way home instead of to New York. A pint glass sat on the ledge beside the speaker as a tip jar. Apparently, any money given went to buy the singer a drink. I went over, shoved in my dollar, and then noticed a picture above it of a wild crowd partying around the karaoke machine. And there, in the center of all the mayhem, were Jack and Troy, with big stupid grins.

A teary smile became my companion for the duration of the trip home.

CHAPTER FIFTY-SIX

Helen

"WELL, THEN, WHY don't you finally come out and live at the ranch?" Clay had said, in his matter-of-fact way. "Cleopatra, Mother, and I are always happy to see you out here, anyway, and you've already said now your ex is gone, you don't need to be in the city."

His logic was sound, so why would I want to argue? He was right, I didn't have a reason to be in the city any longer, and, as much as I'd once loved the apartment, it no longer felt like home. So, two weeks later, I was taking another load up to the ranch in hopes of being ready for tonight's surprise party.

When I pulled through the gates, dusk was already starting to fall, so I hurried down the middle path to one of the small ranch hand bunkhouses Clay and Aster had allowed me to claim. I parked my truck, grabbed a box, and was struck by the dazzling display Mother Nature was throwing my way. While it was always a treat to see these gorgeous displays of color filtering over the city from my highrise patio, it never compared to seeing the sun setting out in the open "big sky country" of Montana.

She's showing off tonight. I truly am where I belong.

Then I heard a horse clip-clopping up the road. Not terribly unusual on a ranch, but Clay had assured me there wouldn't be any hands on board for about another month.

Probably just Clay coming to get me moving before I'm late for the party.

I dropped the box. Something broke, but it didn't matter. Coming up the path was a large man on horseback, silhouetted against the sun falling behind him. I didn't need the light to be able to identify Sir Lancelot's muscular bulk ambling my way, and even blind I would recognize Jack's shape, with his new white hat and that smile of his, sparkles of white flashing out of the darkness.

He waved awkwardly.

I started to cry.

"Wha—what are you doing?" I called out. "You don't ride!" *Oh, Helen. Really?*

"I do today," he said, now close enough for me to see him sitting high, but uncomfortably and a bit hunched over, in the saddle. "I do for you."

"But how? When?" I ran to him, "Never mind! Get down here, you."

He slid out of the saddle, picked me up in his arms, and squeezed me the way I discovered I had been aching to be squeezed. When he put me down, we stood staring at each other while the sun continued to fade.

I refused to let him go for fear it was all a dream, or that he may leave me again. I refused to let him go this time, because—

"So, uh, can the surprise party be me collecting on that raincheck now?" he asked. Lancelot tossed his head.

"Raincheck?"

"Our late night ride. I hear horses have great night vision."

"Oh! Yes. Let's go," I said, and grabbed him by the hand, dragging him to my Cleopatra's stable. "Wait. You did mean now, right? You know I'm not always good at reading people."

"Honey, you've got me all figured out. Yes, I did."

"Okay, then—oops," I dropped his hand, "you hang on to Sir Lancelot and I'll grab Cleopatra, okay?"

"Sure. What about your truck?"

"No, we'll leave it."

He chuckled, "No, I mean, don't you want to unload it first or something?"

"It can wait," I said, and flew through the yard and into the stable to find my girl. "Guess what, my queen, we've got company. Gentleman callers!" I rushed around, putting on my boots and grabbing her saddle, bridle, bags, and everything else we needed for a good ride. I was on autopilot.

Ready to go, we rode out to meet the boys.

Jack had managed to get himself back up on Lancelot, and they pulled up beside us and we began our ride.

The smooth rhythmic sound of the horses' hooves echoed off the dirt road, the only sound competing with the heavy thumping off my heart in my ears. We rode without words, stealing only the briefest glances in the other's direction for fear of disturbing the dream and waking up in our previous reality. This was a moment I had never expected, but my heart had longed for.

Whatever tonight is, Helen, enjoy the moment. Don't overthink it. One night like this is better than you ever imagined.

Soon, we found the marker for the trail. Most never saw it and those that did avoided the difficult terrain and never discovered the beauty at the end which made it my favorite. Single file, we made our way through the darkening field.

The night was warm and alive as the wind whispered through the grasses and shrubs. The world was at peace and I felt as one with the world.

It took about twenty minutes to get to the rise and climb to the top, where the small stand waited. It was a place where Cleopatra and I would stop on our tours, sometimes hunker down in bad weather, or, for me, it was also another place for me to hide out and read, write, or enjoy the stars at night.

We dismounted, tied the horses, and spread a blanket over the small wooden tent platform.

Side by side, we lay watching the stars come out. Every few minutes, we would each steal a glance at the other.

"Is this real?" he asked, the first words to break our silence since we'd left the stable.

All I had in answer was a smile, and I let it shine.

His arm draped over my waist, his hand now on my hip, as he rolled my way. He looked at me with a smile I had never seen before, one he would go on to call "Helen's Smile", as it was only for me.

"Are you okay?" he asked softly.

I nodded, "Yes," and closed my eyes as he finally leaned in to kiss me.

Just the touch of his lips drew out a small moan.

My fingers grazed across the soft stubble he had grown since last we met. I liked it and imagined how it would feel along the inside of my thighs.

We kissed deeply, his hands making quick work of my shirt.

Bad day for buttons, Helen, I thought, as one popped free and fell into the darkness of the blanket.

He's not moving fast enough. I broke the kiss and yanked my shirt over my head and, with a quick flip, released my bra.

I was a mix of raw energy and nervous excitement, my fears wrestling with my dreams. As he leaned in, I placed my hand on his chest. "I need you to understand—I haven't been with another man in many years."

Jack paused. "And I look forward to learning everything about you, about us, together."

His eyes and smile burned bright, and were all I could see in the pale light of the rising moon.

CHAPTER FIFTY-SEVEN

Jack

I'T'S STRANGE HOW life works. At a time when my cock was rock hard, aching for release, and a woman had just bared her chest for me, I paused to think. I realized that the last week of my sneaking up to the Last Chance Ranch, getting to know Clay, and having him secretly teach me to ride, was about more than just trying to escape my past. It was about finding a new me and a new life.

And right now, man, you better not let it pass you by.

Helen tore open my shirt and I threw my hat to the side. She took two fistfuls of the curls that had begun to grow in on the back of my head, pulled me in close and began to kiss my neck, sending shivers through my body.

Gently, I lowered her back onto the blanket.

Compensating for our height difference, I mounted her by straddling her thighs. Much of her was lost in the darkness, but the moon played enticingly over her breasts and I stared in awe at the rise and fall of every uneven breath.

When her hands came up for me again, I moved in for another kiss, but she redirected me to her right breast.

With forced discipline, my tongue softly circled her nipple. I savored the sweet sounds and movements she produced, each one a first experience on a journey I hoped would last a lifetime. My teeth closed gently and she bucked beneath me.

Oops, that was a no. I moved away, about to give some more gentle attention to the left side when she once again guided me, forcefully, back to her right breast. *Ohh, it's like that.* This time my teeth clamped down. She bucked and moaned, her legs swinging wide to wrap around my hips and pull me close. I tugged slightly and got another moan.

Her hands then dove between us, straight down to my belt. Releasing her, I spread my arms wide, hands firmly planted on the platform to create separation and allow her access.

With surprising expertise, my belt was suddenly undone, open, and her hand was inside my boxers stroking the head of my cock.

"Oh God, Helen."

I held that position until my arms began to shake. "I need to move."

"Do it and I stop."

And I found a way to hold on another minute longer. When I finally succumbed to fatigue, my sore shoulder complaining, I rolled off to the left and, true to her word, she stopped.

No problem, I had other things in mind.

Much to my surprise, she took hold of me again, the palm of her hand circling my tip and finding lubrication before sliding down with fuller strokes from head to base.

My plans went on hold.

With every change of position, each shiver or moan, I found myself returning to her eyes. They looked at me in such a way that, for the first time, I felt like I was truly being seen—and it raised every bit of excitement to a whole new level.

Time to show off. In one quick motion, I had her pants undone and around her knees. Leaning in, my tongue gently circled her dark pink areola while my hand found its way inside her panties slowly moving to—

Her voice, deep, guttural, and demanding said, "I want you, Jack. I need you. We have played this slow for far too long. Take me. Fuck me. Devour me. I'm yours. Show me you need me, too."

I didn't need to be asked twice. *She wants the dirty Jack.* Standing up, I scrambled to the end of the platform, lifted her feet, tore off her jeans and panties, and threw them in the direction of my hat. An ankle in each hand, I knelt down and lifted her hips high off the blanket.

She gasped in surprise and excitement, "Oh, fuck."

I pulled her in toward me, her ass resting on my chest, thighs on my shoulders, only the top half of her body still holding any firm ground. I spread her wide and began to lap thirstily, a delicious mix of sweat and excitement. She moaned so loud I'm sure the animals in the surrounding hills ran for cover.

"I need you, Helen."

She moaned again.

I went back for more until her body began to shake. My face still between her legs, I asked, "You need me to stop? Because I'm fucking loving the way you taste, the way you move. Fucking dance for me, baby."

"No, don't ever stop."

"Good," I said, and I went back in until her body became one constant, trembling, vibration with her juices running across the stubble on my chin to cover my chest and her ass. I laid her back down, stood up, let my jeans drop to the ground, and moved to straddle her hips. "Are you watching me, Helen?" I began stroking my cock through my boxers.

I could faintly see her make some type of movement but, even though I was sure she was nodding "yes", I wasn't going to let her off the hook that easy.

"Tell me you see me, baby." Odds were, I was bigger than anyone she had been with before. She had already been stroking it, so she knew. There were times my size was more of a nuisance than anything, but not in times like this. In times like this, I really got to be the hero.

"Yes, Jack. I see you . . . "

"Good. Because every inch of this is for you." I stepped up, now over her chest, removed my boxers, and enjoyed that sweet sound of appreciation.

"Now I'm going to make love to you, Helen. Do you want that?"

"Unh-uh."

"No?"

"No."

Ouch. "Okay, we can just—"

"No making love—*fuck me*. Fuck me the way you've always fantasized. Fuck me like you mean it—"

This side of Helen, the dirty talk, the pure sexuality, was something I had never anticipated. With that response, she had rendered all words meaningless, and my response would be found balls deep inside her.

I got down on my knees between her legs. I slipped on a condom I'd pulled from the pocket of my jeans, and guided the tip to gently glide across Helen's dripping wet, silken lips. I braced myself on top, my face close enough to hers to see her eyes close and a big smile stretch across her face.

"Open your eyes, Helen. Look at me."

She did.

"I want you to always remember this. Know that for as long as you want it—this—me—I'm yours," I said, and as I began to slowly slide, in I watched her eyes get wider and wider. She felt so good. *So hot and wet.*

Her hands on my chest soon became talons digging into my flesh.

It wasn't long before I reached what would be full-depth for tonight. We paused and stayed there for a moment as I let her get used to my size and girth, the only sound our heavy, desperate, breath.

Slowly, I drew back. The power of being the one on top, the one in control of when things really started, the one in control of the pace, made my pulse race.

With smiles, we began.

CHAPTER FIFTY-EIGHT

Helen

THE NEXT MORNING, I danced on air. I was a character straight out of a fairytale, floating on sunbeams. The birds were singing, the flowers were blooming, it was a new day for a new me.

From the moment Jack had shown up last night as my "surprise party"—on horseback of all things—I had felt the world shake. We had stayed on the platform until we wore out the stars and the moon was ready to call it a night. We seized the opportunity to have the sex we wanted, cuddling, talking, watching the magic of the constellations, and just enjoying being alive together. His passion and stamina had been both exciting and liberating. I had always known there was another side of me locked away, a side that only slipped out in my writing. But with Jack, that part had now been set free, and would be encouraged to grow and be further explored. Everything was about to change.

Before dawn, we'd made our way back to the bunk in my new place. We'd slept in, nestled under my comfy duvet, until I was awakened by a knock at the door.

I opened it to see Clay's smiling face. "Mornin'," he said, tipping his hat in usual Clay-fashion. He leaned in to speak privately. I rushed him with a big hug that I couldn't hold back.

"Thank you. Thank you, Clay," I whispered, and gave him a kiss on the cheek.

"You're okay? Not sore with—"

I gave him another kiss on the cheek. "And that one's for Aster."

Catching my breath, I stepped back to let him inside. I felt the need to gush, to tell him everything. *Wait, he probably knows more than you do!*

Instead, Clay took my hand and quietly led me away from where Jack was sleeping upstairs, out past the porch swing to the chairs on the other side of the veranda. We sat down. Clay's face became serious, as he said, "I want you to know, Helen, we like him. He seems like good, decent people and I think this place, and you, will do him a world of good. But," he leaned over to pat me on the knee, "I need you to know that you are still the most important person to us, and if you don't want him here, he's out on his ear faster than he can spit."

I grinned. "Thank you. That means a lot to me. He *is* good— wait . . . out on his ear? *'Here'*? I'm not sure—"

Just then Mr. Perfect Timing, Jack, strolled around the corner. "Mornin', Helen. Mornin', Clay."

Clay stood and they shook hands.

"Just breaking the bad news to her?" asked Jack.

Clay grinned. "Sure was." He gave Jack a second look. "Hey, you got dirt on yer hat," he said, before easing back into his chair.

Jack chuckled and a faint blush went through his cheeks.

I looked at Clay. "I hear you can tell a lot about a man by his hat."

Clay gave me a nod and a wink and we all had a good-natured laugh at Jack's expense.

"Laugh it up, funny people. Go ahead, make fun of a guy who hasn't even had his coffee yet," said Jack.

And then my thoughts snapped back to the big question. "What was that about Jack and this place?" I said, and looked between the two of them for an answer.

"Well, you know how we were getting the other bunkhouse ready for the new ranch hand?" said Clay.

Shocked, the pieces falling into place, I nodded.

"Meet the new ranch hand. He's from Pennsylvania, by way of Texas. He's pretty green, but he may have some potential," deadpanned Clay. "I hear he writes a little, too."

"Howdy, ma'am," said Jack, tipping his hat.

And then it hit me and I jumped from my seat.

"Surprise?" said Jack.

"Hold that thought, funny man," I said, pointing my finger at Jack as I hustled across the porch and around the corner.

Clay snickered after me, "I know that look."

I heard Jack say "yep" as I ran into the house, the door screeching on the hinges. *Darn right they do!* I leapt up the stairs two at a time, ducked into the bedroom to grab my purse from the floor, unzipped it, and dove for my notebook.

I bounced onto the edge of the bed and pushed the button on my pen as I heard footsteps coming up the stairs.

Jack popped his head into the room. "Helen?"

I looked up at him, the grin on my face pushing up against my ears. "Yes?"

"Whatcha writing?"

"I'll be right back down once I get a few words out. You'll see."

And I began. *Conquering a Titan.*

Acknowledgements

Annie: A muse by any other name . . . Your talent, your friendship, and your inspiration leaves me forever in gratitude.

Gill: You motivate and inspire by what you do and who you are. I am always so proud to call you family—even if you hate Jack.

Cheryl: My sister from another mother . . . and father. Your brilliance, passion, commitment, and good heart make our lives better just knowing you. (We need to go for more Schweemies!)

Nadia, Victoria, Sid, Judy: You help me believe, achieve, and overcome obstacles every day. With your help, from the rubble I continue to climb.

Jen: I could never have reached this point without the constant lashes, encouragement, and ever vigilant panda. On to the next one!

The London Writers Society: A brilliant and varied group that always leaves me motivated and remembering what this is all about.

And to all my English teachers who said I was lucky to get whatever grade you gave me, "F" this.

About the Author

Bio, as written by his High School sweetheart after 27 years...and counting!

C. J. Lazar is fiercely loyal, generous, and kind beyond reason. Determination and dedication drive a deep passion for love, life, honesty, music, and laughter.

His bravery against campsite raccoons, and prowess in aggressive monopoly and business, are unmatched. Still fascinated by the human experience, he is indisputably optimistic and strongly opinionated, but welcomes debate and a new perspective at every opportunity. Soft-spoken and thoughtful, he weighs his words carefully, thus his words carry weight.

His abilities as a wordsmith started very young as a Dungeon Master using his creative storytelling to create vivid twists and turns to challenge and engage the players.

His addiction (or perhaps affliction) for reading has created an interesting and descriptive author who tends toward character driven stories with humor (sometimes dark or sarcastic), and always a twist or three. This applies across all genres that he writes . . . and he writes all the genres.

Follow Me Here:

Stay in touch. Share input and feedback while finding out the latest news, releases, and promos.

My Newsletter:
http://eepurl.com/cMGy1X

Facebook:
facebook.com/CJLazarWrites

Twitter:
twitter.com/CJLazarWrites

And my Facebook Group:
facebook.com/groups/1420684244660534

Made in the USA
Middletown, DE
17 June 2017